She'll Never Tell

MAGGIE JAMES

Part One

Olivia – now

CHAPTER 1

Olivia Gilchrist trudged up the stairs to her third-floor flat, her shopping bags heavy in her hands, and inserted her key in the lock. As she did so, she heard a familiar ring tone on her phone. David was calling her. Too raw, too bruised from their conversation the night before, she let it go to voicemail.

She walked into the kitchen to unpack her groceries, one eye on her kitchen clock. Six-thirty p.m. Time to heat up a ready-meal before a night of television. Olivia slid the cardboard packaging from her dinner, pulling open a drawer to find a fork with which to prick the cellophane. At that moment, her doorbell rang. Elena Munro, her neighbour from downstairs, most likely, wanting a chat over a glass of wine.

Instead, when she pulled open the door, two police officers, one male, one female, stood there. One look at their expressions sent Olivia's gut into a tailspin of dread. A police visit never brought anything good, did it? David, perhaps, killed in a car crash; he always did drive too fast. A sob rose in her throat. She'd never get to tell him she still loved him.

'Mrs Gilchrist?' the man said.

Olivia nodded, her mouth dry. 'Yes. What is it? Why are you here?'

'I'm PC Robin Sykes. This is my colleague PC Jackie Wride.' He smiled, although it didn't reach his eyes. 'May we come in, please?'

Olivia found herself unable to speak. Instead, she stood to one side to allow them to pass. The two police officers walked into her flat, and Olivia closed the door behind them, motioning towards the living room with her hand.

'Please sit down.' She gestured towards the sofa, taking a seat opposite them. The question she was terrified to ask forced its way out. 'Is this about my husband, David Gilchrist? Has something happened to him?'

Robin leaned closer, sympathy etched in his expression. 'We're here about your mother, Sonia Harding. Her phone lists you as her emergency contact.'

Tears slid down Olivia's cheeks. 'No,' she whispered. 'Not Mum. Please, not Mum.' The empathy in Robin's eyes told a different story, however. Olivia barely registered the words that followed: *Regret to inform you... tragic accident... already dead when the paramedics arrived...*

'I'm very sorry for your loss,' Robin said. Olivia heard how a passer-by had found her mother's body face-down in the river at Vassals Park. Even as her grief threatened to overwhelm her, Olivia thought how fitting it was that her mother should die in the place she'd loved so much. They'd spent many sunny afternoons together in the Snuff Mills area of the park, watching the metal wheel of the old mill turn, the scent of iron and river water pungent in the air.

'Was it—' Olivia swallowed. 'Her heart?'

Jackie Wride spoke. 'Nobody knows at this stage. But she'd suffered a blow to her head. From a rock in the riverbed.'

Olivia closed her eyes for a moment to picture the scene. Her mother, wearing her usual flat-soled walking shoes, setting off along the path at Vassals. The ground underneath her slippery after a recent rainfall. Her mother's attention distracted by the call of a bird, the ripple of a fish in the water, as her feet skidded in the mud. Followed by her sliding, arms flailing, down the riverbank towards the stone that would prove fatal.

Sonia Harding, stubborn, quick-tempered, often outspoken, but oh, so loving, had died. *Sometimes I hate you.* The awful words Olivia had flung at her mother the last time they met rushed through her head. Angry, accusing, spiteful. She couldn't retract them, not ever.

Grief swelled in Olivia's chest. She opened her eyes to find Jackie staring at her, concern and sympathy mixed in the woman's expression.

'We've referred her death to the coroner,' Robin said.

Confusion hit Olivia. 'But didn't you say she died from a head injury?'

'We can't be sure right now,' Robin replied. 'I appreciate how distressing this is, but a post-mortem will be necessary.'

'But why?' Olivia's voice rose into a wail. Her beloved mother being cut open on a mortuary slab? The idea was impossible, horrible.

'It's standard procedure in cases like this. When somebody dies suddenly and the cause of death isn't obvious.'

'My mother suffered from blocked arteries. She was waiting for a bypass operation. A heart attack, that's what must have killed her. Her doctor can confirm her medical issues.'

'I wish it were that simple,' Jackie said. 'But the exact cause needs to be established. For the death certificate, you understand. We're appealing for witnesses.'

'When was she found?' Olivia's phone vibrated on the coffee table. With a glance, she saw the caller was Elena.

'Just after eight o'clock this morning,' Robin said. 'A man walking his dog called 999, reported he'd found a woman collapsed with head injuries, her face under water. He tried to resuscitate her, as did the paramedics, but they couldn't.'

'You said you were asking for witnesses? What did this man tell you?'

Jackie spoke again. 'He told the emergency services operator he didn't see anyone else around. He waited until the ambulance arrived, then informed the paramedics he needed to leave. We'll put out an appeal for him to contact us.'

'You said she had head injuries.' Olivia's voice cracked. 'Had she been mugged?'

Jackie shook her head. 'No. Her handbag was found beside her in the river. A considerable sum of cash, along with her mobile phone and bank cards, was still inside.'

'Can you think why your mother would have been in that area at that particular time?' Robin said.

'She went to the park early most mornings. Like I said, she suffered heart problems, and walking was her main form of exercise.'

'Did she normally go alone?'

Olivia nodded. More questions followed. She told them she'd last seen her mother yesterday afternoon, that she'd seemed fine. Her usual feisty self.

'This has come as a terrible shock,' Olivia managed, when the questions eventually dried up.

'We appreciate that,' Jackie said. 'And I'm sorry that a post-mortem is necessary. As my colleague here mentioned, it's routine procedure when a sudden death occurs and there's no obvious explanation.'

'How long? Before the results come back?'

'The coroner's office can give you more details. Once the pathologist's examination is complete, he or she will send their report to the coroner. If the result is conclusive, a death certificate will be issued. After that you can arrange the funeral.'

'And if it's not?'

'There'll need to be an inquest. A date will be set, and you'll receive notification by post.'

Jackie's mention of the word 'funeral' opened the dam in Olivia's mind. Sobs racked her body as she buried her face in her hands, not caring about the two police officers. Her sense of loss filled her stomach like a stone, hard and heavy. Without her mother, Olivia was rudderless, unsure of her place in the world.

She noticed the tension in the room, then felt a hand on her arm. When she opened her eyes, she saw Jackie staring at her.

'I'm very sorry for your loss,' the woman said. 'Do you have someone to support you? Is your father around? Any brothers or sisters?'

Olivia, still choked with sobs, shook her head. She had no siblings; never had her lack of them stung more. Her father, Harry Harding, wasn't an option. How could she tell him his beloved wife was dead? Should she even try?

'We'll be on our way now,' Robin said, with a glance at Jackie.

Once the officers had left, Olivia's tears overwhelmed her. She curled into a foetal ball in the armchair, her head a mess of grief. Memories of her mother trooped through her mind. Olivia, aged eight, running to her with a skinned knee after a fall from their apple tree. Herself at fifteen, suffering her first crush on a boy who didn't care. Both times, her mother had known how to turn Olivia's world happy again. So many memories; Olivia sank into them like she would a warm bath.

By the time she'd cried herself out, her eyes felt raw and swollen, her throat shuttered with pain. She pulled herself upright, then a faint sound reached her ears. Footsteps, getting louder. A knock sounded on her door. Elena, of course. Olivia reasoned her neighbour had seen the police go upstairs and heard Olivia's sobs through the thin floor. The woman had come to offer support. Olivia realised she should be grateful, but resented Elena. All she wanted was to be alone.

She tensed, hoping if she didn't respond Elena would go away.

A second knock. 'Olivia?' Elena's voice was tremulous. 'Can I come in?'

Olivia got to her feet. Perhaps it was easier this way. Elena was a good listener; talking to her might help. She walked towards the door, pulled the chain from its latch, and turned the lock. Elena stood before her, her face pale, her hands twisting around themselves. Olivia couldn't quite read her expression. Concern, yes, but Olivia also detected sympathy in the other woman's features. As if Elena already knew. But that was impossible. Neither Olivia nor the two police officers had spoken loudly enough.

'Is everything all right?' Elena asked. When Olivia didn't respond, she continued, 'I heard you crying. Then I saw two police officers leave your flat. What's happened, Olivia? Please tell me.' She moved closer. Olivia allowed her neighbour to draw her into her arms. Elena's hair smelled of lemon shampoo, the same kind her mum had used, causing fresh misery to wash over Olivia.

Elena held her tight, not saying a word, and Olivia found she needed that silence. She became aware of Elena steering her towards her sofa, of being pressed into its depths. Elena sat beside her, her right hand clasping Olivia's left one. Still she didn't speak.

When Olivia was all cried out for a second time, she raised her head. The compassion in Elena's eyes almost undid her.

'Talk to me, Olivia,' Elena's tone was gentle. 'You can tell me anything. What's happened, love?'

Olivia struggled to speak. 'Mum,' she forced out between sobs. 'She's dead.'

Elena's hand tensed against Olivia's. Then the other woman pulled her closer, her palms rubbing circles over Olivia's back. 'Oh, sweetheart,' Elena murmured against her hair. 'I'm so sorry.' She didn't say any more, just held Olivia and rocked her in her arms.

Seconds passed, or it could have been hours. Olivia had no concept of time anymore. She clung to the woman who'd changed from neighbour to friend over the last few weeks. Elena was right. Olivia could tell her anything, and she'd understand. The fact Elena was three decades older, the same age as her mother had been, helped.

'It was a horrible accident,' Olivia said. 'She slipped in the mud and fell in the river at Vassals Park. Hit her head on a rock. The police said—' She repressed a sob. 'That a post-mortem is required to establish the cause of death. Possibly followed by an inquest.'

Elena's response was to hug her tighter. The only sound was that of Olivia's grief.

At last Elena pushed Olivia away. One hand stroked her hair, then Olivia's cheek. 'I'm so sorry,' she repeated. Olivia glanced away, unable to bear the empathy in the older woman's face.

'I realise how much she meant to you,' Elena said. 'How deeply you loved her.'

'She was my world. I can't believe she's gone.'

'That's what it's like when you lose somebody. Life is never the same again.'

Olivia reached over to the coffee table and pulled a tissue from its box. She wiped her eyes, blew her nose. 'I need to talk about her. Is that okay?'

Elena squeezed Olivia's arm. 'Of course.'

Once the memories poured forth, Olivia found herself unable to stop. Underpinning them all was Sonia's love for her daughter. Her mother had told her umpteen times over the years, but Olivia had also felt it in every smile, every hug.

'I just loved the very bones of her, you know?' she said. 'She was my rock. Without her, I've no idea who I am anymore.'

CHAPTER 2

Once Elena had left, Olivia powered up her laptop. What was it Jackie Wride had said about post-mortems? She couldn't remember; the woman's words had got lost in the horror of her mother's death. Olivia needed to get the facts straight in her head, however.

From what she could find on the NHS website, post-mortems were carried out as soon as possible after death, usually within two to three working days, but sometimes within twenty-four hours. More information was available on the coroner's website pertaining to Bristol. Once the pathologist had completed the post-mortem, he or she would forward a report to Avon Coroner's Office, and a staff member would call the family with the results. A copy of the report would be made available if requested.

Olivia copied the email address given and composed a message, identifying herself and giving her contact details, then asked for the post-mortem results to be sent to her. Maybe if she saw the details of her mother's death in writing, she'd be able to accept it better.

She glanced at the kitchen clock. Eleven p.m.; a little late to call David, who was an early riser and normally in bed by ten o'clock, but she couldn't delay telling him. He had a right to know his mother-in-law had died. The two of them were close; Sonia had often referred to David as the son she never had. Her fingers shaking, Olivia picked up her phone.

'Hey.' David's voice was thick with sleep when he answered. 'What's up? You okay?'

For a second, Olivia couldn't speak. Then the words came, awkward, strained. 'It's Mum. She's…' Grief clogged her throat; Olivia closed her eyes, willing the pain to recede. 'She's dead, David.'

A stunned gasp. 'Oh, my God, Livvy. Sweetheart, I'm so sorry. Was it her heart?'

'No.' Sobs choking her voice, Olivia relayed what the two police officers had told her. David's shock was apparent from his brief interjections, his sombre tone. Olivia, wrung dry of emotion, came to a halt at last. Silence for a second or two.

'I'm coming over,' David said. 'You shouldn't be alone. Not at a time like this.'

'No.' Olivia's reply was automatic. She couldn't deal with David. Not then, and especially given the rift in their marriage. She realised she'd been too abrupt. 'It's late, and besides, there's nothing you can do. I'll call you when I get the post-mortem results, and with the date for the inquest, if one is needed. Until then, can you give me some space? Please?'

David agreed, albeit grudgingly. By the time Olivia ended the call, it was past midnight. She also needed to phone Kirsten. They'd been best friends since secondary school; the two of them had bonded over boys, periods, homework, their relationship a constant in Olivia's life. Kirsten adored Sonia, regarded her as a second mother. I'll call her tomorrow, Olivia decided. Along with her aunt Isobel, her mother's sister. Sleep was a must right then.

Later, in bed, Olivia allowed her grief free rein, soaking her pillow with her tears. *Why did you leave me, Mum?*

Followed by a stab of guilt. *Those awful things I said. Now I'll never get to tell her I didn't mean them.*

*****

Olivia's mind flitted back to the day before Sonia's death. She'd finished work early; her fledgling art therapy practice had been slow to take off, so she was rarely booked solid with clients. Her marriage heavy on her mind, she decided to visit her mother. Olivia's childhood home was a five minutes' drive away, and she knew, although Sonia wouldn't admit it, that her mum was lonely. Harry Harding's accident had devastated his wife; Olivia had always considered her parents the poster couple for a happy marriage.

Sonia hugged her daughter, poured her a cold lemonade, then steered Olivia into the conservatory. Inside, the June sun had rendered the air thick and humid. Olivia sat beside Sonia on the wicker sofa, her legs tucked under her, and took a long gulp of her drink. She hoped her mother would help her decide about David.

At first, though, the conversation centred on Harry. 'He recognises me more often now,' Sonia said.

Olivia nodded. 'And his speech is better. Last time I visited, he managed my name. Well, Liv rather than Olivia, but it's still progress.'

'I wish he could come home.' Sonia gave her daughter a penetrating look. 'Husbands and wives should be together, not apart.'

Olivia rolled her eyes, but she was grateful for the prompt. After all, she was desperate to discuss her marriage. 'It's too soon to move back in with David, Mum.'

Her mother pursed her lips. 'You broke his heart by leaving. Look, darling, I understand how badly you want a baby. But you should have stayed. Worked it out as a couple.'

'It's not just our differences over kids, Mum. I don't trust him. Not with Tiffany Cook sniffing around him like a bitch on heat.' Olivia was aware she sounded catty, but her husband's relationship with his colleague had concerned her ever since she met the woman.

Her mother tutted loudly. 'Just because that cheating ex of yours slept around doesn't mean David will.'

Olivia winced at the memory. She'd rather not go there.

'Do you have any evidence David's having an affair?' Sonia said. 'Other than this woman being knockout gorgeous and five years younger than you? Because that's proof of nothing, in my opinion.'

Always so direct, my mother, Olivia thought. 'No. But he talks about her. A lot.'

'From what you've said, their desks are next to each other. They work on the same projects. Of course he mentions her. Listen, darling, I realise I'm stating the obvious, but a baby won't happen while the two of you live under different roofs.'

'Do you think I don't know that?' Frustration seeped into Olivia's voice.

'Of course. But sometimes you act first, think later. The way I see it, you moved out too fast. Like I said, you should have worked it through together.'

Olivia tamped down her resentment. Her mum was only saying what she herself had thought a hundred times. Too quick to walk away, rent the first available flat, all because her pride was hurt. Now Olivia hadn't a clue how to mend her marriage.

'David will come round, given time,' Sonia said. 'After all, he's told you he wants children. Just not yet.'

'But when, Mum? He always puts his career first. Sometimes I think it means more to him than I do.' Olivia brushed away a tear.

Sonia shook her head. 'No way. I've seen the way he looks at you, darling.'

Olivia huffed in exasperation. 'Love isn't everything. I always pictured myself as a mum by the time I hit thirty. The way you were.'

To her surprise, a shadow crossed her mother's face. 'You've plenty of time for that. Back off for a while. Give David some space.'

Olivia's mental hackles shot skyward. 'I'm not being unreasonable, Mum. All I'm trying to do is get him to discuss the issue, but he won't. I can't help thinking Tiffany Cook's the reason.'

'If you want my advice—'

'Oh, here we go.' Olivia pursed her mouth tight. She choked back the words bubbling in her throat. *Presumptuous, interfering...*

Sonia continued as if her daughter hadn't spoken. 'Stop piling pressure onto him. David's got enough on his plate as it is.'

Olivia's anger flared higher. 'Why do you always take his side?'

'I don't! But you need to remember he's chasing a major promotion. His efforts will support both your art therapy practice *and* a family.'

Their conversation exploded into a full-blown argument. The second Sonia said, 'Don't be so sensitive', Olivia jumped to her feet.

'You're so bloody patronising,' she yelled. 'Sometimes I hate you.' Tears stung her eyes as she flounced out the front door.

Now, lying in bed, her mother dead, Olivia despised herself. How stupid, how childish, were the words she'd flung at her mother. Impossible now to retract them. Olivia had no idea how to cope with the guilt.

Or how to forgive herself.

In her head, she turned over what Kirsten might say. 'You're too hard on yourself. People argue. Say stuff they later regret. Doesn't mean they don't love each other.'

Logic told Olivia her friend would be right. She couldn't shake her nagging sense of shame, however.

*****

Olivia spent the days that followed in a fog of self-recrimination. On the fourth day, she'd arrived home early from work, and was sitting with her feet tucked under her on the sofa, memories of her mum running through her head, when her phone trilled. An unknown number was on the screen. Olivia often ignored such intrusions, wary of scam calls, but her grief was causing her to operate on autopilot. 'Hello?' she said, once she'd accepted the call.

'Is that Mrs Olivia Gilchrist?' A female voice, unfamiliar. Some damn telemarketer, Olivia decided.

'Yes, but now isn't a good time—'

'My name's Primrose Batehup,' the woman said. 'I'm calling from Avon Coroner's Office.' A pause. Then: 'I have the results of the post-mortem enquiry into your mother's death.'

Olivia shrank into the depths of her sofa, her grip tight around her mobile phone. 'Go on.'

Primrose cleared her throat. 'The medical examiner has concluded that Sonia Harding died from drowning. Due to the head injuries she sustained following her fall into the river at Vassals Park.'

All the saliva drained from Olivia's mouth. 'Drowning?'

'Yes.'

'So it wasn't—' She moistened her dry lips. 'Her heart condition?'

'No. Mrs Harding suffered a subdural haematoma—that's bleeding in the brain cavity—but my colleague found no evidence of a cardiac arrest prior to the accident.'

Olivia didn't respond. The world made no sense anymore.

'No further enquiries or examinations are deemed necessary,' Primrose continued. 'I'm very sorry for your loss, Mrs Gilchrist.' The woman went on to give some practical details about funeral arrangements, to which Olivia barely listened.

'Can I—' She swallowed back a sob. 'Can I get a copy of the post-mortem report, please? I did request one by email a few days ago.'

'Yes, I have your message on my screen, Mrs Gilchrist. I must advise you that the details can be distressing for relatives to read.'

'A friend of mine is a doctor. She can help me understand the report.'

'Then yes, if you wish, I'll arrange that for you.'

*****

A thick A4-sized envelope landed on Olivia's doormat two days after Primrose Batehup's call. She realised what it was the second she picked it up. Now it lay, malevolent and ugly, on her coffee table. Perhaps this was a mistake.

'You don't have to open it if you decide not to,' Kirsten said.

Olivia's eyes swept over her best friend's face: her pale skin, the freckles sprinkled over her nose. Such a comfort Kirsten had been since that dark day the police arrived on her doorstep.

She set her glass of water on the carpet beside the sofa. 'I can't believe she's gone, Kirst. She was only sixty, for God's sake.'

Kirsten squeezed Olivia's arm. 'I'm so sorry, Liv. Want me to read the report?'

'Please. I can't bear to do it myself.' Olivia handed the envelope to Kirsten. Now it had arrived, she hated the idea of seeing in black and white how her mother had died. She'd already been told about the blow to Sonia's head that caused her to drown, so what difference would the post-mortem findings make? Nothing mattered anymore. Her beloved mother was dead, yet the world continued to turn, uncaring.

Kirsten's fingers ripped open the envelope. She swigged a gulp of coffee, then pulled out the report. Muttered words came from her as she read. *Algae marks on soles of shoes consistent with loss of balance… no indications of foul play…*

A frown puckered Kirsten's forehead. She took another swig of coffee, her eyes darting across the paper. Her fingers shook as she set down the report and met Olivia's gaze.

'What's the matter?' Olivia asked. Kirsten's face had paled, worry etched across it. Her frown had deepened.

Her friend sucked in a deep breath. She jabbed a finger at the report. 'This makes no sense.'

'What? Mum died from drowning, right? Due to her head injury.'

'Yes. The cause of death isn't in doubt. But—'

Grief had stripped Olivia's nerves bare, making her blunt. 'For God's sake, Kirst. Just spit it out.'

'Okay. Here goes. Can I ask—as far as you're aware, were you adopted?'

Shock hit Olivia. She swallowed hard. What on earth was Kirsten driving at?

'Of course not.' Her tone was sharp. 'Mum and Dad would have told me. Sonia Harding gave birth to me. She's—' Too late, she remembered. 'She was my biological mother. Why are you asking?'

She watched Kirsten chew her lower lip. Her friend was clearly struggling to find the right words.

'Because,' she said, 'the post-mortem examination has revealed Sonia never had a child.'

CHAPTER 3

Olivia marched into the reception area of the coroner's office the following day. Her call to Primrose Batehup earlier had warned the woman Olivia expected answers. An apology. That she'd be making a formal complaint.

'Please, Mrs Gilchrist,' Primrose had said on the phone that morning. 'Let me contact the doctor who performed the post-mortem, so he can address your concerns. Just give me some time. Can you do that for me, please?' With reluctance, Olivia agreed. Now here she was, mouth set tight, shoulders squared, anger flaring in her eyes.

Primrose Batehup looked up, spotted Olivia. Her cheeks flushed a dull red when Olivia revealed her name and why she was there. 'I'm sorry, Mrs Gilchrist. I've triple-checked with the pathologist and there's been no error. The post-mortem findings are accurate.'

Olivia clenched her fists. Such incompetence was inexcusable. 'Well, check a fourth time, because I'm telling you now—someone screwed up. Isn't it bad enough that I'm grieving the death of my mother? Now you have the nerve to tell me—' She dragged in a deep breath. 'This is bullshit. Mum deserves better. So do I.'

Primrose got up, moved around her desk. 'Let's sit down,' she said, gesturing towards a pair of armchairs. Not waiting for an answer, she directed Olivia towards the nearest, then seated herself in the other one.

'I realise this is difficult for you,' Primrose said. 'I take it neither of your parents ever said anything about you being adopted? I'm sorry. That must sound like a stupid question. Of course they didn't. That's why this is such a shock.'

Shock didn't even begin to describe it. Olivia couldn't—wouldn't—entertain the idea. If Sonia and Harry Harding weren't her biological parents, why did they never tell her?

She scrambled to her feet. 'You're wrong. Give me a couple of hours, and I'll bring you proof. Like my birth certificate. There's also the physical resemblance. I have my mother's dark hair, my father's height. This has all been a terrible mistake.'

She watched sympathy flash into Primrose's face. The woman laid a hand on Olivia's arm. 'I know how hard this can be.' Her tone was gentle, conciliatory. 'Believe me, I do. I myself was adopted—'

'Don't you dare patronise me.' Olivia's words were fireballs of anger. 'You have no idea what I'm feeling right now. *You* may have been adopted, but I sure as hell wasn't. Like I said, I'll prove it.'

*****

Back home, Olivia went straight to the concertina file in her bedroom where she kept important documents: insurance policies, copies of bills, etc. In it, she was certain, she would locate her birth certificate.

As she did. She knew what she'd find on it, because of course she'd seen the words before. Mother: Sonia Jane Harding. Father: Harold John

Harding. Nothing indicated the certificate was anything but an original document. Olivia had no idea what happened in cases of adopted children, but she presumed their birth certificates would be amended somehow.

In her hands she held proof the pathologist had made a terrible mistake. Olivia needed more, though. She wanted to stand before Primrose Batehup and tell her she'd turned her mother's house upside down and found no trace of adoption papers. Only then would the nagging voice inside her be silenced.

Olivia hated how, ever since her conversation with Primrose, a bubble of doubt, dark and horrible, had mushroomed in her gut. The woman was right; Olivia's complaint would have sparked a thorough check of the findings. Yet the coroner's office was standing by the pathologist's report. That could only mean one thing. The results of the post-mortem were correct.

But how could that be? It made no sense. If it was true, Olivia's world as she knew it would cease to spin, crumble into dust.

She pictured her mother's belly. Smooth, with no puckers or stretch marks. Olivia had seen it every time the two of them sunbathed.

'Just lucky, I guess,' her mother had always said, with a laugh, before changing the subject. Olivia had always believed her; why wouldn't she? Sonia, like Olivia, was slim; she probably didn't gain much weight during pregnancy. Besides, there were oils women could rub into their bellies to prevent stretch marks, right? Their occurrence wasn't guaranteed. Also, Olivia had been a small baby. Another possible reason for her mother's lack of stretch marks.

'You were so impatient to be born, darling,' Sonia had often told her. 'Such an easy delivery. You slid out so quickly, and I was happier than I'd ever dreamed possible. My sweet baby girl, the daughter I'd yearned for, and oh, so beautiful.'

That was the explanation, then. A straightforward pregnancy and birth, meaning her mother's body recovered fast and showed little evidence. Even pathologists got it wrong sometimes.

She grabbed her jacket and keys, then headed out of her flat, hurrying to her car. Her mother's house was close by; Olivia drove the short distance and parked outside. She stared at the peeling paint, the sagging gutters, her childhood home sadly neglected since Harry's accident.

You can do this, she told herself, a bunch of keys clasped in her hand. Her heart heavy, she selected two of them and turned them in their locks. She pushed open the front door and stepped into the hallway.

A stale smell greeted her; the house had gained a shut-in odour already. Olivia walked into the kitchen, deposited her handbag on the table, and opened a window. Then she gathered her courage once more before heading upstairs. She stopped in front of her mother's bedroom. Her father's too, when he lived here. She pushed open the door and glanced around.

The bed was neatly made, her mother's reading glasses perched atop a book on the bedside table. A glass of water stood nearby. Sonia's pyjamas and dressing gown lay folded on one pillow. Her mum could walk in any minute, as though she never left. A whiff of perfume teased Olivia's nostrils: *Obsession* by Calvin Klein. Olivia closed her eyes, breathing her mother in; for a few wonderful, glorious seconds it was as if Sonia Harding still lived.

In a corner of the room stood a filing cabinet. In it Olivia was sure she'd find her mother's will. She tugged open the first drawer. Inside, hanging files were arranged in alphabetical order, each with a descriptive tab at the top. Olivia's fingers rifled through them until she came to the last section, marked 'will'. A thick document lay within. Olivia pulled it out, setting it aside. She'd deal with it later.

She tugged open the second drawer. A plastic tray, divided into sections, containing stationery: pens, rulers, rubber bands. Olivia shut the drawer and opened the third and final one. Tears clouding her eyes once more, she extracted a bundle of papers. Childish finger paintings, all familiar to Olivia. Throughout her childhood they'd decorated the fridge downstairs, her mother reluctant to remove them even when Olivia reached adulthood. She'd only capitulated two years ago when Harry, prior to his accident, fitted a new kitchen.

Olivia ran her fingers over the chalky paint, tears in her eyes. She glanced at the rest of the drawer's contents, her heart tight with grief. Sonia's love surrounded her, all warm and comforting. For a moment she remained motionless, awash in memories.

When she opened her eyes, she stared at her past. Tiny knitted bootees, a pink cardigan, a miniature hair brush, gazed back. Olivia lifted them out, the wool soft against her fingers, and set them on the desk. Underneath lay more baby clothes, all neatly folded. At the bottom of the drawer was a manila envelope, bearing Olivia's name in her mother's handwriting. Her mouth went dry. Could this be it? Proof that she was adopted, which meant her parents had lied her entire life?

She pulled out the contents of the envelope: a red booklet, the words 'my personal child health record' on the cover. Olivia perched on the bed and skimmed through the book. Four tabs split it into sections, the back three covering immunisations, screenings and growth records.

She started with the first, labelled 'child, family and birth details.' From what she could see, the book was given to her mother before she left Bristol's Southmead Hospital's maternity unit. Someone had spilt coffee over the pages and parts were illegible, including Sonia's date of discharge. As far as she could tell, her mother had a normal vaginal birth, no complications, apart from a few stitches. Olivia frowned. That didn't gel with what Sonia had told her, but maybe she'd glossed over any unpleasant details.

Relief flooded Olivia. She'd take the red book, along with her birth certificate, to show Primrose Batehup tomorrow; she'd also insist that a different pathologist should examine her mother's body. Fury sparked through Olivia's veins again.

Okay, she understood people made mistakes, but surely not with something so important?

*****

Olivia thrust her birth certificate under Primrose Batehup's nose the next day, her finger jabbing the paper. 'Look. Here's your proof. Backed up by what you'll find in the red book. Sonia Harding gave birth to me thirty years ago in Southmead Hospital. Whoever performed my mother's post-mortem is an incompetent fool.'

The other woman studied Olivia's birth certificate, then switched her attention to the red book. 'I see what you mean,' she said, her brow furrowed. 'Do you mind if I keep these for a short while, please? I'll get this checked out and come back to you as soon as possible.'

Olivia nodded. Not that anything could change the awful finality of her mum's death. The coroner needed the correct facts, however. It mattered to Olivia as well; that stupid pathologist had turned her world upside-down. She couldn't, for her own peace of mind, allow anyone to claim Sonia wasn't her mother.

*****

The following day, Olivia closed her eyes, leaning back in her chair at the therapy centre where she rented a room. It had been a challenging morning.

Her mobile rang, disturbing the stillness, the sound echoing from the depths of her handbag. Olivia pulled it out, noting the name on the screen:

Primrose Batehup. With an apology, no doubt, and about time.

'Olivia Gilchrist speaking,' she said.

'Hello, Mrs Gilchrist,' Primrose replied. 'Is now convenient to talk?'

'Sure.' She readied herself for the words she was convinced she'd hear. *So sorry... terrible mistake...*

Instead, Primrose continued, 'Would it be possible for you to come into the office? It's concerning the documents you dropped off yesterday.'

The woman must have believed an in-person apology was appropriate. Olivia promised her she'd go straight there after her last client; she needed to collect her birth certificate and the red book anyway. Once the call ended, she reflected on the cautious note she'd detected in Primrose's voice. Embarrassment at the pathologist's incompetence, most likely. Well, she'd listen to the woman, accept the inevitable apology and leave it at that. Somehow, God only knew how, she'd get through her mother's funeral, then try to make sense of a world without Sonia Harding.

CHAPTER 4

Shock hit Olivia like a knife in her chest as a tide of panic rose within her. 'No way. There must be some mistake.'

'I'm sorry,' Primrose Batehup said, with a quick glance at the man seated beside her. She'd already introduced him as Mark Dare, the pathologist who performed Sonia's post-mortem examination. The three of them were sitting around a table at the coroner's office.

'I don't understand,' Olivia said. 'How is this possible? I showed you my birth certificate, the red book. Don't they prove that Sonia Harding gave birth to me?'

Mark Dare cleared his throat. 'I get what you're saying. But a different pathologist has reviewed the results of the post-mortem. There's no getting around the facts, I'm afraid. The woman you identified as your mother never bore a child.'

'How can you—or the other pathologist—be so sure?'

'Giving birth leaves evidence. On the cervix, for example. It stretches considerably to allow a baby to be born, which means it looks different in women who haven't experienced childbirth.'

Olivia remained silent, unable to wrap her head around Mark's words.

'That's ridiculous,' she insisted, a tremor in her voice. 'You've seen my birth certificate. The red book. Both list Mum as my mother. I've checked her paperwork, and found nothing to suggest I was adopted. The only explanation is that I am my mother's daughter.' She mentioned her low birth weight, how her mother had a very short labour.

Primrose Batehup shifted in her seat. 'There's been no mistake, Mrs Gilchrist. The post-mortem findings are accurate.'

Sod her, Olivia thought. Primrose wasn't the one who'd been lied to her entire life, if the report was correct. She didn't dare allow herself to contemplate the implications. Time for that later, once she was alone.

Mark Dare spoke. 'May I suggest a possible explanation?'

Olivia glared at him. 'Go on.'

'That Sonia and Harry Harding adopted you, then destroyed the paperwork. For some reason they chose not to tell you the truth.'

'But why do such a thing?' Olivia remembered the child she was desperate to conceive with David. 'Suppose some inherited illness exists in my birth family? What then?'

Mark shifted in his seat. 'I realise how hard this must be for you. There's a second possibility.'

'Which is?'

'Sometimes adoptions aren't always done through legal channels.'

Olivia stared at him. 'What are you implying?'

'For whatever reason—age, financial problems, for example—a couple might decide they wouldn't be accepted as adoptive parents. So they flout the system.'

'How?'

'Baby trafficking is a genuine issue, Mrs Gilchrist. People can, and do, buy children.'

Olivia shook her head, appalled. 'My parents weren't *criminals*. Why would they buy a child? The idea is ridiculous. And what about my birth certificate? The red baby book?'

Empathy softened the man's features. 'Documents can be forged, Mrs Gilchrist.'

'I don't understand.' Olivia's voice rose high, spiralled around the room. 'Any adoption agency would have welcomed them as parents. They were both thirty, so not too old. Dad had a well-paid job, and so did Mum. Why would they choose the illegal route?'

From the silence that ensued, she deduced neither Mark Dare nor Primrose Batehup could answer that question.

*****

Back in her flat, Olivia opened a bottle of Malbec, poured herself a glass and swallowed the wine in three gulps. She turned Mark Dare's words over in her head. Impossible to dismiss either possibility he'd suggested, given that two pathologists insisted Sonia Harding had never borne a child.

A realisation, so awful she could barely contemplate it, sneaked into her brain. If she was adopted, Harry Harding wasn't her father. She'd lost not just her mum but the man who'd raised her as well.

'No,' Olivia whispered. It couldn't be true. Harry Harding was her father. Wasn't he?

She had his height, mouth, jawline. Mightn't her mum and dad have chosen a child based on its parents' physical characteristics, though? One likely to grow up to resemble Harry and Sonia? But why destroy the paperwork? What reason could they have had to lie?

Olivia had no idea. It seemed the most feasible explanation, however. To hell with Mark Dare's suggestion of an illegal adoption. Her parents would never, ever, have bought a baby.

Shame washed over Olivia. Even if Harry Harding wasn't her biological dad, he was all the family she had left apart from her aunt Isobel, and it had been too long since she'd last visited him. In normal circumstances, she'd see him several times a week. Sonia's death, however, the post-mortem report, the funeral arrangements—with all *that* going on, Olivia hadn't been able to face Harry. To see him so broken, so unlike his former self—her heart would split in two. She couldn't leave it any longer, though.

I'll visit him first thing tomorrow, Olivia decided. She hadn't any clients booked in, so why not?

In the meantime, she needed to call Kirsten.

'Can you come over? Tonight?' Olivia's palm was damp with sweat against her mobile.

'Will pizza or curry be involved? Along with wine and beer?' Then: 'You sound really upset. Is it about your mum?'

'Something weird's happened.' Olivia's voice snagged on the last syllable. She steeled herself, forcing back the tears. If she cried, she might never stop.

'I'll be there in half an hour. With food.' The line went dead. Typical of Kirsten.

Relief poured through Olivia. She stared at her phone. A text pinged through; glancing at the screen, she could see it was from David. Olivia ignored it. She couldn't deal with her husband, or her marriage, just then.

Not long after, her doorbell buzzed. Olivia opened the door and Kirsten pushed past her, carrying a plastic bag exuding a rich curry smell. She dumped the bag on the floor, then turned to Olivia. 'Come here, babe. You look like you've seen your own ghost.' As her friend's arms hugged her, Olivia allowed herself, for a few seconds, to forget all the madness. To be Sonia's daughter again, her mother alive, their awful argument forgotten. The nightmare of the post-mortem report something that never happened.

'So what's up?' Kirsten said, as she peeled herself off Olivia. 'Is this about your mum's death?'

'Kind of. Not directly.'

'You've got me intrigued.' Kirsten retrieved the bag of curry and headed for the kitchen, Olivia close behind. 'You'll feel better with some food inside you. We'll talk after we've eaten, and you can get whatever's bugging you off your chest.' Her friend grabbed two plates from the cupboard and dished rice onto them. She spooned chicken tikka masala on top, then handed one plate to Olivia, eyeing her with a critical gaze. 'You've lost weight, babe. You're looking pale, too. It's only natural that you miss her; so do I. Sonia was like a second mum to me.'

'I wish—' Olivia wiped a tear from her eye. 'That I could ask her to explain.'

Kirsten quirked an eyebrow. 'What, exactly?'

'Let's sit down.' Olivia led Kirsten into the living room and sat on the sofa, her plate of curry on the coffee table. The spicy aroma would normally have proved irresistible, but not tonight. She was wound so tight that her stomach clenched at the thought of food.

Kirsten sat opposite Olivia, her meal on her lap. She forked curry into her mouth, her gaze on her friend.

'I was so convinced the post-mortem report was a mistake,' Olivia said.

Kirsten's fork halted on its way to her lips. She laid it on her plate, which she placed beside her on the sofa. 'You're telling me it wasn't? You didn't get an apology, an explanation?'

'No. The woman at the coroner's office and the pathologist are adamant it's accurate. That can mean only one thing. I was adopted.'

'Oh, babe.' Kirsten sounded shocked. 'I don't understand. Why did your parents never tell you?'

Olivia shook her head. 'No idea. I can hardly ask Dad for answers, can I?'

'If you're right, a record of it must exist somewhere.' Kirsten grabbed her phone. Olivia watched her friend while she tapped at the screen. A minute later, Kirsten frowned. 'Damn. Can you believe this? The UK doesn't have a centralised adoption register.'

'Really?' Olivia felt her hopes deflate.

'Nope. But you can ask the General Register Office to search for adoption records.'

'I'll do that, then. Can you give me your phone, please?'

Olivia skimmed through the information on Kirsten's mobile, then set up an account and password. The results would be mailed the next working day after the request was made, provided that was before four p.m., and if Olivia paid for priority dispatch. Four o'clock was long gone, but Olivia couldn't help that. She'd done all she could for now.

*****

Olivia visited her father the next day at the nursing home where he'd lived since his accident. Guilt stabbed her again when she remembered how long it had been since she last saw him.

'How is he today?' she asked Maria, the chief nurse, after she'd signed in.

'Not good. He seems agitated, distressed, but we're not sure why. But he gets that way sometimes, as you know.'

Olivia did. Most of the time Harry Harding appeared happy enough, until the dark days, a product of his accident, struck. When they did, he became morose, sitting for hours staring out of the window, tears in his eyes. On those occasions Olivia preferred to leave him alone. It was plain he didn't want company, and to see her father that way hurt too much. She'd rather remember the smiling, loving man he'd once been.

She became aware Maria was waiting for a response. 'Something's happened. Can we talk somewhere private?'

Olivia followed Maria into a side room. Once the other woman sat opposite her, she braced herself for the usual effusive condolences after she'd told her about Sonia's death.

To her relief, Maria uttered a brief, 'Sorry for your loss', then addressed Olivia's primary concern. 'I don't think we should tell Harry his wife has died.'

'That's what I thought. But I can't help feeling he has a right to know.'

Maria shook her head. 'He lacks the capacity to understand. It will only distress him further.'

'Won't he miss her, though?' Sonia used to visit her husband every day. Her absence probably explained Harry Harding's current low mood. 'What should I do if he tries to say her name?'

'Tell him she'll be in to see him soon. He won't realise it's not the truth.'

Maria was right. Since his accident, Harry had suffered both retrograde and anterograde amnesia, meaning that he struggled to form fresh memories and had lost many of his old ones. He appeared to live mostly in the present, content to gaze at the flowers outside his window, happy when his wife and daughter visited, although Olivia suspected he sometimes didn't remember who they were. A strangled 'Son…' or 'Liv…', said with a wide smile, showed when he recognised them. Olivia's father found it difficult to speak, due to the accident. He was lucky to be alive, but Olivia often wondered whether she could call his existence living.

'I'll go see him now,' she said.

'I'll be in my office if you need me,' Maria replied.

Olivia made her way down the corridor, the smell of disinfectant strong in her nostrils, towards her father's room. The door was open, the sun streaming through the windows. Harry occupied a recliner beside the French doors, which opened onto a lawn fringed with rose and honeysuckle trellises. His back was to her; all Olivia could see were his hands gripping the recliner's armrests.

She pulled up a chair next to him. 'Hi, Dad.' Her voice was bright with false cheer.

Her father turned to stare at her. His expression was shuttered, withdrawn. Seconds passed.

Harry opened his mouth, but only garbled syllables emerged. Then a flash of clarity. 'L… Liv…'

His smile brightened Olivia's heart. 'Yes, Dad, it's me. How are you today?'

More strangled sounds. 'S…Son…'

Her father clearly yearned for his wife, and Olivia couldn't help herself. The words came, despite Maria's advice. 'I'm sorry, Dad, but I have the most awful news.' She braced herself for what was to come. 'Mum's dead.' When he didn't respond, she continued, 'She died in a tragic accident. I miss her so much.' Tears streamed down her cheeks; she grasped her father's hand. His fingers gripped hers back; she stared into Harry's face, trying to gauge his emotions.

'Son... No...' His eyes were wet with grief. His flesh trembled against hers. On some deep level she sensed he understood her devastation, and matched it with his own. How could he not? They'd both loved Sonia so much, and for so long.

Olivia fumbled in her handbag for a tissue, then wiped her face, blew her nose. With a second tissue, she dabbed at her father's tears. He'd fallen silent, staring at her; Olivia wondered if he'd ever smile again. Despite the circumstances, she felt as close to Harry as she'd always been. In every way that mattered, he was still her father. They sat in silence for a long while, gazing at the roses outside. Sonia's favourite flower.

*****

Olivia found an envelope marked 'General Register Office' on her mat when she arrived home from work the next day. She tore it open eagerly, only to find a single sheet of paper. Its words dashed her fragile hopes into tiny pieces. *Regret to inform you... no records relating to the adoption of Olivia Rose Harding... if we can be of any further help...*

She'd been so sure. Only one option remained. As Mark Dare had suggested, her adoption must have taken place below the radar. That meant discovering the truth would be much harder. Maybe even impossible.

She still had no idea why her parents would have resorted to such a measure. It made no sense.

Olivia wiped away a tear. She'd never felt more helpless. Or alone.

*****

'Sorry to impose,' Olivia said later, as she cradled her steaming mug of coffee. 'I just need some company.' Kirsten was in London for a wedding; Olivia was reluctant to call David, so five minutes ago she'd knocked on Elena's door. She'd already decided not to divulge the post-mortem findings to her neighbour; the horror of them was still too raw. Likewise with the letter from the General Register Office.

A smile from Elena. 'Happy to help. You can come down whenever you like.' She leaned forward in her seat. 'The move from London to Bristol hasn't been easy. I get lonely at times. So you're doing me a favour.' Elena had already told Olivia the gist of her situation: recently widowed, no children. How she was renting the flat below Olivia's while she searched for a house to buy in Bristol, the city where she was born.

'We haven't known each other long, but I can talk to you,' Olivia said. 'We're both hurting. Both lost someone we loved.'

'It's worse for you, I think. Yes, Peter and I were married for twenty-two years. He was a good husband—kind, faithful, loving. He got colon cancer in his fifties, though; I nursed him the best I could, but he succumbed anyway. By the time he died, we'd grown apart; I was more of a nurse than a wife. Whereas you—' She smiled, and for a moment Olivia didn't see sadness in her eyes. Only compassion. 'You were close to your mother, weren't you?'

Olivia choked back a sob. 'She was my rock. I could talk to her about anything. Boys, sex, all the usual girlie stuff.'

When Elena didn't reply, Olivia shot her a glance. 'I hope I'm not treading on sensitive ground. You told me once—' Olivia cleared her throat. 'That you didn't have children with your husband.'

Elena placed her empty mug on the coffee table, her gaze averted. Her hand shook as she did so. 'You're right. We didn't have kids.'

Olivia noticed Elena's voice sounded strained. Had she unintentionally upset her friend? Before she could apologise, Elena spoke. 'Do you need me to do anything? Funeral arrangements, that kind of thing.' Her cheeks flushed. 'Sorry. I'm not trying to intrude. Just help.'

Olivia was touched by the other woman's solicitude. 'I'd rather deal with it all myself, if you don't mind. But thanks for the offer.' She took a sip of coffee. 'I've already booked the funeral. Might be best to consult a solicitor pretty sharpish about Mum's will, too.'

'She made a will? That's good. So many people don't.'

'Mum always believed her heart issues might mean she died early.' Grief squeezed Olivia's chest. 'She drew up a new will after Dad's accident, the one that caused his brain damage.' She glanced at Elena, shocked to see her neighbour's face had grown pale. 'What's wrong? You don't look well.'

'Nothing. I'm fine. You said your father suffered a head injury?'

Time to be honest about her father's accident. So far, when Elena had enquired about him, Olivia had deflected her questions, reluctant to go into painful details. 'Yes. A drunk driver crashed into Dad's side of their car, spun it across the road and into an oncoming lorry. Mum was okay apart from bruises and several cracked ribs, whereas Dad—' Olivia's voice trembled. 'He survived, but needed intensive care and a long time to recuperate. Parts of his brain sustained permanent damage. His memory, both short and long-term, is shot to pieces.'

'Oh, Olivia. I'm so sorry.' Elena's face was still chalk-white, her expression strained. 'That's tragic. He was such a lovely man.'

Olivia was taken aback. 'You make it sound like you once knew him.'

'Did I? Silly me.' Elena shook her head. 'From the way you spoke about him, it's obvious you love him. That's all I meant.'

Her neighbour's choice of words still seemed odd, but Olivia let it pass. 'He'll need permanent care for the rest of his life. Luckily, Dad received a large insurance pay-out after the accident, and Mum left him well provided for in her will.'

Olivia's phone trilled with an incoming call. David's name appeared on the screen. She swiped a finger to reject the call.

'Your husband?' Elena asked.

Olivia nodded. 'Yes. I've asked him to give me space, but he still contacts me a lot. He probably wants to ask about the funeral arrangements.'

'Is there a chance you'll get back together? Oh, God, that's none of my business. Sorry.' Elena looked so mortified that Olivia couldn't find it in herself to be annoyed.

''Don't get me wrong,' she said. 'I miss David. I just can't deal with him right now.'

Elena reached out a hand to grip Olivia's arm. 'Give it time. You're grieving. If David loves you, he'll understand.'

CHAPTER 5

A cold, damp day at Canford Crematorium. Olivia hurried from her car towards the building to avoid the drizzle. She was early, but a small group of people were already huddled under the porch. Olivia spotted David among those gathered. She managed a smile as she approached her husband.

David stepped forward and drew her into an embrace. At first Olivia was reluctant, mindful of the shaky state of their marriage, but knew she needed the comfort. She pressed her head against his chest, breathing in the warmth and safety he offered. 'I miss her, David. So much.'

'So do I, Livvy. It's hard to believe she's gone.' He pulled back to stare at her. 'You don't look well, sweetheart.' He traced the darkness under Olivia's eyes, his fingers gentle, tenderness in his gaze.

Olivia turned away, afraid his compassion might break her. 'I'm okay. It's just—' She waved a hand towards the crematorium. 'Well, you know.'

David drew her into his arms again. 'Yeah. I do.' He pressed a kiss into her hair. 'We should be together, Livvy. Not apart. Especially at a time like this.'

'Don't, David. Not here. Not now.' The ghosts of old arguments about babies and Tiffany Cook hovered in the air between them. To her relief, her husband didn't persist. Instead he released his hold on her, and the loss pained Olivia more than she'd ever admit.

The double doors of the crematorium swung open, and a man emerged. Olivia recognised him as being from the funeral company she'd engaged. Relief passed over his face when he spotted her. 'Mrs Gilchrist? We're ready now. If you'd like to follow me?'

Once inside, Olivia made her way to the front row of seats and sat down, David beside her. Over the next few minutes the room filled until there was standing room only. No surprise there. Her mother had been—*was*—much loved.

Somehow she made it through the service without crying. Unable to bear the thought of making small talk about her mother over canapés, she'd not arranged a wake.

Afterwards, outside again in the cold and damp, David gripped her arm as she walked to her car. Olivia realised what he intended to say before the words left his mouth. 'Call me,' he said, his tone urgent. 'Please, Livvy. You don't have to go through this alone.'

'I need time.' Hurt flashed into David's eyes, but Olivia steeled herself, unwilling to give him false hope. All she wanted was to mourn her mother and discover the truth about her birth.

She realised she was being unfair to her husband. He had no idea what the post-mortem had revealed; Olivia hadn't found the courage to tell him. In an instant, the rock of pain in her gut melted, and she smiled at him. How selfish of her to keep her grief to herself. She wasn't the only one hurting. So was David.

'Coffee?' she enquired.

His expression lifted. 'That little cafe in Westbury-on-Trym? Bean Feast, right? The one with the wacky artwork?'

'Sure. See you in there.' Olivia walked away, wondering what she'd done, but it was too late to change her mind. Seeing David had made her realise how much she'd missed him, however. The strength of his arms, the smell of his shampoo, the warmth of his body. Perhaps hope existed for their marriage, if she could persuade him to become a parent. Not to mention banish the spectre of Tiffany bloody Cook. Her mother had certainly thought Olivia was making a fuss about nothing over *that*. Maybe it was time to take the first step towards reconciliation. Besides, she needed to tell him about the post-mortem results.

Five minutes later she parked her car outside Bean Feast. She spotted David at a table near the window, a steaming mug in front of him. As she pushed open the door, twin odours of coffee and baked goods assaulted her nostrils. She slid onto the chair opposite her husband, a smile on her face.

'It's good to see you again,' she said. 'Even if it is under difficult circumstances.'

David reached across the table to take her hand. 'Can I get you anything? Cappuccino, espresso?'

Olivia shook her head. Coffee was the last thing on her mind. 'How are you holding up? I know how much you loved her.'

He shrugged. 'Your mother's the first person I care about that I've lost. Guess I should count myself lucky, huh?' He drew in a breath. 'It's weird. I always thought grief was linear. Like, it starts off bad, then diminishes over time, all in a nice straight tidy line. But it's not like that. Not at all.'

He was right. Some days Olivia awoke to sunshine streaming through her curtains, and she'd have a good day. Other times pain sliced her like a ragged shard of glass the moment she opened her eyes, and cut ever deeper until sleep closed them.

'There's something I should tell you,' she said. 'About Mum.'

'What? Fire away.'

Olivia sucked in a deep breath. She told him the post-mortem results, how the pathologist stood by his findings. 'I don't understand any of it,' Olivia finished, a sob blocking her throat. 'My birth certificate states she's my mother. I've not found any trace of adoption papers. Besides, if I was adopted, why didn't Mum and Dad tell me? Why the secrecy?'

David's fingers squeezed tighter around her hand. 'Have you thought of contacting a tracing agency?'

Olivia stared at him, thunderstruck. She hadn't considered that possibility.

'I had a mate in college who learned after his parents' death that they'd adopted him,' David continued. 'The discovery hit him like an express train; he drank like a fish for weeks. Once he'd got over the shock, he contacted one of those agencies. And ended up reconnecting with his birth mother.'

'But what information can I provide? If my birth certificate shows Sonia Harding's my mother?'

David shook his head. 'No idea, Livvy. But it's a start.' Her heart contracted at the tenderness in his tone. 'I can't imagine what you're going through.

To discover you're not Sonia's daughter has to hurt like hell. That's why I suggested you dig further. But, Livvy—' His expression grew sombre. 'Just remember you may not like what you find. Whatever circumstances led your birth mother to give you up, they probably weren't pretty.'

Olivia's gut clenched with dread. David was right. Was she prepared to deal with whatever she might encounter?

The answer was yes. Because she had to. She had no choice. Better to uncover the truth than to languish in doubt and ignorance.

'Listen, Livvy.' David's voice shook her from her thoughts. 'The house is too big, too empty, without you. Come home, sweetheart. We'll work things out. Together.'

Olivia sat back in her seat, breaking the contact between them. Love for her husband washed over her; pain pricked her heart at what she was about to say. 'I can't, David. Not right now.'

'Then when?'

'I don't know. Just give me time, okay?' She dropped her gaze. 'Besides, it's not just Mum's death that's bothering me.'

David didn't respond, but his eyes revealed his hurt. His fingers played with a sachet of sugar. 'You still think I cheated on you.'

'Can you blame me? With that damn Tiffany Cook always on the scene—'

'I work with the woman, Olivia.' His voice had turned steely. 'She's a colleague, nothing more. One I like and respect, but that's as far as it goes. I've told you this a million times, but you refuse to listen.'

'That's because—'

'Because your ex-boyfriend slept around, while swearing you were his one and only. Yeah, that sucks. But don't you dare tar me with the same brush.' He stabbed an angry finger towards Olivia. '*He* might be a cheating bastard, but I'm not.'

Olivia didn't respond at first. 'I want to trust you,' she eventually managed. 'But it's hard. Matthew promised again and again that he'd change, and like a fool I believed him.'

'You're punishing me for that dickhead's mistakes. How is that fair?'

David was right, of course. The wounds inflicted by Olivia's ex ran deep, however.

'You've no reason to be jealous. Come home, Livvy. Please.'

Panic stabbed through her. She'd lose David if she didn't make their marriage a priority, but how could she? First, she had to find herself.

'I can't. Not yet. It's not just about Tiffany Cook. We also split up because I want children, whereas you—' Olivia swallowed hard. 'I can't discuss kids, not while I've no idea who I am. I need to discover my roots, where I came from. My birth mother, if possible. Give me time. That's all I ask.'

David's gaze slid onto his coffee cup. 'Fine. But don't leave it too long, Livvy.'

'I won't.' An uneasy silence settled around them, and Olivia sensed the conversation was over. For now.

'I'll see you soon,' she said, once they were outside Bean Feast.

Olivia drove to her flat, parked up and switched off the engine. Instead of going inside, she sat in her car, gathering her thoughts. She'd worry about David later. Right now, on the day of her mother's funeral, Sonia was all she could think of.

How do I move on from this, she wondered. Her mum's death weighed on her each second of every day, along with a nagging sense of abandonment. Sonia Harding had been a fantastic parent, yet they didn't share any genes. Then who had given birth to her? Handed her over for adoption?

She had no answer. David's suggestion of using a tracing agency was sound. She knew she'd do it. It was just a question of when.

With a sigh, Olivia pulled her car key from the ignition and stepped outside. Minutes later she was in her flat. A quick bite to eat, then she'd check if Elena was free for a chat.

Olivia headed to the kitchen, about to open her freezer, when voices reached her from the flat below. They sounded angry, although she couldn't discern the words. One was Elena's, the other male. Olivia listened, unsure what to do. Whoever was with Elena didn't seem friendly.

A door crashed back on its hinges. Heavy footsteps thudded in the stairwell, getting ever fainter as they headed towards the exit. Olivia hurried downstairs, only to find Elena's door wide open. A gasp of horror escaped her as she ran into the living room.

Elena lay crumpled like a rag doll on the floor, her limbs at weird angles, her skirt rucked up around her waist. Her face was pale and sweaty, her eyes closed. A pool of blood had seeped from her head, staining the carpet an ugly red. The corner of the coffee table was also bloodied.

'Oh, my God. Elena, can you hear me?' Olivia felt for a pulse at her friend's neck. To her relief, she found one, strong and steady. She ran upstairs to retrieve her phone, cursing the fact she had no idea whether Elena's flat had a landline. Her fingers shook as she stabbed 999 into the keypad. 'Ambulance, please,' she said, once the operator responded.

Paramedics would, she was told, attend as soon as possible. Olivia rushed downstairs and into Elena's bathroom, where she grabbed a towel and placed it under her friend's head. Smears of blood marred the white fabric, but the wound was no longer bleeding. Elena's eyes fluttered open, her gaze vacant and unfocused. Unintelligible sounds issued from her mouth.

'Shush. You're going to be okay, Elena. Everything will be all right.' Except that Olivia had no idea whether that was true. Where the hell was the ambulance? Why hadn't the paramedics arrived?

Elena's eyelids drifted shut again, and she fell silent. Olivia noticed a whiff of body odour tainting the air. Not from Elena, who always smelled of soap and shampoo. Must be from the unknown guy. Who was he? What the hell happened here?

She knelt beside Elena, her hands reaching to pull down her friend's skirt, when her attention was caught by Elena's stomach. Thick silver lines radiated across her belly either side of her navel. The flesh was loose and puckered. Olivia stared in confusion at the stretch marks. What she was seeing were, most likely, the remnants of pregnancy. But how could that be? Hadn't Elena claimed to be childless?

At that moment she heard footsteps climbing the stairs, accompanied by voices. The ambulance must have arrived. Olivia dashed to the front door. 'Hurry,' she said, pointing to the living room. 'She's in there.'

Events after that merged into a blur. The paramedics, one male, one female, went about their business with quiet efficiency.

'Best to get her checked out in hospital,' the man said. 'That's a nasty head wound.'

Olivia rode in the ambulance with Elena, her thoughts a mess as she clutched her friend's hand. A prayer played repeatedly in her head. *Please let Elena be okay.*

At the Bristol Royal Infirmary, hospital staff whisked Elena out of sight; Olivia sank into a chair, exhaustion overwhelming her. She couldn't do this alone. With shaking fingers, she pulled her phone from her bag and walked outside into the late afternoon air. David. She needed David.

He answered straightaway. 'Hey, sweetheart, what's up?'

He didn't hesitate once Olivia told him. 'I'll be there right away.'

Olivia returned to the reception area to sink back on her chair. Thank God for her husband; he hadn't let her down, even though David had never met Elena.

Fifteen minutes later he hurried into the entrance lobby, his eyes roaming the busy space. Olivia ran towards him, tears streaming down her cheeks; he threw his arms around her in a fierce hug. For a moment neither of them spoke.

David broke away. 'What happened?'

Olivia told him. 'I think she was attacked by the guy who was shouting at her. She must have hit her head on the coffee table on her way down.'

'You need to inform the police.'

'Of course. But right now Elena needs me.'

'I'll go make some enquiries. Someone, somewhere, will know how she's doing.' At that moment, a doctor approached them.

'Mrs Olivia Gilchrist? Elena Munro's emergency contact?'

Olivia nodded. 'Yes. How is she?'

'She's suffered a mild concussion. We're keeping her in overnight for observation. We'll do further tests and scans tomorrow, but, all being well, she should be able to go home afterwards.'

Thank God. 'Can I see her? Is she conscious?' Urgency threaded through Olivia's tone.

The doctor shook his head. 'Visiting hours are almost over. Besides, she needs to rest.'

*****

Later, once home, Olivia thought back to when she first met Elena Munro. Back then, she'd just moved into her flat. She'd only encountered a couple of her neighbours, and while they'd been polite, they hadn't wanted to chat. Elena proved different.

They became friends easily. Olivia, still in her pyjamas, was pottering in her kitchen when she heard furniture being moved in the flat below. It had stood empty throughout the short time Olivia had lived there; maybe she should say hello, introduce herself. She showered, got dressed, and went downstairs. As she neared the bottom step, a woman emerged from flat number three. Somewhere in her late fifties, perhaps early sixties. Greying hair cut into a bob, her expression strained.

When she didn't speak, Olivia took the initiative by stepping forward. 'Hi. My name's Olivia. I live in flat number four.'

A strange look stole across the woman's face, but she managed a smile. 'It's good to meet you. My name's Elena.'

'I take it you're moving into number three?'

Elena's gaze slid to the floor. She must be shy, Olivia thought. 'Yes. Perhaps you'd like to come in for a cup of coffee sometime? Once I've got everything sorted?'

'That would be lovely. Thank you.' Olivia had no idea how quickly her friendship with the older woman would blossom.

Later that evening she was curled up on her sofa, her heart heavy at the prospect of being alone; Kirsten was away at a medical conference. Elena's knock on the door saved Olivia from her solitude. 'I hope I'm not intruding,' her neighbour said, a bottle of wine in one hand, after Olivia invited her inside.

'Trust me—you're not.'

Elena left in the early hours of the next morning, a smile on her face and happiness in her eyes. 'Tonight's been wonderful,' she told Olivia. 'Let's do this again soon.'

After that, their friendship progressed rapidly. They shared a cup of coffee the next evening, and most days afterwards. When Olivia arrived home from work, Elena often opened her door to greet Olivia with a cheery, 'Fancy a brew?' It became a ritual, along with a bottle of wine at the weekends. Olivia told herself Elena was lonely, in need of company. So was she; despite the age gap, she loved being with Elena. Conversation between them mostly flowed like the wine they drank, and when it didn't a comfortable silence prevailed. They needed each other; it was simple as that.

Guilt sometimes nibbled at Olivia at the one-sided nature of their relationship. She'd spilled her guts to Elena about her marriage to David and her devastation at her mum's death. Elena, however, had revealed little about herself.

'My life hasn't been that interesting,' she'd said one evening. 'I grew up in Bristol, but spent years in London, married to Peter, working in one of his many jewellery shops. There's not much else to say, I'm afraid.'

'No kids?' Olivia regretted the question the instant Elena's expression grew shuttered. Perhaps Elena's husband hadn't wanted babies.

Elena shook her head. 'Peter and I never had children.'

'Were you and he unable to?' How insensitive. 'I'm sorry. I shouldn't have asked that.'

A closed-off look stole over Elena's face again. 'I would love to have been a mother. But it was not to be.' She cleared her throat. 'That reminds me. Can I ask you a favour?'

'Sure.'

'Would you be my ICE contact? If anything happens to me?'

For a second Olivia couldn't recall what the acronym signified. Then it clicked. 'You mean In Case of Emergency, right?'

'Yes. I don't have anyone else to ask.'

'Of course I will.'

'Thank you.' Elena reached into her handbag to pull out a pen. She rummaged through the contents some more and produced an old till receipt, which she gave to Olivia. 'Could you scribble your number on that, please? I'm not very good with technology. If I try to add you to my contacts in front of you, I'll get all flustered, and mess it up.'

Olivia repressed a smile. She jotted down her number, then handed the pen and scrap of paper back to Elena.

'Gosh, is that the time?' Elena said. 'I should go. Thanks for a lovely evening.'

Olivia stood up. 'You know you can talk to me, right? About anything.'

'Of course.' Elena's smile didn't quite reach her eyes. She's not like me, Olivia thought; Elena clearly preferred not to discuss being childless. She made a mental note to be more considerate in future.

CHAPTER 6

Olivia found little time to dwell on her friend the day after Elena's hospital admission. An unusually full schedule of clients left her barely time to think. She presumed the hospital must have discharged Elena by now; a shame she couldn't have driven her home, made sure she was okay.

To her surprise, her friend didn't greet her as usual when Olivia walked up the stairs after she'd finished work. Elena's door was open again. Through the gap Olivia heard whistling, then a muttered curse. Like before, the voice was male. Olivia froze. Was Elena in danger? Had her attacker returned?

She grabbed her phone in case she needed to call the police. More words reached her ears as she edged closer. 'Come on… pick up, damn you…'

To her relief, Olivia recognised the voice: their mutual landlord, Barry Price. Tension drained from her shoulders as she walked into Elena's flat.

'Hello?' she called. 'Barry? It's me, Olivia.'

Barry appeared in the doorway of Elena's kitchen, his mobile clamped to his ear. He didn't bother with preamble. 'Did you know about this? Have you spoken to her?'

Olivia stared at him. 'Know about what? What do you mean?'

'She's gone. Done a runner.' Barry's lips curled in contempt. 'At least her rent was paid up to date. And I can't find any damage.'

Olivia glanced around. Everything looked normal in Elena's kitchen: the fruit bowl piled high, a mug in the sink. Her gaze travelled to the living room, visible through the open door. A magazine on the coffee table. Elena's cardigan slung over the arm of the sofa. 'I don't understand,' she said.

'You heard me—she's upped and left. I got a text this afternoon, saying she won't be back. She's left all her stuff here, too. Clothes, books, everything. As you can see.'

Olivia couldn't believe what she was hearing. Thoughts ran through her head: the likely attack, the shouts she'd overheard. Was Elena too frightened to return to her flat? Olivia could understand that, but why the abrupt departure? Why leave all her things behind?

And—if she was her friend—why not tell Olivia?

She was still clutching her mobile in her hand, the screen dark. Once Olivia awakened it, she spotted a notification. A text she'd missed, from Elena.

Hi, Olivia. This will come as a surprise, but I'm returning to London, so we won't see each other again. I know this leaves Barry in the lurch, so could you do me a favour, please? I've taken what I need, so can you pack up the stuff I've left? Keep anything you want and give the rest to a charity shop. All the best. X

The detached tone of the message stunned Olivia. She'd been wrong; this woman wasn't her friend. Elena must have returned home after her discharge from hospital. And didn't wait around to tell Olivia in person. *We won't see each other again... could you do me a favour... all the best.*

Friends didn't say goodbye so casually. After all their cosy evenings together, Olivia only merited a text, and a cold, impersonal one. She knew she shouldn't care, but she did.

Barry strode back into the hallway. He waved a hand towards the kitchen. 'If you want any food, take it. As to the rest of her stuff, she said in her text you'd sort it.'

Olivia bristled at Elena's presumption that she'd help. She would, however.

'Yes. This weekend.' There seemed nothing else to say.

Once Olivia was upstairs in her flat, she curled up on her sofa, her knees hugged to her chest. How could she have misjudged Elena so badly?

She picked up her mobile and composed a quick text. *You could at least have said goodbye in person.*

Olivia waited, but didn't get a response. Well, screw Elena. She was better off without her.

*****

It wasn't until later, after Olivia had eaten a reheated lasagne, that she remembered what she saw as Elena lay on her living room floor. The stretch marks on her abdomen, the puckered flesh. Had Elena lied about not having children?

Her words drifted into Olivia's brain, as clear as the day Elena said them. *Peter and I never had children... I would love to have been a mother. But it was not to be...*

Olivia couldn't fathom a reason for Elena to deny having given birth. There seemed no reason to lie.

The irony didn't escape Olivia. Sonia Harding had been a devoted mother, claiming Olivia as her own, yet that proved false. Now here was Elena, adamant she hadn't borne children, but her stretch marks and crinkled belly indicated otherwise. Or perhaps she'd just lost a lot of weight.

Olivia decided it didn't matter either way. She'd pack up Elena Munro's stuff, then forget her.

*****

Olivia set to work boxing up Elena's possessions the following Saturday. She began in the kitchen, transporting any usable food up to her own flat. Next came the bathroom. Inside the wall cabinet she found, tucked behind a bottle of aspirin, a packet labelled 'Cipramil 20mg', along with Elena's name. Olivia had no idea what the medication was for and didn't care. She tossed the packet into a rubbish bag, along with the aspirin.

Elena's living room came next. It was sparsely furnished apart from a few ornaments, the pictures on the walls, several books and DVDs on the shelves. Soon Olivia had filled two storage boxes, and the one containing the books was especially weighty. Pulling out her mobile, she sent David, whom she'd already informed of her neighbour's defection, a quick text. *I'm at Elena's place, boxing everything up. Some of the stuff is too heavy for me to move. Any chance you could lend a hand?*

Another immediate response. *Sure. But only if you buy me a drink afterwards.* Followed by *:-)*.

Olivia smiled. Yes, she could manage that.

She glanced at her watch. She'd been working for less than an hour; the only area that remained was the bedroom. She shot David a quick text. *Come over at seven. We'll load up your car, then go to that new wine bar in town. Does that sound good?*

Sure does, David replied.

Olivia took the remaining storage boxes and opened the door to Elena's bedroom. She folded and packed Elena's clothes, then cleared out her chest of drawers. Two boxes, one large, one small, were stacked inside the wardrobe; Olivia decided to leave those for last. She removed more arty prints from the walls, filled another storage container with books and knickknacks, and stripped the bed. Then she eyed the two boxes still in the wardrobe.

Olivia leaned in to grasp the top one. To her relief it weighed almost nothing, and she slung it on the mattress. Then she pulled the other box towards her, its bottom sliding over the wooden floor of the wardrobe. Olivia knelt down, placed her arms around it, and lifted.

To her horror the base gave way. The box was one of those cheap self-assembly cardboard jobs, in poor condition, and held together with packing tape. Several sketches and watercolour paintings now lay strewn across the carpet.

Olivia ran upstairs to her flat and grabbed scissors and a roll of duct tape, intending to make good the damage. Back in Elena's bedroom, she repaired the box, then turned to the mess on the floor, picking up the sketch closest to hand, clearly done by a talented artist. Her gaze travelled over the pencilled lines, which depicted a ruined building with an archway in the middle. Under its curve lay a bleeding heart, transfixed by a dagger. Next to it was a baby, naked and alone. The initials MB were in the lower right-hand corner. Olivia flicked through the rest of the pictures. Each contained the ruined building, the archway, the heart. All had the initials MB.

Olivia was all too familiar with the anguish that seeped from every pencil line, each brush stroke. She'd seen it all too often with her art therapy clients.

She straightened up, rubbing her back. Only then did she notice the sole painting still hanging on the wall, and moved nearer to examine it. It was a finished version of the sketches, also signed with the initials MB. The emotion, though, was ten times deeper. Olivia shivered. Who was MB, and what was their connection to Elena?

Most likely she'd never know. Olivia replaced the sketches and paintings back in the box, which she put in a storage container. She removed the painting from the wall and placed it on top of the other artwork. As she did so, she noticed an envelope lying in the bottom of the wardrobe underneath where the boxes had been. She reached in to get it, and froze.

On the front was her maiden name, Olivia Rose Harding. Not in Elena's handwriting, but one that was all too familiar. Her eyes traced over every loop and whorl. She'd seen it on countless birthday and Christmas cards, shopping lists, etc. It belonged to Harry Harding.

Olivia stood in Elena's bedroom, not moving, the envelope clutched in her hand. Underneath her fingers she detected a small bulge; whatever was inside wasn't a letter, or even paper. The envelope was unsealed. She stared at her father's handwriting, unable to fathom what this meant.

Her mouth grew parched with fear. So long as she didn't look inside, her world would remain the same. When she did, everything might change, and Olivia had no idea whether she was ready.

Time ticked by on Elena's bedside clock. Still Olivia hesitated.

Then, her fingers trembling, she pulled the flap free and drew out the contents. She stared at what lay in her palm.

A curl of baby hair, tied at the blunt end with a small pink ribbon. Given that Olivia's name was on the envelope, it must be hers, but why did Elena Munro have it in her possession?

Her neighbour's abrupt departure, the lock of hair—none of this made any sense.

Olivia picked up the second, smaller box and hesitated, her fingers poised to flip off the lid. She presumed that was where the envelope had come from, and she knew she had to return it there. To do so would expose herself to what might lie inside, however. Please God, no more shocks.

She perched on Elena's bed and pulled herself up so that her shoulders rested against the headboard. The box sat on her thighs, the envelope still in her hand. Olivia leaned her head back and closed her eyes. She wondered whether she should call David and tell him to come over right away. Nope, not a good idea. She needed time to process what she'd discovered.

Olivia reached for her phone and tapped out a quick text. *Taking longer than I thought to box everything up. Not sure I'll finish here tonight. I'll call you to rearrange that drink.*

His reply pinged through almost immediately. *Shame. Was looking forward to seeing you.*

Olivia moistened her dry lips. She set the envelope containing the lock of hair down on the bare mattress. Then, after pulling in a deep breath, she opened the box.

The contents were sparse, just one envelope. Unlike the other one, this had been sealed, but slit open along the top. Inside was a letter, which Olivia pulled out. A jolt of shock ran through her as she flipped it open and recognised, for a second time, her father's handwriting.

I never intended to hurt you. Some relationships are not meant to be, and while I will always be grateful for what you've done, I can never love you the way you want. So take care of yourself, and be happy.

Harry

Olivia read the words over and over, trying to make sense of them. The letter wasn't dated or addressed to anyone, yet Elena must have been the recipient, surely? Olivia recalled the other woman's words: *He was such a lovely man.* Despite Elena's denial, she'd clearly once known Harry. A one-sided infatuation with him before he married Sonia, perhaps?

That didn't explain Olivia's baby hair being in her wardrobe, however.

A thought edged into Olivia's mind. She recalled the way Elena sought her out, seemed eager to establish a friendship. Was it mere coincidence that she'd moved into the flat below, or did the woman have a hidden motive?

Might Elena—Olivia gasped at the idea—be her biological mother?

Impossible to get the notion out of her head. The post-mortem results, Elena's stretch marks, the lock of hair...

But why leave so abruptly? Send Olivia such a cold, impersonal text?

It didn't take long for Olivia to decide she was being stupid. Clutching at straws in her desperation for answers. How foolish of her. Of course Elena wasn't her mother.

She replaced the letter back in the box and closed the lid. Her brain felt like a steel hand was wringing it dry of emotion; she couldn't deal with this. Olivia grabbed the box of paintings, locked the door of Elena's flat behind her and went upstairs. She dumped the box in her living room, then put on her shoes and coat. She exited the building and walked without caring where she was going. Hands thrust in her pocket, she meandered from street to street, her thoughts a mess. It wasn't as if she could ask Elena the answer. Her brain concentrated on one thing: her lingering suspicion that she might be Elena Munro's daughter.

The facts pointed that way. Much as she was reluctant to admit it, Olivia now accepted that Sonia Harding didn't give birth to her. Whereas Elena had lied about not having a child and possessed a lock of Olivia's hair, along with a letter from Harry Harding. Olivia couldn't escape the growing conviction that Elena was her biological mother.

The wind ruffled her hair and blew cold against her cheeks. It was now seven o'clock, and while the evening was still light, a noticeable chill had settled in the air.

A terrible thought occurred to her. Olivia was born eight years after Sonia and Harry Harding's wedding. If Elena was her mother, then Harry had cheated on Sonia. But how could that be? Her parents' relationship always seemed rock solid. Did nobody stay faithful anymore?

Harry's letter indicated Elena was once in love with him, though; Olivia might be the result of a quick fling. Then, for whatever reason, Elena chose not to keep her daughter, but allowed her to be brought up by the man she loved. An undercover adoption, none of it documented.

Even that didn't answer all her questions. What about Olivia's birth certificate? The red book? Both recorded Sonia, not Elena, as Olivia's birth mother.

Mark Dare's words drifted back to her. *Documents can be forged, Mrs Gilchrist.*

It all proved too much. Tears filled Olivia's eyes and spilled down her cheeks. Why did her father cheat on the woman he adored? Why hadn't Elena wanted her daughter? Olivia's world had tilted on its axis; nothing would ever be the same again.

David. She needed her husband. Olivia wiped her eyes, and walked home.

CHAPTER 7

David came over straightaway after Olivia's frantic phone call. His arms were warm and strong around her as they sat on her sofa; Olivia rested her head on his shoulder while her grief poured forth. 'I can't believe any of this. If I hadn't found that letter, the lock of hair, I wouldn't have known. Elena Munro is my mother. She has to be.'

David pulled her closer. 'It seems that way, yes. Have you decided what you're going to do? Is there anyone you could ask to find out the truth?'

'No.' Her father was an impossibility, although Olivia knew she'd try anyway. 'Apart from my aunt Isobel, but we're not close.'

Her husband eased himself away, but kept one arm around her. 'You look exhausted, Livvy. Why don't you get some rest?' He stood up, pulling Olivia to her feet. 'I could stay with you. Just for tonight.'

Olivia was tempted. With so much weighing on her mind, she knew sleep wouldn't come without a struggle. Whereas if David was beside her—it was possible she might forget, for a few hours, the devastating discovery she'd made.

'I'll need to get up early tomorrow, though,' David said. 'Work's hectic right now, and Tiffany and I—'

'Tiffany and you *what*?' That bloody woman again, right when she and David were making headway with their relationship. Well, she wouldn't stand for it.

'For Christ's sake, Olivia.' David's jaw was tight with tension. 'You know I collaborate with her on various projects. I'll say it again. She's a colleague, nothing more.'

'I want to believe you. But—'

'Your ex cheated on you. I get it, I really do. You have to move past that, though. Learn to trust me.'

Before she could reply, he continued, 'Because if you can't, our marriage won't survive. How would *you* feel, being constantly accused of something you haven't done?'

He was right, of course. Either she had faith in him, or divorce was on the cards. Olivia's heart lurched at the awful thought.

'I love you, Livvy.' To her relief, David's tone was gentle again. 'Let me stay tonight. Please?'

Temptation almost overwhelmed Olivia, before common sense prevailed. The truce she was forging with her husband was fragile, and liable to crack under pressure. David staying the night, the two of them making love—that would imply reconciliation, but Olivia still harboured doubts over Tiffany Cook. Then there was all the weirdness over her birth mother. She shook her head. 'I love you too. But it's too soon. I need time. And space.'

A hint of frustration crossed his face. 'I understand. My patience has a limit, however. Don't stretch it too far.' He picked up his jacket and car keys. 'I'll call you tomorrow.' A brief hug, then he was gone.

Olivia called Kirsten to update her, then took a shower and brushed her teeth. Time for bed. Contrary to her expectations, within ten minutes she was asleep.

*****

Olivia wrapped up work early the next afternoon, then headed for her father's nursing home. 'How is he?' she asked Maria after she walked through the door.

'You're in luck. He's having a good day.'

Harry Harding's gaze turned to his daughter as she entered his room, and recognition dawned in his eyes. Olivia smiled at him. She'd already persuaded herself she'd jumped to the wrong conclusion. Harry couldn't have been unfaithful to the wife he adored. Didn't the letter prove his indifference to Elena, rather than his love?

'Hi, Dad,' she said, pulling up an armchair. Harry's chair was in front of the patio doors. The morning sun highlighted the sag of his jowls. He appeared older every time she visited, and hurt stabbed her.

'Li… Li…' Her father's smile soothed away Olivia's pain. She chatted with him about her art therapy business, Kirsten, the weather, careful to avoid any mention of David or Sonia. Olivia remained undecided about whether to broach the subject of her birth, aware Harry might get distressed or not understand. In the end, she decided it was worth a shot.

Olivia drew her chair closer and took hold of her father's right hand. 'Dad,' she said. 'You know I love you. So much. And I have something to ask you.' Their usual code would have to suffice. 'Remember, it's one squeeze for yes, two for no.'

His smile grew wider. Encouraged, she plucked up her courage.

'I don't want you to get upset, Dad, but I need to know. Was I adopted?'

She waited, her heart heavy in her chest. The smile faded from her father's face. Distress lurked in his eyes. His hand lay slack in hers. The double squeeze she'd hoped for didn't come.

'Is… Is…' A blob of drool hovered on his lips. Olivia was unsure what he meant—her aunt Isobel, perhaps? Or was Harry attempting a sentence?

Olivia squeezed his arm. 'It's okay, Dad. Forget I said anything. Doesn't that honeysuckle look gorgeous?'

Her father refused to be deflected. 'Is…' he repeated. Then: 'Cam… camer…'

Olivia strained to hear what he was saying. Another syllable followed the 'er', but it was mumbled, unintelligible. Then the answer clicked into place in Olivia's head. Before his accident, her father had been a keen amateur photographer. The word he was searching for was 'camera'.

How did that help her, though?

'Cam… Li…' Her father's strangled attempts at speech sounded anguished. Were those tears in his eyes? Guilt stabbed Olivia; she should never have asked. Time to put this right.

She adopted her best and brightest smile. 'Everything's fine, okay? There's nothing for you to worry about.'

He stayed silent, but the tension ebbed from his face. 'Camer…' he repeated, his voice trailing away, before his eyelids closed. Soon his soft snoring filled the room.

Olivia stood up, leaned over to kiss his forehead. 'I love you, Dad,' she whispered, even though Harry couldn't hear.

In her car, she sat behind the wheel, thinking things through. Harry must have retreated to his memories of photography, his distress in some way attributable to that. Olivia started the engine and drove away. She'd get his camera to take with her on her next visit. Her father couldn't use it, of course, but seeing it might make him happy.

It had also given Olivia an idea. The walls of her childhood home were lined with framed photos: Olivia as a baby, growing up, her parents at various events. What if she compiled them into an album? Gave him something he could browse through while enjoying the happy memories the photos evoked?

Olivia pulled into the driveway, retrieved her key and entered her parents' house. Harry had used the smallest bedroom as an office, with his photographic equipment in boxes on shelving. She located his favourite camera and set it aside. While she was here, she might as well collect all the photos. Later, she'd call her aunt Isobel. Perhaps Izzy would provide some answers.

*****

Once she'd eaten, Olivia gathered her courage to phone the woman she'd only met three times, and not for several years. Izzy was younger by a decade than Sonia and somewhat of a mystery. She was night to Sonia's day, her life a mix of drugs, booze and travel, her rucksack always packed and ready for Izzy to fly somewhere new. Right then she lived in Rome, but that could change at any time. No wonder the sisters never got on. Sonia, with her insistence on routine, planning and order, annoyed the hell out of Izzy, and the antipathy was mutual.

Olivia grabbed her mobile and placed the call. Her aunt answered straightaway. 'Hey, doll! How are you?'

To Olivia's relief, Izzy's voice wasn't thick with alcohol. That was unusual, but Izzy had been the same during their last conversation, when Olivia phoned her about Sonia's death. They made small talk for a while; Olivia learned her aunt was clean and sober, had a place in a halfway house, and worked part-time at a local art gallery.

'I have to ask you something,' she said when a suitable lull in the conversation presented itself. 'I need the truth, please. Was I adopted?'

A sharp intake of breath reached her ear. 'Of course you weren't. Why on earth would you ask?'

'You're sure?'

'Yes. I recall Sonia phoning to tell me she was pregnant. We'd not spoken for ages, and I remember how delighted she sounded. I was in France. Paris, to be exact. There was this exhibition…'

'Aunt Izzy.' Her aunt could reminisce for hours if Olivia didn't cut her short. 'What about when I was born?'

'Harry called me two weeks after the birth. I wondered at the delay, but I guess parenthood must be hectic, especially with a newborn. He told me how beautiful you were. He had such pride in his voice.'

'Did you speak with Mum?'

'I'm not sure. It's a long time ago. What's all this about?'

Olivia told her about the post-mortem report. 'I thought at first they'd made a terrible mistake. But they didn't.'

'It makes no sense,' Izzy said. Olivia could tell she'd shocked her aunt. 'Why would Sonia lie?'

'I've no idea. Does the name Elena Munro mean anything to you?'

'No. Should it?' A pause. 'Who is this woman?'

'She may be my birth mother.' Olivia told her aunt about Elena's stretch marks, the lock of baby hair.

'Can't you ask her? I realise it might be difficult, but—'

'She's disappeared. Moved out, isn't replying to my texts.'

'Oh, sweetie.' The empathy in her aunt's voice brought tears to Olivia's eyes. 'Listen, I've no idea what to say. As far as I've always known, your mother had a normal pregnancy and birth. No question of adoption, not that I'm aware of. None of this makes sense.'

'Why hide the fact I was adopted? That's what I can't fathom.'

Silence for a while. Then: 'How much did Sonia tell you about her childhood?'

Olivia tried to recall. 'Not a lot. She didn't seem close to her mother, or her father, whereas I adored Granny Susan and Granddad Jack.'

'Our parents loved us,' Izzy said. 'They were always there when we needed them, but it was never enough for Sonia.'

Olivia wasn't surprised. Her mum, bless her, had been difficult at times. 'Why not?'

'I'm guessing she never told you. That she was adopted.'

Her aunt's words stunned Olivia. 'No. I had no idea.'

'Sonia didn't like to talk about it. She resented our parents because they weren't her biological ones. She hated me even more.'

'Why?'

'Because your Granny Susan was my birth mother, even if she wasn't Sonia's. Mum had fertility issues, hence Sonia's adoption. Then, when Sonia turned ten, Mum conceived naturally.' A sigh from Izzy. 'She always believed Mum loved me more. That wasn't true.'

Olivia stayed silent. She tried to imagine the bitterness Sonia must have felt. In the light of recent events, it wasn't hard to do.

'Did she ever try to find her biological mother?' she asked.

'Yes. It didn't go well.' Izzy cleared her throat. 'Turns out she was fifteen when Sonia was born. Her parents were drug addicts with a tendency towards violence. They cared more for their next fix than for their daughter. By the time Sonia tracked her mother down, the girl had taken the same path. Stick-thin, addicted to heroin. She yelled at Sonia to get lost and never come back.'

Olivia's heart ached for her mum, along with the woman who so cruelly rejected her own child. Hadn't Elena spurned her, albeit in less dramatic circumstances?

'Sonia suffered a breakdown afterwards,' Izzy continued. 'Dark moods dogged her for a long time. They worsened when her birth mother died from a massive overdose. Sonia had been keeping tabs on the woman from a distance.'

Olivia brushed away a tear. 'I had no idea.'

'That's Sonia for you. Seems she kept a lot of secrets. More than I'd realised.'

'Is that why she never told me I was adopted? Because she hated the fact she was adopted herself?'

Her aunt released a long breath. 'Perhaps. One thing I do know: she loved you very much. I can only assume she wanted to protect you from the same pain she suffered.'

'Wouldn't it be easier just to tell me the truth?'

'Try to see it from her point of view. Sonia always felt adoption carried a stigma. The woman—no, girl—who gave birth to her handed her over to strangers. Sonia never recovered from that early rejection.'

Olivia fell silent. Given her own hurt, she could empathise with her mother's pain. 'How come she also fooled you into believing she was pregnant?' she said at last.

'I was abroad, remember.' A sigh. 'I always found it sad that Sonia struggled to conceive. She never said anything, of course.'

'How did you find out?'

'Your father told me. I visited one time I was back home, hoping to patch things up between Sonia and me. She'd been crying, her face all red and blotchy. Harry took me aside and explained she'd got her period that morning. How they'd been trying for a child, but no luck. The doctors couldn't find any problem. That's why, when Sonia called to tell me she was pregnant, I was overjoyed. It seemed like a miracle.'

'Except it was all a lie.' Olivia could understand Sonia's reasons, but she was still hurting.

Fresh resolve flooded her. She needed to find Elena. Elena was the key to everything.

*****

Olivia sat on Elena's bed the next evening, wiping perspiration from her brow. All Elena's possessions had been boxed up, several storage containers now stacked against the wall. Barry had persuaded Olivia, via a cash incentive, to clean the flat for him. She was hot, sweaty and cranky, housework not being her natural forte. Time to wrap up here.

Olivia moved over to the window to open it, the smell of cleaning products strong in the room. She stood there for several minutes, sucking in gulps of fresh air and watching people in the street below.

Had any of their worlds had been shaken to the core, like hers had?

Don't complain, she chided herself. She had her health, her career and a husband who loved her. With any luck, they could repair their marriage.

Her stomach rumbled, reminding Olivia she'd not eaten that evening. She'd dig some food out of the freezer, open a bottle of wine, and watch trash television—what better way to unwind? As she turned to leave the room, however, something caught her eye.

Two shoeboxes, on top of the wardrobe, pushed towards the back. Even at this angle, Olivia could barely see them; it wasn't surprising she'd missed them before. With a sigh, she grabbed the chair from Elena's dressing table and positioned it in front of the wardrobe so she could stand on its seat. She dragged the first box towards her and lifted it down. Its surface was thick with dust, although someone had opened it recently, as evidenced by finger marks in the grime. Olivia seized a cloth and wiped it clean. Then she flipped open the lid. An envelope lay face down, its flap tucked inside. Olivia pulled it out, turned it over, and her breath hitched in her throat.

Her father's handwriting again. A name: Cameron James Harding. Along with a date, the same as Olivia's birthday.

No, no, no. She must be hallucinating, except that she wasn't. The lumpiness under her fingers betrayed the envelope's contents. Her hands shook as she opened it, already knowing what she'd find. A lock of baby hair, a shade darker than her own, this one bound with a blue ribbon.

All the oxygen whooshed from the room. An iron grip squeezed Olivia's lungs, the second shoebox now forgotten. She stared at the tiny curl of hair as though it might come alive.

Her recent visit to her father flashed into Olivia's head. She'd been mistaken; he wasn't asking for his camera. He'd never done so before, had he? No, he'd only mentioned it after Olivia brought up the subject of adoption. Somewhere in Harry Harding's damaged brain the memory of Cameron survived.

She was one of twins. Unknown to her, she had a brother, Cameron James Harding, and Olivia, stunned at the realisation, let the lock of hair fall to the floor, then sank to her knees beside it. Sobs welled inside her, almost causing her to choke. Hadn't she always longed for a sibling? But where was he, this Cameron James Harding?

Olivia placed the lock of hair in the envelope and set it back in the box. She walked into the bathroom, unwound some toilet roll and blew her nose, flushed the tissue and washed her hands. She returned to Elena's bedroom and found the storage box containing the letter from Harry Harding. Olivia read it through again. The letter hinted at a relationship, sure, but wasn't conclusive evidence that Harry was her father.

She ran through in her head what little she knew, or suspected. Twin babies, born to Elena, probably fathered by Harry Harding. Their mother, unable to cope, deciding on an undercover adoption.

Why the secrecy, though? And why split the twins up?

Perhaps her brother had died soon after birth. Or else Elena took Cameron for herself and gave her daughter to Harry and Sonia.

Olivia threw the letter back in the box and collapsed on the bed, huddled in a foetal ball. Would she ever uncover what happened thirty years ago?

*****

Too anguished to sleep that night, she tossed and turned in bed, the two envelopes of hair now in her bedside cabinet. At three o'clock, eyes gritty and temper rising, she reached for her phone. She was in no mood for politeness.

Are you my mother? Why didn't you tell me? Did I once have a twin brother?

She waited, although she knew Elena wouldn't reply. Her fingers tapped out more questions. *Is he alive? Do you know where he is?*

The silence from Olivia's mobile mocked her. She wondered whether Elena had deleted or blocked her number.

Nothing she could do about that. She'd assume the opposite, and keep texting the woman she believed was her mother, just in case.

You should have told me I had a twin. If he's alive, wherever he is, I'll find him.

She would, too. Cameron was out there somewhere, and Olivia was determined to track him down. Along the way she might rediscover Elena, and learn the reason for her abrupt departure. Although after the way the woman had behaved,

Olivia wasn't sure she wanted any future connection. What kind of person gave away her daughter, then returned decades later, only to abandon her a second time?

CHAPTER 8

Olivia nibbled a slice of toast the next morning, her eyes on her mobile phone. No response yet from Elena, but then Olivia hadn't been expecting one. A sob rose in her throat, matched by the acid in her gut. She and Sonia had had their issues, but Olivia had never doubted Sonia's love for the daughter she raised as her own. Elena, though? No, Olivia didn't see love in the woman's behaviour. Only selfishness.

She set down her toast, unable to stomach food. A glance at her oven clock told her it was eight minutes after ten on this damp Saturday morning, the rain on the kitchen window urging Olivia to crawl back to bed and sink into sleep.

The doorbell buzzed, startling her from her thoughts. For a second, she considered ignoring her caller; there was nobody she cared to see right now. What if it was Kirsten, though? Her friend didn't often drop by unannounced, but Olivia was reluctant to miss her if she had. She hauled herself to her feet, glad she'd bothered to shower and dress, and padded into the hallway.

When she pulled open the door, it wasn't Kirsten standing before her. A woman, probably in her late fifties, her brown-grey hair pulled into a loose topknot. Her expression was hesitant, yet full of… hope, perhaps? Olivia took in the white blouse teamed with blue linen trousers, both with crisp creases. A navy handbag, matching boat shoes, an expensive jacket. She'd never seen this person before.

For a second, neither of them spoke. Then: 'Hi. Um, this is awkward. Are you Olivia Gilchrist?'

Olivia nodded. 'Can I help you?'

'Yes. Well, I hope so.' The woman smiled, but it seemed forced. 'I realise you don't know me, but I'd prefer not to talk on your doorstep. Can I come in?'

Irritation prickled through Olivia. 'That depends. Who are you? What do you want?'

An awkward laugh. 'Sorry. I should have started with that. My name is Rebecca Brady.'

Olivia stared at the woman. 'Is that supposed to mean something to me?' She was aware her behaviour was rude, but didn't care. All she wanted was to crawl back to bed.

Olivia watched the woman's throat move as she swallowed. She was clutching her bag so tightly her knuckles were white. 'Did Elena never mention me?'

'No.'

Rebecca Brady stepped closer. 'I'm her sister.'

*****

Olivia handed her visitor a mug of coffee. She settled herself on the sofa opposite Rebecca, who was perched in an armchair, her eyes fixed on her host.

'Do you know where she is?' Olivia said.

'No. I was hoping you might. She talked about you a lot. That's why I'm here.'

Olivia's laugh was bitter. 'I can't help you. She texted me, telling she was moving out. Didn't say where she was going.'

Rebecca frowned. 'That's Elena for you. Blows hot, then cold. I'm guessing she acted all friendly at first, right?'

Tears pricked Olivia's eyes. 'Yes. She seemed lonely. Eager to talk, make friends with me. We got on so well. At least, I thought we did. But that text—it was hard, impersonal. Like we were strangers.'

'That's par for the course.' Rebecca set down her mug. 'Let me tell you about Elena. Would it surprise you to hear we're twins?'

Olivia couldn't see much physical similarity, and Rebecca looked younger, less careworn. It provided more evidence that Elena was her biological mother; twins clearly ran in the family.

'Not identical, of course,' Rebecca said. 'I favour our mother, whereas Elena takes after our father. We have very different personalities, too. My sister is, shall we say, unstable. One of the classic symptoms.'

'Of what?'

Rebecca chewed her lower lip, her expression uncertain. 'She's never been diagnosed. Refuses to admit there's a problem, won't see a doctor. I'm pretty certain, however, that Elena has borderline personality disorder.'

Not something Olivia knew much about, although she'd heard of it. 'What's that?'

The other woman shifted in her seat. 'Elena suffers from emotional instability. Her moods veer all over the place; high one day, down the next. Pretty tough to deal with, I can tell you. She's impulsive, dangerously so. Treats people terribly, too.'

'In what way?'

'It's all or nothing with Elena. Her relationships burn hot, until she pulls the plug on them.'

'What about her husband? She told me she was married for twenty-two years. His name was Peter. She moved from London to Bristol after his death.'

'Elena's never had a husband. If she claimed she did, she lied.'

Like she did about not having kids, Olivia thought. 'What causes borderline personality disorder? Is it inherited?'

'Some experts claim genetics play a part. Most say that childhood abuse often features. Our parents were good people, though. Nothing like that happened. I've no idea why Elena is the way she is. I've often wondered about the reason. And always come up with a blank.'

'That must have been tough on you.'

'I've tried to help her over the years. Urged her to get counselling, psychotherapy, whatever. Elena won't listen, just screams at me how I'm out to ruin her life.' She wiped her eyes with a tissue. 'But I'm not. I love my sister.'

For a moment there was silence. The question Olivia ached to ask throbbed through her head.

'I'm worried sick,' Rebecca continued. 'She'll contact me eventually, of course. She always does. In the meantime—God knows what might happen.'

'You say Elena's never been diagnosed. She's not on any medication, then?'

'Only for depression. She'll admit to that, but not to anything else.'

Olivia remembered the packet of Cipramil she'd found in Elena's bathroom. Antidepressants, according to Kirsten. 'How long? Before she gets in touch?'

Rebecca shrugged. 'Your guess is as good as mine. Might be a couple of weeks. Or she could leave me hanging for months. The longest has been two years.'

Fear stabbed deep into Olivia. Two years? Elena might not be anybody's idea of the perfect mother, but her mental state wasn't her fault. Olivia recalled the times they'd spent together, the closeness she'd felt with Elena. She needed to reconnect with her, talk with the woman who gave birth to her, ask her about Cameron. Understand why Elena handed her children over for adoption. Although, given what Rebecca had said, the reasons were easy to surmise.

Olivia dredged up her courage. The dread churning in her gut forced her gaze to the carpet. If she looked at Rebecca, her bravado might desert her. Her throat dry, she managed to say, 'There's something I have to ask you.'

'You can ask me anything,' Rebecca said. 'But first—may I hug you?'

Startled, Olivia could only nod. Rebecca crossed the floor to sit beside Olivia, then took her hand. Without a word, she pulled her into a stiff embrace. Olivia, her head on Rebecca's shoulder, stared at the carpet, her body rigid. The other woman's arms tightened around her until Olivia's lungs protested.

'I didn't dare hope—' Rebecca's voice was hoarse with emotion, her breath warm against Olivia's hair. 'Now here you are. All grown-up. So beautiful.'

I was right, thought Olivia. Elena was her biological mother, Rebecca her aunt. The key to Olivia reconnecting with Elena.

For a second, Sonia's face appeared in her mind, asking: *What about me?*

I'll always love you, Olivia answered in her head. *But Elena gave birth to me. To my twin brother, too. He's out there somewhere, and I need to find him.*

At last she found the words. 'Elena's my mother, isn't she?' Now she'd started, she couldn't stop. 'I found the locks of baby hair she kept. One from me, the other from Cameron. Do you know where he is? Why did she have us adopted? Please—'

Rebecca's body went rigid. The other woman pulled back, her face ashen. Olivia stared at her, unsure how to react.

A tremor rocked Rebecca's voice. 'You're wrong.'

'You mean Elena's not my mother?' Sour disappointment flooded Olivia. She'd been so sure.

'No. She's not.'

Tears trickled from Olivia's eyes. Rebecca's words had cast her adrift again. Made her roots a mystery once more. So who…?

'I am,' Rebecca said.

For a second Olivia didn't respond. She was frozen, unable to comprehend. 'What do you mean?' she managed at last, her voice a whisper.

Rebecca took Olivia's hands in hers. 'I've dreamed about this moment.'

'I don't understand.' Olivia was desperate to pull away from Rebecca's grasp but also never to let go. She swallowed a sob. 'You're my mother?'

Rebecca nodded. 'Yes. Yes, Olivia, I am.'

'But—'

'I realise this is a shock. I never meant you to find out this way.'

'So why—'

'I had it all planned. How I'd write you a letter, explain why I had you adopted. But Elena—'

'What does she have to do with this?'

'I'll tell you everything, I promise. I'm sorry it's taken so long.'

Olivia swallowed. 'Can I hold you? Please?

Rebecca disengaged her hands from Olivia's, her expression inscrutable. For a second she didn't reply. Then: 'Of course.'

Olivia pulled her into a hug. She allowed herself to sink into the embrace, let everything go. This was the woman who had given birth to her. The scent of Rebecca's hair drifted into her nostrils, and Olivia closed her eyes, breathing her in.

When Rebecca released her, a smile warmed the older woman's face. Once again it appeared a little forced. 'Thank you. My daughter in my arms again—it's all I ever wanted.'

'Tell me.' Olivia's voice cracked with emotion. 'Why did you have me adopted? Where's Cameron?'

Sadness crossed Rebecca's face. 'Oh, sweetheart. Let me explain. I was careless, and I got pregnant, and I was so scared. It's not just Elena who suffers from depression. The black dog's haunted me all my life, on and off.'

'You experienced postnatal blues?'

'Prenatal as well. My mind sank into a horrible place. Then I found out I was having twins. Fear overwhelmed me.'

'What about—' Olivia sucked in a breath. 'The father? Didn't he care?'

'No. Sorry, Olivia, but he wasn't a good man. When I told him I was pregnant, he yelled at me to get rid of the baby. He had no idea I was carrying two, of course.'

'What was his name?'

'Peter Munro.'

Olivia's head was spinning. 'That's the man Elena said she married. She claimed he owned a chain of jewellery shops.'

Rebecca shook her head. 'Like I said, Elena's never been married.'

'Tell me about my father. Please.'

'There's very little to say. He died in a knife fight before you were born.' Her voice was strangely detached.

Olivia was unable to reply. She'd hoped so much Harry Harding had fathered her, not some random stranger.

'After the birth I couldn't think straight,' Rebecca continued. 'I remember almost nothing about back then. My parents swooped in and took over. They arranged the adoption, not me. By the time the fog in my head cleared, my babies had gone.'

'But—' Olivia was confused. 'My birth certificate. On it, my mother's name is Sonia Harding, not yours. I searched everywhere, but didn't find any adoption papers. Everything is as it would be if I hadn't been adopted.' She recalled Mark Dare's words. *Documents can be forged, Mrs Gilchrist.*

'I wish I could tell you what happened, but I can't,' Rebecca said. 'All I know is that you went to a loving couple who would give you a wonderful life. My parents refused to say anything else.'

'Why not?'

'They were too worried about my mental health.'

'But what about Cameron? Why did your parents split us up? Do you know where he is?'

'Olivia—'

'I always wanted a brother or sister. So much.'

Rebecca grasped Olivia's hands. 'Listen to me, please—'

'He's out there somewhere. I'm going to find him.' Olivia was on a roll. 'I wonder if he looks like me? It'll be weird at first, meeting him, but—'

'Cameron is dead.'

The world ceased to spin, fell silent. Olivia, her mouth a slack 'O', stared at Rebecca. 'No,' she whispered.

'He died a few minutes after I gave birth to him,' Rebecca said. 'Cameron had heart and lung problems, was much smaller than you. He was too weak to survive.'

'No. He can't be dead.'

'His death spiralled me into hell. I couldn't eat, sleep, function. My parents had to have me sectioned in a mental hospital.'

First her mum, now her brother. Olivia was too numb to cry.

Rebecca squeezed Olivia's hands, then let them drop. 'I'll make us a cup of tea. I think we both need it.' She headed towards the kitchen.

Olivia listened as the other woman opened cupboards, clinked spoons into mugs. Her brain had frozen, except for one thought: *At least I've found my mother.* It brought little comfort. Cameron's loss cut too deep.

Minutes later Rebecca breezed back into the room carrying a tray, which she set on the floor. She handed Olivia a mug. Olivia set it on the side table. Too dark, too strong. Besides, she wasn't interested in tea. She had questions.

'I need to know,' she said. 'Those locks of hair. How come Elena had them if she's not my mother?'

Rebecca's smile held sadness. 'It's like I told you. My sister doesn't operate the way most of us do. People with borderline personality disorder display disturbed patterns of thinking; they twist the way they see the world to suit their delusions. Elena's a textbook case.'

'What do you mean?'

'She didn't give a damn about you, or your brother, or me after your birth. Too wrapped up in herself. Recently, though, she's become obsessed with motherhood, babies, kids. She had a child decades ago that she gave up for adoption, but later discovered she couldn't have any more.'

'Why not?'

Rebecca looked embarrassed. 'Elena slept around a lot in her twenties. Had numerous abortions. She ended up getting chlamydia, but didn't bother seeking treatment. By the time the symptoms got too painful to ignore, the infection had done significant damage. Her doctor told her it was unlikely she'd ever conceive. Just as well. I love my sister, but I don't always like her. She'd have been a disaster as a mother.'

'I still don't get it.'

'Elena convinced herself she'd given birth to you and your brother all those years ago, not me. She stole the locks of hair from me, refused to give them back. My most precious possession, all I had left of my babies, gone. She got angry, told me I was the delusional one, not her.' Rebecca wiped her eyes.

'I'm sorry.' The words seemed so inadequate.

'Where are they? The locks of hair?'

'In my bedroom. I'll go get them.' Olivia walked from the room.

From their hiding place in her bedside cabinet, she extracted the two envelopes. How she wished she'd had the chance to know her brother. His hair was all she had of him, and Olivia was reluctant to let it go. Rebecca's claim was greater than hers, though.

Back with Rebecca, she handed over the envelopes. The other woman opened Cameron's straightaway, her fingers rubbing the soft strands. 'It's so silky,' she said, wonder in her voice. Her expression radiated pure joy.

Hope sparked in Olivia. Rebecca would have proved a loving mother, given the chance. It wasn't too late, though. They could still forge a relationship, claw back some of what they'd lost.

'Elena stole this from me,' Rebecca said, still caressing Cameron's lock of hair. 'I'd like it back, please.'

'Take it. It's yours.'

Rebecca replaced the hair in its envelope, which she tucked inside her handbag. She didn't seem to have noticed the one containing Olivia's hair. Hurt stabbed Olivia. Don't be petty, she chided herself.

'You can have mine too,' she said.

Rebecca appeared startled, but soon collected herself. 'I'm sorry. If I'm more focused on Cameron's hair, it's because it's all I have of him.' She laid the other envelope on the coffee table. 'You and me, though—we have the chance for a fresh start.'

'Yes.' Something was puzzling Olivia. 'Why do the envelopes have Harry Harding's handwriting on them?'

'Who's Harry Harding?'

'The man who raised me, whom I still call Dad.'

Rebecca shook her head. 'No idea.'

'He also wrote Elena a letter. Well, I presume it was to her, although he didn't mention her name. Saying how he couldn't love her the way she wanted. What's that all about?'

'I wish I could tell you, but I can't. We'll probably never find out what happened.' Rebecca glanced at her watch. 'I should get going.'

'When will I see you again?'

'I'll call you. I'd give you my number, but I can never remember it. I'm hopeless with technology. I can manage texting, but that's it.' She laughed. 'I got yours, along with your address, from Elena's phone. She let slip something, you see. Made me suspect she'd tracked you down. How, I've no idea. Not that it matters. The moment you opened the door, I knew I'd found my daughter.'

'Call me now,' Olivia said. 'That way I'll have your number.'

Rebecca looked uncertain, but pulled out her phone and tapped the screen a few times. Olivia's mobile trilled from the coffee table.

'When will you ring me?'

'Soon. But promise me one thing. Well, two.'

'Of course. Anything.'

'Number one. If Elena contacts you, let me know. The second? Remember what I told you. She's mentally unstable, twists everything to suit herself. Whatever she says, don't believe it.'

CHAPTER 9

After Rebecca left, Olivia retreated to her bed, still fully clothed, and dragged the duvet over her head, the darkness a makeshift womb. Grief and elation battled inside her. A few weeks ago Olivia had believed herself the natural-born only child of Sonia and Harry Harding. Now she was Rebecca Brady's daughter, with a dead brother and biological father, and her aunt, Elena Munro, suffered from a personality disorder. Nothing would ever be the same again.

She wanted to cry for Cameron, but the part of her that was grieving for him felt numb. Figures drifted through her head: her birth weight of four pounds, two ounces, as recorded in the booklet found among Sonia's possessions. A healthy bouncing baby girl, if a little premature. In contrast, Rebecca had said Cameron was too small to survive. Olivia hated herself for that. She'd killed her own brother by stealing his nourishment in the womb.

Kirsten's voice floated into her head. Olivia could well imagine what her forthright friend would say; she realised she was being illogical but couldn't help it. She pictured Cameron as a male version of herself, taller, with similar eyes, the same smile, and pain seared her heart.

'I wish I could have known you,' she whispered into the dark.

The air under her duvet was hot, stale, but Olivia didn't care. Her thoughts turned to her biological father. Peter Munro didn't care about Rebecca, or his kids, so why should Olivia bother about him? Harry was her dad. They might not share any genes, but he was her father in every way that mattered.

Olivia's phone rang in the living room. Rebecca; it had to be. She tossed off the duvet and sprinted to get it, disappointed when she saw David's name on the screen. She let his call ring out, and he didn't leave a voice mail message. No problem. She'd catch up with him later.

Back under her duvet, she turned over in her head the meeting with her mother. Olivia realised their conversation had missed out so much: where Rebecca lived, her job, whether she was married, had other children. Olivia sat bolt upright, the duvet still hugging her shoulders. Perhaps she had half-brothers and sisters. Too caught up in her shock at Rebecca's revelations, she'd been too stunned to ask.

She would, though. The next time they met.

Doubt niggled in Olivia's gut. Something was bothering her about Rebecca. She ran through their conversation for what seemed the thousandth time before it hit her. Rebecca appeared chilly, remote, despite her initial display of affection. A little 'off' somehow. Shouldn't a woman meeting her long-lost daughter be more excited, happy? Even Rebecca's hugs seemed cold. As did her attitude towards her sister. Rebecca said she loved Elena, but her eyes had told a different story.

Perhaps that was understandable, given Elena's personality disorder. Rebecca must have struggled through tough times with her sister while battling her own demons, capped by Elena stealing the locks of hair. I need to cut her some slack, Olivia told herself.

What about Rebecca's attitude towards her daughter, though? Hurt stabbed Olivia at her biological mother's lack of warmth. Why take Cameron's hair but not hers? How come Rebecca didn't try to find Olivia herself? Instead she'd relied on Elena's efforts. And waited thirty years to do so.

I'll demand answers, Olivia decided. When we next meet up.

She struggled to sleep that night, falling into an uneasy doze after three o'clock. On waking she was groggy and irritable. Olivia trudged through work, her eyes and ears glued to her phone when she wasn't with clients. Every time it beeped, hope surged through her, only to be dashed.

Kirsten sent a text just after four o'clock that afternoon. *Hey, bestie. Not seen you for ages. Wanna go for curry tonight?*

Olivia hesitated, unsure. What if Rebecca got in touch? She'd phone later, surely?

She typed out a reply. *Can't make tonight. Tomorrow? I have some news.*

Within seconds, her phone pinged. *Raj Tandoori at 8? What news? Tease :-)*

Olivia smiled. She was certain Rebecca would be in touch later. *You'll have to wait :-)*

She got through the rest of the day on autopilot. That evening she tried to eat but her stomach rejected the idea of food; Olivia made do with a slice of toast and left half on her plate. She perched on the sofa, her eyes fixed on her phone. Ring, she willed it in her head.

She listened to the kitchen clock, audible through the open door, as it ticked the minutes away. Seven o'clock came and went. So did eight. Nine.

Olivia chewed her fingernails, her nerves strung tighter than trapeze wire. Why hadn't Rebecca called?

By half-past nine, she surrendered to temptation. With unsteady fingers, she tapped out a text. *Hi. Need to speak to you. Can we meet again? Please?*

Her mobile remained silent.

Give her time, Olivia persuaded herself. This couldn't be easy for Rebecca.

*****

By seven o'clock the following evening, Rebecca still hadn't called or texted. She knows where I live, Olivia told herself. Even if she'd lost her phone, she could still get in touch.

She'd talk to Kirsten later over their curry at Raj Tandoori. Her friend would know what to do.

Olivia took a shower, opened her wardrobe and selected whatever clothes were closest to hand. Just as she was pulling on an old T-shirt, her phone beeped. She tugged her top into place, then rushed to her bedside cabinet. A new message, the sender Rebecca. Elation flooded Olivia.

Seconds later she sank onto her bed, tears spilling from her eyes. With shaking hands she brushed them away. Her breath came sharp and shallow, heading towards panic. The hurtful words on her phone screen mocked her.

I don't think meeting up is a good idea.

Perhaps Rebecca needed time. Well, of course she did. Olivia waited until her breathing was under control, then typed out a text.

I understand if you don't want to right now. How about next week?

Minutes passed, each one a knife in Olivia's heart. Then: *It's too hard for me to see you. Too much time has passed. I can't be a mother to you, not after so long.*

No, no, no. Screw giving Rebecca time. She'd had thirty years, hadn't she? *You can't mean that. I need to see you.*

Her phone remained silent. Olivia's fingers jabbed at the screen. *Why are you being like this? We could meet for half an hour. That's not too much to ask.*

Still no response. Please, Olivia chanted in her head. She propped herself against her pillows, her gaze on her phone. The text messaging service on her mobile didn't show the usual bouncing dots when somebody was composing a message, but Rebecca would reply soon, surely? The woman was her biological mother; it would be too cruel to leave Olivia hanging.

Five minutes passed, then ten. Still no response. Olivia closed her eyes, leaned back against her headboard. Emotions swirled through her: hurt, grief, confusion, topped by anger. She deserved better.

Her mobile beeped, startling Olivia from her funk. Bolt upright again, she seized her phone, only to be disappointed when she saw it was Kirsten. *Where are you? Not like you to be late.*

Oh, God, she'd forgotten all about their curry at the Raj. Her fingers flew across the screen.

Any chance you could get us a takeaway and come here instead?

Seconds later, a response arrived. *Sure. You OK?*

Olivia tossed her mobile to one side and closed her eyes. More minutes passed. Another beep from her phone.

Rebecca's name was on the screen. Olivia's fingers shook so hard she struggled to open the message.

I'm sorry, but I can't see you again. Although I didn't show it I found our meeting very difficult. It brought back painful memories. I can't put myself through that a second time. Please don't contact me again.

A howl of misery burst from Olivia. She flung her phone across the room; it crashed against the wall, landing on the carpet. Her arms around her knees, Olivia curled into a ball, too numb to cry.

Hours seemed to pass before her doorbell buzzed, yet it could only have been twenty minutes. Olivia dragged herself to her feet, every cell in her body protesting. Concern flew into Kirsten's expression after Olivia opened the door. Her friend took one look at her, then pushed past and dumped the bag of takeaway food on the hall table. Her arms wrapped around Olivia and pulled her close.

'What the hell happened?' Kirsten demanded when Olivia broke free. 'You look like shit. Is it David? Did he tell you I ran into him in town?'

'No. He called yesterday, but I didn't pick up and he didn't leave a message.'

Kirsten bit her lip. 'Look, it might be nothing. But I spotted him outside the Llandoger Trow pub earlier. Chatting to a woman who looked exactly how you described Tiffany Cook.'

Olivia's hackles rose. 'Tall, about twenty-five, long blonde hair?'

'Yes. And they seemed pretty chummy. Standing close together, only had eyes for each other, etc.'

Painful memories rushed through Olivia. The lies, the subterfuge, she'd endured on discovering her ex in bed with another woman. So much for David and Tiffany being nothing but colleagues. No wonder she found it hard to trust men.

The grief Rebecca had inflicted hurt more, however. 'I can't bother about David right now. You won't believe what's happened. God, Kirst, I don't know where to start.'

'Good job I do,' Kirsten said. 'There's not a lot lamb biryani with a side of tarka dahl won't solve. Sit down, babe. I'll warm the plates and bring the food through.'

Olivia's stomach clenched. 'I'm not sure I can manage anything to eat.'

She was aware resistance was futile. Kirsten had already disappeared into the kitchen.

Her friend reappeared minutes later with steaming plates piled high, followed by cutlery. 'God, that smells good. Get some food down you and then we'll talk.'

Olivia managed a couple of forkfuls before her stomach rebelled. Tears filled her eyes, and a sob swelled in her throat. Kirsten glanced up, noticed her distress. 'Oh, babe,' she said, before coming to sit beside Olivia. She wrapped an arm around Olivia's shoulders and pulled her close. 'Talk to me,' she said.

So Olivia did. It poured from her—the knock on the door from Rebecca, the revelation that they were mother and daughter. The coldness Olivia noticed, along with the hurtful messages. Kirsten's mouth fell open with shock. Her friend interjected from time to time, asked the occasional question. When Olivia finished, silence settled over the room for a few seconds.

'Wow,' Kirsten said. 'I'm not sure what to say. The timing stinks, coming so soon after your mum's—I mean Sonia's—death. Can you be certain Rebecca's telling the truth? About being your mother, I mean?'

'Why would she lie?'

'No idea. But people do.'

'From what she said, it's Elena who's the liar.'

Kirsten's forehead puckered. Olivia knew that look. She waited.

'Maybe,' Kirsten said, 'Rebecca's the one telling porkies, not Elena. Think, Olivia. While Elena was your neighbour, did you spot any evidence of a personality disorder?'

Olivia shook her head. 'I'm not a trained psychiatrist, though. And this borderline personality thing—it sounds like it makes people pretty manipulative. Convincing, too, when they want their own way.'

'Did Rebecca provide any proof to support her claim she's your mother?'

'No.'

'You need to dig deeper, Olivia. If Rebecca misled you about one thing, then she might have lied about other stuff too.'

'Like what?'

'About your twin brother being dead.'

Olivia stared at Kirsten. She was right, of course. 'But why would Rebecca lie about being my mother?'

'Perhaps she's the crazy one, not Elena. It could be Rebecca who has borderline personality disorder, which she's projecting onto her more stable sister.'

'What if—' A horrible suspicion had sneaked into Olivia's brain. 'Suppose that, instead of being concerned about Elena like she claims, Rebecca had something to do with her leaving Bristol? You've got to admit—it's weird how Elena just upped and left. Right after someone attacked her.'

'But you heard a male voice in her flat. Not a woman's.'

Olivia chewed her lip. 'I don't have a clue what's going on, Kirst. Except that Rebecca doesn't seem on the level. You know what hurt? Hoping that the man who raised me might be my biological father, that my parentage wasn't a total unknown. Then Rebecca told me some random guy got her pregnant.'

'She might have lied about that as well.' Kirsten squeezed Olivia's arm. 'Don't get your hopes up, though. The odds that Harry's your dad seem low.'

'So how do you explain his writing on the envelopes containing the locks of hair?'

'I can't. Not in any way that makes sense.' Kirsten got to her feet, dragged Olivia up with her. 'Let's see if we can find answers.'

'Where?'

'Among Elena's stuff. I bet you slung most of it in boxes without looking, right?'

Olivia hesitated. She wasn't sure whether she could cope with much more.

'Come on, babe. Don't you want the truth?'

Yes, she did. Olivia rummaged in her handbag to find the keys to Elena's flat. She followed Kirsten down the communal stairwell.

Inside the flat, the air was cold, unwelcoming. Olivia walked into the bedroom, her eyes on the stack of boxes. Elena, she thought. Where are you? More to the point, who are you?

Kirsten plumped herself on the bed. 'So what else is there to sort?'

Olivia remembered the second shoebox on top of the wardrobe, the one she'd forgotten after discovering her brother's lock of hair. 'Not much. Only that.' She gestured towards it. Kirsten pulled up a chair, climbed on it, and took down the box.

'Could you… I can't…' Olivia said.

Kirsten understood at once. She patted the space beside her on the mattress. 'Sit here, babe. I'll do the honours.' Her fingers worked the knotted string around the box's middle.

Once that was done, she opened the lid. Inside was a stack of envelopes; Kirsten selected one and pulled out the contents. A Christmas card, holly and mistletoe festooned across the front, along with 'To The One I Love' in golden cursive.

Kirsten flipped it open to read the message. '"To my darling Elena, the best wife ever. All my love, Peter." Followed by three kisses.'

Olivia snatched the card from her. 'Rebecca told me a guy called Peter Munro fathered me.' Confusion sounded in her voice. 'She also said Elena never married.'

'This card says otherwise. More proof Rebecca Brady fed you a pack of lies.'

'Maybe not about everything. If Elena's my biological mother, her husband might be my dad.'

'But why did Elena tell you they didn't have kids? How come they gave their babies up for adoption? And if Rebecca misled you, if Cameron's alive, not dead, why split the two of you up?'

'I've no idea, Kirst.'

Olivia pulled another envelope from the box. A birthday card, inscribed with a similar loving message. Peter Munro had clearly adored his wife. From the number of cards, it was obvious they were married for many years, which fitted with what Elena told her.

Kirsten flipped through the rest of the cards. All were to Elena from Peter Munro. When she reached the last one, she paused.

‘This one’s different,’ she said. She handed the envelope to Olivia. ‘Isn’t that your dad’s handwriting?’

Olivia froze. On the outside was Elena’s name, penned in Harry Harding’s distinctive script. It wasn’t a card, either; inside was a letter. She pulled it out to read.

Dear Elena,

What you said today disturbed me. I hope you understand that giving the babies to Sonia and me is the best way forward. The only one, in my opinion. We had an agreement, remember. You said it yourself—you can’t look after one child, let alone two. Cameron and Olivia will have stability, security and love. They will want for nothing, I can promise you that.

You’ll receive the rest of your money after the babies leave hospital. I wish you all the best, but what you asked of me earlier is impossible.

Yours, Harry

Olivia remained frozen, the single sheet of paper clutched in one hand. She couldn’t fathom what the words meant.

‘May I read it?’ Kirsten asked. Olivia handed her the letter.

‘This raises more questions than it answers,’ her friend said a minute later.

‘She sold me.’ Olivia’s tone was dull. The letter had hit her hard, right when she thought she couldn’t hurt anymore.

'Oh, lovey. Come here.' Olivia allowed Kirsten to draw her into a hug.

'You know what I think?' Kirsten said. 'Elena was a surrogate. One who found it hard to give her babies up once they were born.'

Olivia hadn't considered that possibility. 'But she did. Me, at least.' She recalled what Rebecca had told her. 'Perhaps Cameron did die after all.'

'Maybe.'

'We know Elena got married. Rebecca lied about that.'

'But didn't Elena say she'd not had kids?'

'Her stretch marks tell a different story.' Olivia thought back. What had Elena once said? *I would love to have been a mother. But it was not to be.*

'She never said specifically she'd not had children.' Olivia understood Elena's words might have another interpretation. One that fitted with a surrogate being expected to honour the agreement she'd made.

'Harry might be your dad after all,' Kirsten said. 'The reason you didn't find any adoption papers.'

Olivia shook her head. 'But why is Sonia named as my mother on my birth certificate and in the baby book? And how come they never told me the truth?'

Kirsten sucked in a breath. 'I suspect it was because of the money.'

'What do you mean?'

'In the UK, it's illegal to pay for a surrogate pregnancy. Legitimate expenses are permitted, but nothing else. I get why they'd want to keep it under wraps. Give me a second, will you?' Kirsten grabbed her phone. A few minutes later, she handed it to Olivia. 'Look at this article. If Elena was a surrogate, her name should be on the birth certificate as your mother. Not Sonia's.'

Olivia read it, then gave the phone back. 'What can I do, Kirst? How do I uncover the truth?'

As always, Kirsten proved the practical one. 'There's a simple way to check if Cameron's alive. Remember the account you set up at the General Register Office? Use it to search online for his death certificate.'

'You do it. I can't.' Olivia chewed her fingernails as Kirsten's fingers tapped her phone after Olivia had logged into the site. Several minutes passed. Kirsten's brow furrowed, then she handed Olivia her mobile.

'There's no death certificate for any Cameron Harding of the right age. But I did find this.'

Olivia stared at the screen. She was looking at a mirror image of her birth certificate, apart from the name, Cameron James Harding. Sonia and Harry were listed as Cameron's parents. Same date of birth, same registrar.

'Rebecca lied. It seems your brother might still be alive,' Kirsten said.

CHAPTER 10

'How do I find him, Kirst?' Olivia couldn't stop crying. 'I have a brother out there somewhere, and I need to locate him.'

'I don't know, babe,' Kirsten replied. 'But we'll sort it. Together.' She stood up, stretched, yawned. 'Coffee would be good.'

'How about we go back upstairs and I'll get the kettle on?'

Once in her flat again, Olivia busied herself in the kitchen. When she returned, a mug in each hand, Kirsten had the box of paintings from Elena's bedroom in front of her. Her fingers traced over the top one, which showed the ruined building from a distance.

'This looks familiar,' she said.

'You recognise it?'

'I think so.' Kirsten pulled out the painting, propping it on her lap so she could study it more closely. 'God, this is raw, isn't it? That's a bleeding heart, yeah?'

Olivia nodded. 'Whoever painted that—they suffered huge emotional pain. I can't help feeling it's significant.'

Kirsten pointed at the MB in the corner. 'You said Elena's surname is Munro, right?'

'Yes. But the initials are MB, not EM, Kirst.'

'What if Elena's short for Madelena? I bet Elena's maiden name began with B, and she painted these pictures before her marriage, while still raw with grief.'

'Oh, my God. You could be right. It all fits. She used to be Madelena Brown, Bates, whatever—'

'Brady, if Rebecca and she really are sisters and Rebecca never married,' Kirsten interjected. 'I bet Elena was once Madelena Brady.'

Olivia pointed at the baby under the archway. 'Is that Cameron, do you think?'

Kirsten blew out a breath. 'It's possible. But I don't understand the link to the castle.'

'The building's a ruined castle? You said you recognised it?'

'It looks like the one at Tynemouth. You went there with me years ago.'

'I remember.' Olivia had been fifteen, holidaying with Kirsten and her parents. They owned a small cottage on the coast between Blyth and Whitley Bay, and Tynemouth's castle and priory had featured on a day trip. Kirsten used to visit there every year with them.

Kirsten grabbed her mobile, tapped a few times, then turned the screen Olivia's way. 'Yeah. That's Tynemouth Castle.'

'I don't get the connection either,' Olivia said. 'Elena was Bristolian. Still had a trace of the accent, despite having lived in London for years. She never mentioned the north-east.' A thought occurred to her. 'Rebecca's accent was more northern. They didn't sound alike.'

'Well, some link exists. We just have to find it.'

Olivia stared closer at the painted figure of the baby. An idea, wild but possible, was forming in her mind. 'What if Elena abandoned Cameron? At Tynemouth Castle?'

Kirsten looked shocked. 'But why would she? Anyway, he was born in Bristol. What reason could she have for dumping him three hundred miles away?'

'I don't know,' Olivia admitted. She stared at the painting again, then picked up her mobile. She paused. If she was right, Elena had abandoned Cameron thirty years ago, before newspapers went digital. This might not be as easy as she'd hoped.

Her fingers shaking, she typed 'finding old newspaper articles'. The British Newspaper Archive came up first.

Kirsten collected their mugs. 'I'll make a fresh brew. This is stone-cold.' She walked into the kitchen.

Olivia remained fixated on her mobile. She created an account, then filtered her search to the north-east. From the drop-down menu she selected 'Newcastle Evening Chronicle' and the year of her birth. In the search bar she tapped in, 'Abandoned baby Tynemouth Castle'.

And there it was. A headline screamed at her. Dated a week after her birthday.

'Oh, my God,' she said, as she read.

NEWBORN BABY ABANDONED IN TYNEMOUTH

A local woman told yesterday how she found a baby boy abandoned in a rubbish bin during a morning walk in Tynemouth village.

Police began a search for the baby's mother following thirty-year-old Amy Sutcliffe's discovery of the child at seven a.m.

Ms Sutcliffe said she was strolling towards Tynemouth's Front Street in the direction of the castle when she thought she heard a cat crying. On further investigation, she discovered the sound was that of a baby, not an animal, and coming from inside a rubbish bin outside a residential property. The child had been wrapped in a shawl and zipped inside a closed holdall.

Paramedics rushed the baby to the maternity unit at North Tyneside General Hospital, where he was found to be in good health. Staff there estimate him to be around a week old.

Amy, who works in local government, said, 'I was shocked when I realised I'd found a baby. He was clearly distressed. It's lucky I heard his crying and was able to help.'

The owner of the property outside which the child was abandoned, eighty-four-year-old Arnold Murray, said he was equally shocked. 'It's all very upsetting. I was asleep in bed when the ambulance arrived. Thank goodness someone found that poor bairn before the bins were collected.'

Police later carried out house-to-house enquiries in the area.

Acting Inspector Steven Davis appealed for the mother to contact the police. He said: 'She may need medical attention and we would ask her to please come forward.'

Horror filled Olivia. 'I don't get it,' she choked out between gulps of air. 'How could she do something so cruel?'

Kirsten came in with their coffee. 'What are you talking about?'

She'd forgotten her friend hadn't read the article. Olivia handed Kirsten her phone.

'Wow,' Kirsten said, shaking her head after she returned it to Olivia. 'I don't know what to say.'

'That's Cameron. Has to be. She threw my brother away like he was trash.' Anger seared Olivia.

'It makes little sense.' Kirsten pulled the other pictures of Tynemouth Castle from the box. 'This place gets a lot of visitors. The painting indicates he was left where he'd be found by staff at the castle. Under shelter, too. And the sorrow depicted doesn't fit with Cameron being thrown in a rubbish bin.'

'Yes, it does. At least to me.' Olivia's fury meant she was on a roll. 'Rebecca didn't lie about everything. Elena's delusional, all right.'

'What makes you say that?'

'The fact she can't acknowledge the truth. She zipped her baby, a helpless week-old child, into a holdall. A closed one, meaning he only had a limited air supply. He could have died, Kirst. Either from lack of oxygen or by being crushed after the bin was emptied into the collection lorry. So she convinced herself she abandoned him somewhere safe.'

Kirsten looked doubtful. 'From what you said, she never gave you any hint her mental state was shaky, apart from those antidepressants you found.'

'Perhaps she's as good a liar as her sister.'

'There's always the possibility the baby in the bin wasn't Cameron. That this is all a giant coincidence.'

Olivia shook her head. 'I don't believe that for a minute. The dates, the location—it all ties in. Elena abandoned my brother.' She warmed to her theme. 'I don't want a bitch like her in my life. Mum and I may have had our differences, but she loved me, always wanted the best for me.' A visceral longing for Sonia welled inside Olivia, her grief so pure it was almost painful.

Kirsten grabbed Olivia's phone again. She tapped and scrolled before handing it back. 'I can't see any mention of the mother coming forward. The baby must have been adopted.'

'Of course Elena didn't come forward. She threw her child away, Kirst. The heartless bitch.' Her friend's words sank in. 'Oh, my God. You're right. Cameron's out there somewhere. I just have to find him.'

*****

The following evening, Olivia glanced around Elena's bedroom, now bare apart from the furniture. Her job there was done. All Elena's belongings—the cards, the letters from Harry, her paintings of Tynemouth—were in Olivia's flat. One day, Olivia decided, she'd discover what happened thirty years ago. Perhaps even meet her brother.

She walked through the rest of Elena's flat, checking for anything she'd missed. Olivia paused in the living room, remembering Elena's rucked-up skirt, how the dough of her belly was striped with stretch marks. She pulled out her phone to tap out a quick text to Elena. *Call me, please. It's important.*

She waited, but her mobile remained silent. The sun streamed through the windows, highlighting the dust on the coffee table. Something else, too; a glint caught Olivia's eye. The object was tiny, nestled in the carpet's pile. She bent down to pull it free.

A gold earring, shaped like a rose in full bloom, lay in her hand. Words rushed into Olivia's head, a conversation with Sonia not long before her death. *Remember the gold rose-shaped earrings your dad gave me? One's gone missing. They're on a wire hook, and I must have flicked it out somewhere. I've searched everywhere but can't find it.*

A dull ache pulsed behind Olivia's eyes. As far as she knew, Sonia had no idea that her daughter's biological mother—if that was what Elena was—had sought her out. Olivia didn't recall mentioning her new friend to her mum much, except in passing and with few details.

The earring in her palm said otherwise. Sonia Harding had been to Elena's flat. Why, though? And how had her mother known about Elena?

Maybe, Olivia thought, she was making something out of nothing. Yes, the two women met up. The earring was proof of that. Olivia could understand why Sonia would want to talk to Elena, given the clandestine adoption. Maybe she'd spotted

Elena one time when visiting Olivia, and got scared that Elena might reveal the truth to her daughter. Yes, that must be it.

Olivia stared at the earring. More confirmation that she needed to find either Elena, Rebecca or both. The two women held the key to the mystery of her birth. And maybe Cameron Harding's whereabouts.

Part Two

Elena - before

CHAPTER 11

Thirty years ago, Elena never intended to get pregnant. Babies were cute, but reserved for the future. Right then she was single, stuck in a tiny flat and didn't earn much. On the positive side, she enjoyed her job as a teaching assistant, loved the part of Bristol where she lived, and best of all, she had Sonia. Elena couldn't imagine life without her gal pal. Sure, Sonia could be bossy, but oh, so kind beneath her blunt exterior. Pretty, too, the honey pot around which many male bees buzzed. Elena had never been jealous of her, however. Until Harry Harding.

Elena knew straight away Harry was different to Sonia's previous boyfriends. Sonia couldn't stop talking about him, her cheeks flushed, excitement in her eyes, and Elena realised her friend had fallen hard for the guy.

Elena's own feelings for Harry Harding took time to grow. So long, in fact, that by the time she grasped she was in love with him, her heart was a helpless hostage, powerless to resist. He wasn't conventionally handsome. Tall, dark-haired, with brown eyes so deep she could tumble into them and never find her way out. His nose, however, was hooked, his lips big and fleshy. No, he wasn't good-looking, but Elena had never cared about appearances. Harry fascinated her in a way no man ever had before. So solid, stable and kind. Different to the other guys she'd known. She ached to meet a man like Harry.

She rarely dated, though. Elena was less confident than Sonia, more mousy, too reserved. Oh, she'd had boyfriends, the odd fling here and there. None ever lasted long.

Sonia's wedding to Harry followed a year later. She confided in Elena how she was already trying to get pregnant. 'You'll be our first child's godmother, of course. Harry's not bothered whether we have a boy or a girl, but I've always wanted a daughter,' she said, her eyes shining. 'I just adore little girls. So cute.'

Elena suspected another reason existed for Sonia's preference. They never discussed Sonia being adopted but Elena knew the wound had cut deep into her friend. Every time she'd tried to discuss it with Sonia, she found herself angrily shut down. A little girl would, she thought, help heal the hurt.

For the first time ever, she resented Sonia. Her friend had everything Elena didn't—loving parents, a sister, good looks, a husband. Why were some people so blessed? But then she remembered Sonia's breakdown after her biological mother overdosed on heroin. The depression that followed. Perhaps her friend wasn't so lucky after all.

Especially, it seemed, when it came to babies. Several years passed, and still Elena wasn't a godmother.

One evening she called, unannounced, at Sonia and Harry's house. Elena told herself it was because she'd not seen Sonia all week and her friend had seemed withdrawn when they last met. Sonia had explained her period arrived that morning. 'I'm losing hope,' she'd told Elena. 'The doctors can't find anything wrong.'

'Hello, you!' Harry exclaimed when he saw who his visitor was. 'Sonia's not in, I'm afraid. Gone to a yoga class at the church hall. She shouldn't be long. Want to come in and wait?'

Elena nodded. She did, very much.

'I'll get the kettle on,' Harry said. Elena followed him into the Hardings' kitchen.

Minutes later they were seated at the oak table, mugs in hand. Elena sipped her coffee. 'Just what I needed.'

Harry smiled, but it didn't quite reach his eyes. She noticed the tension around his mouth, the pallor of his skin. He looked like he wasn't sleeping well, and Elena experienced a lurch of compassion within her belly.

'Are you all right?' she asked.

Harry set his mug down. 'Just tired.' His gaze met hers; Elena watched his Adam's apple rise and fall as he swallowed. 'Actually, that's not true. Sonia and I are going through a rough patch. It happens, I guess.'

This was news to Elena. Sonia hadn't said anything along those lines, apart from about her failure to conceive. 'Is it the baby thing?'

When he didn't reply, she tried again. 'Do you want to talk about it?'

Harry shrugged. 'Yes. No. Hell, I don't know. Maybe.'

Elena laughed. 'Well, that covers all possibilities.'

The sound of a key in the front door indicated Sonia was home. Her friend hugged her, and Elena berated herself for her traitorous thoughts. Harry was out of bounds, she reminded herself. So why couldn't she stop wondering how his lips would feel against hers?

*****

Elena's world imploded the next day. She was eating breakfast when her mobile rang; the caller was her aunt Linda. They hadn't spoken since the funeral of Elena's father years ago.

Linda informed her, in clipped tones, that she'd found her sister, Elena's mother, dead in bed. Two bottles—wine and sleeping tablets, both empty—were on Kathy Baxter's bedside cabinet. No note, although suicide seemed a distinct possibility. Her alcoholic mother had battled depression most of her adult life. Or perhaps she just got careless with her pills. Elena would never know.

'She's at peace at last,' Sonia said, when Elena told her about Kathy's death. Elena couldn't argue with that.

She persuaded herself she didn't care. Her mother had failed her daughter when fifteen-year-old Elena needed her most. Why grieve for the woman?

'Because, deep down, you're that little girl whose mum drank too much,' Sonia said. 'Somewhere inside, you still love her. Want things to be different.'

Her friend was right. Elena found herself unable to get out of bed the next morning; her world dissolved into racking sobs that continued throughout the day. Thank God it was the school holidays, so she was off work. In her head, she was five, and her mother's alcoholism hadn't escalated the way it did during Elena's teenage years. Her father hadn't yet… She cut *that* thought dead straightaway.

Elena stayed in bed for two days. Eventually she threw back the duvet and took a long shower. Once she'd dried her hair, she pulled on a top she'd not yet worn. With it went her shortest skirt, teamed with ankle boots and a leather jacket. Mascara, eyeliner, blusher, lip gloss. Elena surveyed her reflection in the mirror. She didn't recognise the woman staring back.

She caught the bus into Bristol's city centre and walked into the first bar she found. Oblivion was what she sought.

Her strategy worked; Elena retained little memory of that night. Jumbled images, all blurred, jostled in her head. Herself, drinking shots and chasers, surrounded by men. A taxi ride, a guy beside her in the back seat. Stumbling through his flat to get to his bedroom. Elena, naked underneath him. Alcohol might have killed her mother, but that night it proved her friend. For a few hours, at least, she held her grief at bay.

Until the morning. Elena awoke, her mouth a sandpit, a sledgehammer at work in her head. Next to her, the man lay snoring, his mouth open. His sour breath turned her stomach. Shame slammed into her as she eased herself off the bed. Her eyes scanned the floor, searching for a discarded condom, but without success. Two minutes was all she needed to dress, grab her handbag and tiptoe from the room. Once outside, she took the bus home, downed a pint of water and crawled into bed.

*****

A week later Elena spotted Harry in the street, his head down, hands thrust in his jacket pockets. It was early evening, and Elena was returning to her flat after buying groceries. She hurried after Harry, her breath hitching in her chest as she grabbed his arm. He swung round, startled, then pasted a smile on his face. 'Hey, you,' he said. 'How're you doing?'

'Fine.' Elena stared at the man she loved. Harry's skin was sallow, dark circles underpinning his bloodshot eyes. His hair looked unwashed, his shirt wrinkled. Elena's belly lurched again. She longed to take him home, love him, and never let him go.

'Do you have time for a coffee?' she asked.

Harry nodded. He walked with her to her shabby flat. He didn't speak as she filled the kettle, set mugs on the table, spooned coffee into them. Elena sat opposite him but remained silent. She knew he'd unburden himself before long.

'Sonia's talking about divorce,' Harry said at last.

Shock raced through Elena. To her shame, a sliver of hope followed. 'Why?'

'The baby thing. She's convinced she's let me down. How I won't love her unless she makes me a father.' He shook his head. 'She's being ridiculous, of course.'

'What about IVF?'

'Sonia's convinced it won't work. Too concerned about low success rates and the intensive hormone treatment required.' A sigh. 'That's why she's been so down. You must have noticed.'

Elena had. She'd asked Sonia what was wrong, but received a curt brushoff. In hindsight, it made sense. Sonia's infertility cut too deep for her to talk about. 'Do you know what the problem is?'

'No. We went for tests, got the all-clear for everything. It's a mystery why Sonia hasn't got pregnant.'

'What about adoption?' But Elena already knew the answer.

Harry sighed. 'She won't even discuss it.'

He looked so careworn, so defeated. A jolt of love rocked Elena; without thinking, she reached across to clasp Harry's right hand. He was so absorbed in his misery he didn't appear to notice. Oh, the warmth of his skin against hers. Elena indulged in a fantasy, one in which she was married to Harry and had just told him she was pregnant. Her husband's eyes were wet with joy as he moved around the table to take her in his arms. They kissed, and—

'We don't make love anymore.' Harry's words shook Elena from her daydream. 'Sorry. I know that's too personal to share. Even before, it was all temperature charts and calendar dates. Now she says there's no point if she can't get pregnant.' His tone was bitter. 'I've told her it's called 'making love' for a reason. But she won't listen.'

Elena stayed silent, unsure how to respond.

'I should go,' Harry said. But he remained seated, their hands still joined. He glanced at them, and she saw the exact moment the shock hit him. He tried to pull away, but Elena held firm. She knew her love for him must be shining from her eyes. She'd repressed her feelings for so long, but no more.

Realisation bloomed in Harry's expression. 'Elena,' he whispered.

'Let me take care of you.'

'This is wrong. We can't do this.'

Elena released his hand to walk behind his chair. She wrapped her arms around him, rested her chin on his shoulder. Her heart thudded so hard she was certain the whole world could hear it.

Harry stood up, shoving himself away from the table. The motion was so abrupt Elena staggered backwards. Then she was in Harry's arms, his mouth on hers, and rational thought fled from her brain. Within seconds they were in Elena's bedroom.

The sex was everything she'd dreamed of. Elena had always pictured Harry as a tender lover, and he proved her right. I'm making love for the first time, Elena thought. Before, sex had always been clumsy, unsatisfying. She was too inhibited, too damaged, to relax.

To her dismay, she realised sexual release was Harry's focus, not love. The result of weeks—months?—of deprivation, she assumed. Confirmed by the first words out of his mouth once they were lying, spent and sweaty, on Elena's bed.

Harry turned his back to her. 'This was a mistake.'

Hurt hit Elena hard. They'd been so good together, hadn't they? 'You don't mean that.'

Still facing away, he got out of bed and gathered up his clothes. 'Yes, I do. Time for me to go home.'

To *her*, Elena thought, sour resentment welling inside. 'Stay. Please?' She had no pride left, it seemed.

'You know I can't.' Harry sat on the bed to pull on his socks. 'Like I said, sex was a mistake.' He shrugged on his shirt.

When Elena didn't respond, Harry turned to her, saw the distress in her face, took her hands in his.

'I'm sorry if I've hurt your feelings,' he said. The compassion in his words almost destroyed her. 'But I love Sonia. You and I—we got carried away, that's all.'

Anger flashed through Elena. 'You used me.'

'Sonia must never know.'

'She won't hear it from me.' Elena hated herself. She'd been a fool.

'It's a one-off. Can't happen again.'

'I get that. Just go. Please.'

Once he'd left, tears of self-disgust slid down Elena's face. Sonia didn't deserve such a betrayal. Elena recalled the tightness of her friend's hug years ago, after the ugliness with her father. Back then Sonia had held her close, never saying a word; somehow her silence conveyed everything necessary. Elena shoved the memory back inside the box in her mind where it lurked. She couldn't go there.

It was only later, when she was preparing for bed, that a thought occurred to her. She wasn't on the pill, and Harry didn't use a condom.

Elena persuaded herself it would be fine. She'd need sheer bad luck to get pregnant from that one occasion. Well, two, if she counted the guy from the bar. Right?

*****

Elena didn't worry, not at first. Her periods had always been erratic; sometimes she got one every three weeks, other times she went six months without bleeding. Her breasts were sore, but she'd experienced that before prior to menstruating; she told herself it was nothing to worry about. Her period was probably about to arrive at last. Except that it didn't.

The sex with Harry took place mid-summer, but it wasn't until the week before Christmas that Elena realised she was pregnant.

She was having a fry-up for breakfast one Saturday when the truth hit her. Elena had been comfort-eating, burying her grief over Harry under greasy takeouts and huge meals. She lifted a forkful of sausage to her mouth, then stopped when she felt a flutter in her belly. It was the weirdest sensation, like a butterfly was struggling to get free. She held her breath, waiting, and then it came again, this time stronger. New life was moving inside her, but Elena persuaded herself it was indigestion.

Unbidden, something a colleague once told her sneaked into her mind. Suzanne loved to chat and spent one lunch break telling Elena about her pregnancies and giving birth, not holding back on the more unpleasant details. Elena remembered what Suzanne said about feeling her babies move inside her. 'It's the most beautiful experience,' she told Elena, a rapturous look on her face.

Was pregnancy possible? Yes, of course, given that she'd had unprotected sex at least once, possibly twice. Maybe her recent weight gain wasn't due to her calorie intake. How could she have been so damn stupid?

Elena shoved aside the plate of fried food, no longer hungry. Her mind on autopilot, she shrugged on her coat and shoes, grabbed her keys and handbag, and hastened to the nearest rank of shops, where there was a pharmacy. She purchased a pregnancy test, embarrassment tinting her cheeks, then scurried home.

The test sat on her bedside cabinet all day. Elena was too terrified to open it and read the instructions. Instead, her mind roved over possibilities. If she was pregnant, she was too far gone for an abortion; the idea horrified her anyway. But how would she ever cope? She had no partner, she lived in a flat so small it was hard to turn around without hitting the other wall, and she didn't earn much money. And what about her mental health?

Like her mother, Elena suffered from depression. The dark feelings had arrived in a few months after her periods started, but she couldn't blame her hormones. Her father? That was a different matter. Mostly she functioned pretty well but the darkness was a low-grade hum in the background, always there. Since Harry's rejection, however, the blackness had intensified. Some weekends she spent both days in bed, the duvet pulled over her head. How on earth would she ever cope with a baby? She was, she told herself, a prime candidate for postnatal depression.

There remained the question of who was the father. Which one got her pregnant? Her drunken night of sex, or the one-sided lovemaking with Harry?

On Sunday morning Elena awoke to the realisation she had to sort this one way or another. She reached for the pregnancy test, ripped open the carton and read the instruction leaflet. Minutes later she was in her bathroom, holding the plastic stick in her stream of urine.

She didn't dare look for another half hour. Instead she made a piece of toast, forced herself to eat it and washed it down with a cup of coffee. Then she sat on her bed, took a deep breath, and reached for the plastic stick.

Elena stared at it. Two blue lines gazed back. She was pregnant.

Oh, God. What on earth was she to do?

She only had two options. Either have the baby and manage somehow, or offer it for adoption. Elena pictured herself with a screaming newborn, a tiny scrap of life dependent on her for everything. Panic overwhelmed her, and she reached her bathroom just in time to vomit up her breakfast.

Elena tried to convince herself it would be all right. She wasn't some giddy schoolgirl; she was almost thirty and in good health. No reason existed not to have this baby, be a wonderful mum. Deep inside, a voice in her gut warned otherwise. *Your own mother was a piss-poor parent, and she had a husband. What makes you think that you, single and barely making minimum wage, can do better?*

Was adoption a viable alternative? Elena wasn't sure. She knew how badly it had scarred Sonia.

Elena's depression swamped her, and she crawled into bed, too numb to cry. Her mind a blank, she settled into a restless doze.

When she woke up, it was dark. Her stomach growled, reminding her she'd vomited up her breakfast, and she stumbled into the kitchen to fix herself a bowl of cereal. As she spooned cornflakes and milk into her mouth, she accepted the inevitable. She couldn't have this baby, so adoption was the only option. Elena pictured her son—she saw herself giving birth to a boy, not a girl—with adoring parents who'd give him the life she couldn't. A well-off couple, unable to have kids of their own, with love to spare. Yes, that was the answer.

Sonia and Harry, perhaps. Sonia's refusal to consider adoption ruled out that option, however. As did the thought of Elena seeing her child whenever she visited Sonia. She'd have to lie, too, about the possibility Harry was the father. Sonia deserved better.

Elena sat on her bed again and picked up the test stick. At some point she'd need to go to her doctor, get checked over, and start antenatal classes. Christmas was looming, however, and she told herself she'd wait until the New Year; she was unlikely to get an appointment earlier, anyway. A week or two extra wouldn't matter.

Elena wasn't concerned about the situation at work. She doubted her request for maternity leave would prove welcome, but as the law stood, the school had no choice. What bothered her more was the question of Harry.

He'd be able to do the maths when he heard about her pregnancy. Elena wasn't spiteful enough to wish to jeopardise his marriage to Sonia, so she'd have to lie. She planned to claim the father was an ex-boyfriend with whom she'd reunited for a while, but who didn't want to be involved in his child's life.

The truth was—she had no idea who had fathered her baby.

CHAPTER 12

'Is something wrong? You seem very distant.'

Elena's stomach lurched with dread. Oh, God, Sonia had found out. No, that was impossible. If she knew, she'd be slapping Elena, not looking concerned. Besides, how could Sonia know? The sex only happened once, and Harry wouldn't have said anything.

As always, guilt stole over Elena. She loved Sonia like a sister, but had been a crappy best friend to her. Friends didn't sleep with each other's husbands. Her cheeks flushed at the thought of Harry Harding, their time together in bed. Despite her remorse, she'd do it again in a heartbeat.

She realised Sonia was waiting for an answer. 'Oh, nothing. Just a bit tired.'

'You should talk to your doctor. Maybe you're anaemic.' Sonia eyed her friend with a critical gaze. 'Don't take offence, but you've put on a lot of weight. Might be a thyroid issue.'

'Or overeating.' Elena gestured towards the biscuits on the coffee table.

'You're sure nothing's wrong?'

'I'm positive.' Elena was desperate to deflect Sonia. 'What about you? You seem different these days. Happier.'

'I am.' Sonia smiled. 'Life's good right now.' She didn't elaborate, and Elena felt a rush of hurt. Sex with Harry had driven a wedge between them, even if Sonia remained unaware of Elena's treachery. Elena's guilt meant she'd become distant with Sonia, which had a rebound effect. The two of them didn't communicate well anymore. She couldn't remember the last time her friend had confided in her.

Sonia left not long after, saying she needed to buy milk. As soon as her friend was out of the door, Elena called Harry. She couldn't bear the secrecy a minute longer.

'I need to talk to you. Please.' Elena's grip tightened around the phone handset. It was four o'clock; Harry was still at work, but she was hoping he'd drop by on his way home.

'What about?' Harry sounded wary.

'I'll explain when I see you.' Elena drew on her remaining reserves of courage. 'It'll only take a few minutes. Please.'

Silence, followed by a heavy sigh. 'OK. I'll come round about five-thirty.' With that, he ended the call.

A knock sounded on Elena's door at the arranged time. She hurried to open it, smoothing down her skirt and tucking a stray strand of hair behind her ears. Harry offered her a forced smile as she waved him inside. She stepped aside to allow him to pass.

'Coffee?' she enquired, as he strode into her kitchen. With a shake of his head, he pulled out a chair and sat down.

'Why did you ask me to come round?' he said.

To Elena's horror, she burst into tears. She sobbed noisily, dabbing her eyes on a piece of kitchen roll, not caring how she looked. Once she'd got herself under control, she risked a glance at Harry. Concern showed in his expression.

'Tell me what's wrong. Please.' He reached out to squeeze Elena's arm. 'I realise we've not spoken to each other for a while. But I care about you. I can't bear to see you like this.'

She gave her eyes a final wipe and blew her nose. 'I'm pregnant,' she blurted out. 'The baby is yours.'

A stunned silence followed Elena's words. She kept her eyes on her hands, still wrapped around the piece of kitchen roll. The tension in the room thickened. At last Elena glanced at Harry. His face was ashen. His fingers drummed a staccato beat on the table as his gaze bored into his lap.

In her head, Elena justified her words. The baby was most likely Harry's. She couldn't be certain that she and the other guy hadn't used condoms; they might have done, but she had almost no memory of that night. With Harry, she knew contraception didn't happen. He was the father of her child, surely?

'Say something,' Elena prompted. Harry didn't respond.

'I wasn't going to tell you. I'm sorry it came out this way.'

'Are you sure?' His voice sounded as if his throat was closing over. 'Have you done a test?'

'Yes. I've not seen my doctor yet, though.'

Harry looked at Elena, confusion in his expression, and her heart melted. Harry Harding had buried himself deep in her soul, and she wasn't sure he'd ever leave.

'I don't understand.' His brow wrinkled as his fingers continued to tap out a beat on the tea-stained wood. 'It's been, what, six months since we had sex.' He shook his head. 'I've noticed that you'd put on weight. Sorry, that sounds rude. How come you've not seen your GP?'

This is going to sound stupid, Elena thought. 'I didn't realise. It's not unusual for me to go a long time between periods. And I was comfort-eating, so that explained the weight gain. It wasn't until I felt the baby move I wondered whether I was pregnant. I did the test and—' Elena spread her hands wide in a gesture of appeal, the sodden kitchen roll dropping onto the floor. 'It was positive.'

'But we only had sex once.' He grimaced. 'I suppose one time is all it takes.'

'Yes.'

Harry shifted in his seat. 'I need to think. About what to do.' Desperation sounded in his voice, shooting another pang of love through Elena.

'I don't mean to make things awkward for you,' she said. However much she loved this man, she wouldn't be a marriage wrecker. 'Sonia's like a sister to me. I'd never want to hurt her. I realise what we did was wrong.'

'Yes, it was. Sonia and I—well, we've never been happier. I don't mean to upset you, but it's the truth.'

Surprise hit Elena; she didn't know how to respond. Hadn't their marriage been falling apart a while back? Why hadn't her friend told her things had improved? But then, she remembered, Sonia rarely confided in her now.

'I love you,' she said. She hadn't meant to, but somehow it slipped out.

Harry's panicked expression shattered any lingering hopes she might have harboured. As did his words. 'Don't say that. Please. I can't be with you that way. You get that, right?'

'Sorry.' How embarrassing. Humiliating, too. She'd only herself to blame, though.

'You seem so different these days. So does Sonia,' she ventured. 'What changed between you two?'

'We had an honest heart-to-heart discussion, poured everything out. Decided being together mattered most, even if we never have children. I'm still trying to persuade Sonia to consider adoption. But she's adamant it's not an option.'

'Do you think you'll convince her? Given time?'

He sucked in a long breath. 'I'm not sure. She's desperate for a child, would make a wonderful mother. Yet I'm concerned about how she'd cope with the adoption process. She's correct in saying it won't happen overnight. Even if we're approved, we need to find the right child. That could take even longer.'

Elena nodded. She knew Sonia would find the wait difficult. Impossible, even.

'Will you be okay with a baby?' Harry said. 'You still haven't told me what you're going to do.'

'I can't be a mother.' There, she'd admitted it.

Shock filled his expression. 'Don't tell me you're considering abortion. You're not flushing our child down the drain like its life means nothing.' His hands clenched, their knuckles white.

Elena shook her head. 'No way. I couldn't. Besides, it's too late for that.' The floodgates opened, and words poured from Elena's mouth. 'But I'm certain I'll never cope. I don't earn enough money. This place is too small. Like Sonia, I've suffered with my mental health. I'm terrified that I won't be able to love my baby. Or take care of it.'

'You'll be fine—'

'Don't patronise me.'

'I mean it.' He swallowed hard. 'I'll support you financially. You needn't do this alone.'

She gulped back a sob. 'I'm going away for a while. Where doesn't matter.'

'And then what?' Harry's fists remained clenched, his mouth set in a grim line.

'I'm doing this for Sonia's sake, not mine. She must never know I'm pregnant. And I can't hide it much longer.'

'I get that.'

'Once the baby's born, I'll put it up for adoption.' The second the words left her lips, she realised how Harry would react.

'No!' His eyes were blank pools of shock. 'You can't.'

She had to make him understand. 'It's the only way. This is the best solution for everyone, don't you see?'

'No. Have you considered—'

'I've already told you I'll never be able to cope. Our child deserves better than a mother who's not sure if she can love it. Who has nothing to give a kid.'

'Elena—'

'And what about you and Sonia? You said you've never been happier. If you give me money, don't think she won't find out. Then all hell will break loose.'

Harry leaned across the table. 'Sonia and I could adopt the baby. He or she is half mine, in case you've forgotten.'

'But then she'd discover the truth. About us, I mean. Besides, she's against the idea.'

'She need never know I'm the father. Not if we don't tell her.' Harry stood up. 'I have to go. Sonia's expecting me home. Promise me you'll think about it, okay?'

Elena nodded, but inside her the certainty grew. Adoption, somewhere other than Bristol, was the best solution.

*****

By later that evening, Elena's mood had lightened. She'd resigned herself to the fact she needed to move away, find somewhere to live, then give birth. After that, she'd make enquiries about adoption. Once she'd entrusted her baby to the care of Social Services, she'd search for another job and put the past behind her. New Year, new start, and all that.

Elena refused to contemplate the possibility that she might fall in love with her child. That couldn't happen, because she wouldn't be keeping her baby, would she? One glance around her shabby flat reminded her how little she earned. Impossible to give her son the life he deserved.

She'd reckoned without Harry.

*****

Two evenings later, Elena lay on her sofa, her bulging belly making getting comfortable difficult, and persuaded herself everything would be all right. Even if, deep down, her instincts told her otherwise.

A loud knock startled her from her thoughts. Elena swung her legs onto the floor and walked to the door to yank it open.

Harry stood before her. Beside him, Sonia. Her best friend's expression was thunderous.

'We have to talk,' Sonia said as she pushed past Elena, who was too stunned to speak. Harry must have told Sonia the truth.

Elena stood aside, motioning Harry into the tiny living space. Her mouth was dry, her stomach tight with tension.

Sonia and Harry commandeered the sofa, while Elena perched on a chair opposite them. Shame flushed her cheeks as she stared at her friend. Sonia's left hand lay in her husband's right one, their fingers entwined. How stupid, how childish, her former fantasies seemed. She'd been a fool.

Elena watched Sonia's gaze travel over her pregnant belly. For a second she spotted fury in her friend's face. She didn't blame Sonia.

'Right now I hate you,' Sonia said, her mouth twisted with dislike. Tears pricked Elena's eyes.

'We're no longer friends,' Sonia continued. 'I can't bear to look at you. Coming here was hard. Harry's admitted he had sex with you.'

'I'm sorry—'

'I realised something was wrong the moment he got home a couple of nights ago. It's taken me this long to worm it out of him.' Sonia snorted. 'It hurt like hell, but he's assured me it was a one-off, and I believe him.' She glared at Harry, who squeezed her hand. 'But he also told me you're pregnant. With his baby.'

'I never meant—'

'Shut the hell up.'

Elena quailed at Sonia's tone. She turned to Harry, mystified. 'Why on earth did you tell her?'

He glanced away, his face pale. 'We want a fresh start for our marriage. No secrets. I had to come clean, don't you see?'

'Never mind all that,' Sonia cut in, her gaze on Elena. 'I've come up with a solution to this mess.'

Elena's mouth fell open. 'I don't understand.'

'Harry tells me you're planning to put the baby up for adoption.'

'Yes. I'll never be able to cope—'

'He and I want to give it a home.'

Elena had no idea what to say. She knew her plan to offer their child for adoption hadn't sat well with Harry.

'I can't conceive naturally,' Sonia said. 'Or I haven't so far, anyway. This is the best solution. For everyone.'

'But how will that work? You, me, Harry, the baby?'

Sonia's voice was hard enough to cut glass. 'You won't be around. Our friendship ended the second you opened your legs for my husband.' She almost spat the words at Elena.

Elena knew she deserved Sonia's hate. Tears stung her eyes at her treachery. Sonia had supported her during her darkest moment to date, and this was how Elena repaid her?

'I understand,' she whispered.

'Nobody must know,' Sonia continued.

Elena was confused. 'Is that possible? For me to hand my baby to you and Harry without involving Social Services?'

Sonia pursed her lips. 'I very much doubt it. And I can't risk them knowing. What if they're bothered about the mental breakdown I suffered? My bouts of depression?'

'Sonia's worried they might decide to give the baby to a different couple,' Harry said. 'She'd never cope with the disappointment.'

Sonia nodded. 'Our problem is, if we try to adopt a child through the usual channels, it might take years. Plus, there's no guarantee we'll get a baby, and I want that. More than anything.' She brushed a tear from her eye. 'I need a newborn in my arms. I crave the sleepless nights, the crying, the dirty nappies. All of it. And you're my best hope.'

Elena understood. This way Sonia was guaranteed a baby, and without the wait.

'That's why the adoption needs to happen under the radar. No paperwork.' Sonia leaned forward, resting her forearms on her knees. 'Here's what we'll do.'

*****

'The real reason I want this? Because the baby will be half Harry's,' Sonia told Elena before she left with her husband an hour later. 'Any other child we adopt won't carry his genes. And I've never been keen on the idea of IVF. This way everyone wins. Right?'

Elena nodded.

'I promise I'll love this baby as if it were my own. He or she will have the best of everything. But I can't have you sniffing around my husband, worried you'll sink your claws into him again. You get that, don't you?'

Sonia was right. This was the perfect solution. But could Elena follow through?

'I'll return tomorrow,' Sonia said. 'So I can hear what you've decided.'

After they'd gone Elena undressed and crawled into bed, stupefied. The money Sonia had offered was generous. Half after Elena agreed, the rest once she handed over her child. The idea gripped Elena and refused to let go. She rubbed her swollen belly as she considered her options. Sonia had made it clear she expected Elena to leave Bristol. Hadn't she wanted a fresh start? This way she'd get it, and with a decent cash sum to boot.

The baby kicked, causing doubt to wash over Elena. Over the past few weeks, she'd become intrigued by the idea of motherhood. Despite herself, she was bonding with the tiny person inside her. She realised cracked nipples, sleepless nights and dirty nappies came with the territory, but didn't care. Part of her craved a child.

The realisation both thrilled and terrified her. From what she'd heard, most women fell in love with their babies at first sight. How could she hand her son over to Sonia if that happened?

Hours later, Elena wasn't any nearer to reaching a conclusion. At last, she drifted into a restless sleep, but the instant she awoke she knew the answer.

She'd accept Sonia's proposition, have her baby, then give him to her former friend after the birth. What choice did she have? She was in no position to care for a child.

'You're doing the right thing,' Sonia said the following evening, when Elena, still beset by doubts, informed her of her decision.

CHAPTER 13

That night Elena couldn't sleep, tortured by misgivings. Had Sonia forced her into a hasty decision, one she'd later regret? She ran though the facts. Their friendship was over. Harry would never love her. A child might fill the void in her heart. Other women managed as single parents. Why shouldn't she?

You made a promise, she told herself. Sonia wanted a baby too, and would love Harry's son, give him the best of everything.

It didn't work. Elena wasn't sure she could hand over her child so easily.

On impulse, Elena called Sonia the next evening. 'What do you want?' Sonia's tone was curt.

'Can we talk?'

Silence for a second. Then: 'What about?'

'I can't tell you over the phone. Could you come here? Please?'

Sonia grudgingly agreed. Elena waited, her heart hammering all the while.

Thirty minutes later, a knock sounded at her door. Sonia strode in, her expression stony. She didn't sit down; instead she stood, her hands gripping the back of a chair. Elena leaned against the wall, uncertain and scared now Sonia had arrived.

'What did you want to discuss?' her former friend said.

Elena drew in a breath. 'I'm not sure. About you adopting my baby.' She cringed as fury filled Sonia's face.

‘We had an agreement.’ Sonia’s tone was pure ice.

‘I know. But—’

‘But nothing. You promised me.’

‘You’re right. It’s hard, though. The idea of giving up a child.’

‘So is infertility.’

‘I’m sorry—’

‘You owe me this,’ Sonia said. She frowned, her mouth a tight line. For several seconds she was silent. Then: ‘I need to think. Alone.’ She headed towards Elena’s bathroom.

Sonia didn’t emerge for ten minutes. When she did, her expression was granite-hard. She strode up to Elena, grabbed her arm and shoved her backwards until Elena’s head hit the wall. Sonia’s face was so close Elena could smell coffee on her breath. She recoiled at the hatred blazing from Sonia’s eyes.

‘Here’s what’s going to happen,’ Sonia said. ‘You’ll honour our agreement. You’ll hand over your baby to me after the birth. Then you’ll leave Bristol. I never want to see your ugly face ever again.’

Elena tried to shrink away, except there was no room. Sonia had always been blunt, but never cruel, not like this. She didn’t recognise this woman.

‘Because if you don’t,’ Sonia continued, ‘I’ll tell everyone the truth. About what you did.’

Elena found her tongue. ‘What good will that do? I’ve every right to keep my child if that’s what I decide.’

‘I’m not talking about the baby.’

Elena blinked. 'What, then?'

Sonia brought her face even closer. Her eyes were chunks of ice. 'Get this through your head. If you don't give me your baby, I'll go to the police.'

Elena, too shocked to respond, stayed silent. Sonia's lips curved in a triumphant grin.

'I'll tell them about our conversation.'

'I don't understand,' Elena whispered.

'You remember, don't you?' Sonia said. 'The one in which you admitted murdering your father.'

Elena stared at her, her mouth open.

'Don't think I won't do it. Because I will, in a heartbeat. I'll say you got drunk, told me his death's been on your conscience for years. That you shoved him off the balcony after he raped you.'

Elena flinched in horror. The word plunged a knife deep into her heart.

'He had a high level of alcohol in his blood, didn't he?' Sonia continued. 'Making it easy for you to pitch him over the edge. I'll tell them you swore me to secrecy, but that I'm not prepared to cover up a murder.'

Still Elena couldn't speak.

'It's close enough to the truth. He *did* rape you. You were angry. Very angry, in fact.'

'Yes,' Elena whispered. 'I was.'

'You told me you hated him.'

She did. She remembered the words clearly.

'So you took revenge. In the only way you could.'

Memories swirled through Elena's head. Her father's breath, hot and boozy. The weight of his body crushing hers. Herself, huddled on her bed afterwards, bewildered and enraged. Yes, she'd hated her dad for what he'd done. But she didn't kill him.

'You have five minutes to decide,' Sonia said.

Elena needed to be alone. As if in a dream, she walked into her bedroom and closed the door. Echoes of that night roared through her brain. The shame she'd felt. She'd never wash it away.

*****

In Elena's head, she was fifteen again, back in her childhood home, a scruffy sixth-floor flat in a rundown part of Bristol. Her father, Gerry Baxter, was an alcoholic. So was Elena's mother Kathy, although both managed to hold down jobs. Mostly they ignored Elena, who raised herself as best she could. She was all alone in the world.

Except for Sonia. Elena, reserved and thin-skinned, was drawn to Sonia's bullish temperament; what the other girl saw in her, she wasn't sure. Somehow, though, their friendship worked. Elena found in Sonia's parents the love and stability lacking in her life. Soon she was spending most of her time at Sonia's. Neither Gerry nor Kathy noticed. Or cared.

As Elena turned from girl to woman, she observed how her father's gaze often strayed to her budding breasts. The heat in his eyes made her cringe. Soon he was touching as well as staring. Kathy, of course, remained oblivious. Elena told no one, not even Sonia. Shame became her constant companion.

Elena was fifteen when her father, furious at being fired from his job, raped her in a drunken rage. She didn't sleep afterwards, the horror of Gerry Baxter's body on hers too raw, too recent. Shortly after six a.m. the doorbell rang. Muffled voices reached her.

Kathy threw open the door. 'You'd better get out here.'

When Elena walked into the living room, two female police officers were with Kathy. 'Is this your daughter?' one of them asked.

Her mother nodded. Elena listened, numb, as the officer spoke. Gerry Baxter was dead. His body was found earlier, broken and bloody after falling from the balcony of their flat into the communal car park. Elena's brain remained frozen. Last night, as her father raped her, she'd wanted him dead. Now she'd got her wish, and she was glad.

The coroner recorded an open verdict, deeming it impossible to know whether Gerry Baxter's death was accidental, due to the high level of alcohol in his blood, or suicide. Elena told herself she didn't care either way.

A month later, she broke down in front of Sonia. Sonia was prattling on about a boy she fancied, but Elena wasn't listening. In her head, her father was raping her again. Then his body smashed against hard concrete. Before she could stop them, tears poured down her cheeks.

Sonia stopped mid-sentence to stare at Elena. Then she pulled her into her arms. 'You're crying about your dad, right?'

Elena nodded. Sonia's hair smelt of flowers and love, and Elena's pain receded a little.

'You miss him, don't you?'

Elena pulled away. Her hands twisted in her lap. She shook her head.

'I don't understand,' Sonia said. 'I know your dad drank too much, but—'

'He raped me.'

'What?'

'The night he died. I tried to stop him, but he was too strong.'

'Whoa. Back up, will you?' Elena risked a glance at Sonia. Concern filled her friend's face. 'Your father *raped* you?'

'Yes. He'd been touching me for years. Nothing worse, not—well, you know. Until he got fired.'

'You should have told me. Or Mum.'

'I couldn't. I felt too ashamed. Oh, Sonia, it was so awful.'

'You shouldn't deal with this alone. Could you talk to Mrs Davis, maybe?'

The school counsellor. She'd barely exchanged two words with the woman. Elena shook her head. 'You can't ever tell anyone. Not even your mum.'

Sonia's hands squeezed Elena's. 'I won't. That's a promise.'

'I hated him,' Elena blurted. 'I wanted him dead.'

Sonia stared at her, her mouth slack with shock. 'You don't mean that.'

'Yes, I do. That night—I was so angry, and then he died. It's like I murdered him.'

'But you didn't. I know you, Elena. You couldn't have killed him.'

'No. But I wanted to.'

*****

'Time's up,' Sonia said, as she knocked on Elena's bedroom door.

Elena had already decided she had no choice. Sonia was stronger than her, always had been. After so long, Elena doubted a prosecution would ensue, or even an investigation. No evidence existed, and it would be her word against Sonia's. She couldn't take the risk, however. The mere thought of being questioned by the police terrified her. An interrogation would break her, the same way Gerry Baxter broke her years before. Sonia had realised this, of course, and used it to manipulate her.

Elena stared at her. Sonia's face was a slab of granite. Devoid of pity.

She had to try, however. 'You'd tell the police I murdered my father? When you know damn well I didn't?'

'As I said, in a heartbeat.'

Elena shook her head. 'I thought you were my friend.'

'Likewise. Then you slept with my husband.'

Elena knew she was defeated. She had no ammunition left with which to fight.

'You win,' she said. 'I'll give you my baby.'

CHAPTER 14

Elena's chest was tight with nerves, but her task was simple: to keep the appointment Sonia had made with her GP. A different doctor, one who'd never seen Sonia, following her former friend's move to a new medical practice. No way would the busy reception staff remember what Sonia looked like, not when a week had passed since she filled in the paperwork. She'd given Elena a rundown of her infertility problems so Elena could play along. Elena doubted that would be an issue. Sonia's old medical records probably hadn't been transferred yet. All she had to do was to go inside, give her name as Sonia Harding, so that Sonia's notes would show she was pregnant. Sonia had been very clear that that was how she wanted it.

'You'll be late if you don't get a move on.' Sonia's tone was cold, but Elena didn't blame her. It couldn't be easy for Sonia to spend time around her.

She got out of the car and slammed the door, heading towards the entrance. The reception area was welcoming, a whiff of antiseptic in the air. Elena plastered a smile on her face.

'My name is Sonia Harding. I have a ten o'clock appointment with Dr Williams.' How easy it was to lie. The baby inside Elena kicked, hard, and she gasped as she took a seat.

The surgery was running late, according to the receptionist. Elena's mouth dried as she waited. She tried to reassure herself that it'd be okay. Sonia and she had already rehearsed her story. All Elena had to do was play her part.

After she'd been waiting for forty minutes, the announcements board lit up and a voice boomed through the speaker. *Sonia Harding to room four, please. Sonia Harding to room four.*

Elena rose on cotton-wool legs and headed towards consulting room four. A chrome plaque was fixed to the door, bearing the name 'Dr R Williams.' She knocked, then pushed it open.

Dr Williams was an older man, somewhere in his fifties, glasses, bald. His expression was harried, and Elena's fear multiplied.

'Come in, Mrs Harding.' He gestured towards a chair. 'Sorry for the delay. Today's been hectic. What can I do for you?'

So it was that easy. Elena took a deep breath. The words she'd rehearsed with Sonia tumbled from her lips.

'I'm here to request antenatal care. Rather late, I know, but I didn't tell my other doctor I was pregnant.' Her gaze fell away. This was where things might get awkward.

She glanced at Dr Williams. He was frowning, and panic surged in Elena.

'May I ask why?' he said.

Elena managed a small smile. 'I didn't realise for ages. My periods have always been irregular, and I've been suffering with depression. My marriage was on the rocks, you see. I was miserable, so I turned to food. I thought I was gaining weight because of too many takeaways. It never occurred to me I might be pregnant. I've done a test, however, and it's positive. And now—' Elena forced another smile. 'My husband and I are back together. So here I am.'

Dr Williams stared at her, and Elena was terrified he'd rumbled her. Then he glanced at the clock on the wall, clearly concerned about his backlog of patients. He asked some questions about her pregnancy, and Elena's fear ebbed away. When she left minutes later, she had a referral to Southmead Hospital's antenatal team.

Phew. She'd done it. As far as Sonia Harding's medical records now showed, she was pregnant. Elena had been told she'd soon receive notification of her first scan date. Her legs shaky, she pushed open the swing doors and made her way back to Sonia's car.

'Well?' Sonia said, after Elena got into the passenger seat.

'Everything went fine. The next step is to have a scan at Southmead. You'll get a letter to inform you of the date.'

'Great. I'll come with you, of course.' They drove to Elena's flat in silence.

Sonia pulled up outside. 'My husband and I will give you the first half of your money later today.' She emphasised the words 'my husband' so that Elena got the message. Harry wasn't hers, never had been, despite the fact his son—Elena was still convinced her child would be a boy—occupied her womb. This was a business arrangement, nothing more.

Try telling that to her heart.

*****

Not long afterwards, Elena found herself in a waiting room again, this time at Southmead Hospital's antenatal unit, Sonia seated beside her. She flicked through a copy of *Homes and Garden*; as she stared at the photos of gorgeous houses she would never own, Elena reminded herself why she was doing this. Harry and Sonia would give her son the life he deserved. She couldn't.

A woman in blue scrubs came through the double swing doors, a clipboard in her hands. 'Sonia Harding?' she said, her eyes scanning the waiting area. Sonia dragged Elena to her feet, a wide smile on her face. 'That's us. I'm Sonia's friend, here for emotional support.'

'Hello, Sonia.' The woman smiled at Elena. 'My name is Hannah, and I'll be doing your scan today.'

They followed Hannah into a side room. Elena stared at the examination table, the machines that surrounded it, and fear jolted through her. The train she was riding had hurtled out of control; all she could do was hold tight and pray.

Hannah nodded at Sonia and gestured towards a chair. 'Your friend can sit there. This shouldn't take long.'

After a few questions, all of which Elena answered as if she were Sonia, Hannah directed her behind a screen so she could undress. Elena removed her skirt and knickers, set them to one side, and walked to the table, positioning herself on it. Hannah turned away from her computer monitor and came over.

'Right,' she said. 'I'm going to rub some jelly over your tummy. It'll feel cold, but some women like the sensation. I'll be running this—' she waved a probe that was connected to the machine at Elena—'over your bump, which will transmit pictures onto the screen. They'll allow me to see how your baby is doing.'

Elena lay back on the table. Hannah smoothed the icy gel over her belly and got to work with the probe.

'Ah, there we go,' she said, her voice all sing-song. 'A nice, clear picture. Let me just—' A frown puckered her brow as she moved the wand.

'Is everything okay? Is the baby—well, you know—properly formed?' Elena detected panic in Sonia's tone.

Hannah set down the probe. Her face broke into a grin. 'Want to look at the screen?'

Sonia immediately rushed over. 'Show us.'

Hannah turned the monitor their way. The image was dark, grainy, but clear enough. Two babies lay nestled in Elena's womb. One kicked its tiny foot; Elena gasped as she simultaneously felt the movement.

'You're having twins, Sonia,' Hannah said.

Elena stared at the fuzzy image. Now she understood why she'd grown so big so soon.

'Oh, my God,' Sonia said. Elena glanced at her; Sonia's face was pale, but her eyes radiated happiness.

Elena grew conscious that Hannah was waiting for a response. 'That's wonderful.'

'Yes, it is.' Sonia's smile was so wide it would surely break her face. 'Harry will be over the moon.'

'Would you like to know the sex of your babies?' Hannah asked.

'No,' Elena and Sonia said simultaneously. 'I want it to be a surprise,' Elena said, after a glance at Sonia.

Hannah smiled, then typed on her keypad while Sonia and Elena gazed at each other. Sonia took Elena's hand and squeezed it. 'Thank you,' she mouthed, and for a second their old connection resurfaced. Then Sonia dropped Elena's hand, and the moment was lost.

Hannah wiped the gel off Elena's stomach, then gestured towards the privacy screen. 'Get dressed, please, Sonia, so we can have a quick chat.'

Elena complied, then walked back to take the seat next to Hannah's desk. Before she could speak, Sonia butted in. 'What does this mean in practical terms? Are there any special complications involved in having twins?'

Hannah smiled at Elena. 'You're fit and healthy, so there shouldn't be too many problems. You needn't worry; we'll monitor you all the way.' A few more exchanges between Hannah and Sonia—Elena was still too dumbstruck to respond—and then they were done.

Sonia didn't speak until they were in her car. 'I've been doubly blessed,' she said, her voice thick with tears. 'I persuaded myself that one baby was fine. Didn't dare hope for more. Now, though? I'm delighted.' She blew her nose, wiped her face. Her cheeks were red and blotchy, but flushed with excitement.

Elena stayed silent, and fear replaced joy in Sonia's face. 'You're not having second thoughts, are you?' Her expression turned hard. 'Remember what I told you. About the police.'

As if Elena could forget. 'You've nothing to worry about. In three months you'll be a mother to twins. And I'll be out of your hair.'

*****

That evening Elena had just eaten a dish of pasta and meatballs when her doorbell rang. She set her plate aside, wondering who it could be.

Her visitor turned out to be Harry. No sign of Sonia. He smiled, albeit with a trace of nerves. 'Can I come in?'

She stared at him. 'Where's Sonia?'

He averted his gaze. 'She doesn't know I'm here. I told her I was returning some tools to a friend.'

This didn't feel right. Elena wasn't sure she was comfortable with Harry lying to Sonia, not after the tentative bond the two women had established that afternoon.

She gestured for him to enter, then closed the door. 'Can I get you a coffee?' she asked.

Harry shook his head. 'I won't stay long.' He perched on the sofa, and Elena joined him. Only a few inches separated them, but the emotional gulf was immense. Were it not for the fact she was carrying his babies, they might as well have been strangers.

'Why are you here?' she said.

'To thank you. For making me a father, for what you're doing for Sonia.' Harry glanced at Elena's belly. 'May I?' Without waiting for a reply, he traced his fingers over the curve of her stomach, his expression rapturous. Right on cue, Elena felt a kick within her; Harry jerked away, as if he'd touched a hot coal.

'Was that—?' Incredulity in his voice. Elena smiled, then guided his hand back to her belly. A whole series of kicks ensued this time. Harry didn't speak, but awe and wonder battled in his face. They sat like that for a few minutes, neither of them speaking. Elena could feel the warmth of Harry's palm through her clothing. When the kicks ceased, he withdrew his hand.

'Twins,' he said, his voice hoarse.

'Yes.'

'Two babies.'

Elena laughed. He was excited; well, of course he was. He'd make a great father. She recalled Harry's touch on her stomach and allowed herself a guilty fantasy. The two of them, married. Harry attending the next scan instead of Sonia.

For a second time, her feelings slipped out before she could rein them in. 'I love you.'

Harry leapt off the sofa as though he'd been scalded. 'Don't say that. Never again, you understand?' His words burned Elena like fire.

When she didn't respond, Harry walked to the door. 'I need to get going. You won't mention to Sonia that I was here, will you?'

She shook her head, her face hot with shame.

'She wouldn't understand. I had to feel the babies move, however. I couldn't do that in front of Sonia.'

Once Harry had gone, Elena slumped back on the sofa, her head a mess. Hadn't Harry already made it very clear he loved Sonia, not her? She needed to get that through her thick skull, and fast.

His indifference was made plainer still by the letter she found pushed through her door the following day.

I never intended to hurt you. Some relationships are not meant to be, and while I will always be grateful for what you've done, I can never love you the way you want. So take care of yourself, and be happy.

Harry

He was right, of course. Elena resolved to focus first on the birth, then life in a new city. She persuaded herself everything would turn out fine. Wouldn't it?

CHAPTER 15

Despite her immense belly and aching back, Elena remained in good health for the rest of her pregnancy. When she reached her thirty-fifth week, she went into labour one cold and damp morning. She'd just had breakfast and was standing at the sink in her kitchenette, washing her cereal bowl, when a warm gush flooded her legs. Throughout the night she'd had sporadic pains, but convinced herself they were Braxton Hicks contractions. She stumbled into her bathroom to get a towel to mop up the mess. Her mind was in overdrive; even at that point, she couldn't believe this was happening.

Once she'd cleaned herself up, Elena opened her wardrobe to retrieve the bag she'd packed in preparation. She glanced at the envelope of cash given to her by Sonia, the first half of the money she'd been promised. Best to take it with her, in case her flat got burgled while she was in hospital. Elena tucked the envelope inside her holdall, along with Harry's letter. Despite the rejection it contained, she couldn't part with it. Then she called Sonia.

She and Harry arrived at Elena's flat soon afterwards. The plan was that Harry would stay with Elena throughout the birth, the way he would if the real Sonia Harding was in labour. It had been Sonia's suggestion, even though Elena knew she hated the idea.

Sonia's face betrayed her panic when Elena opened the door. 'Oh, my God, you've gone into labour too soon. Something's wrong.'

'Try to relax, darling,' Harry said. 'How many times must I tell you? Thirty-seven weeks is considered full-term for twins. So Elena's only two weeks early.'

'I hope you're right. I can't lose these babies, not now.' Sonia's face was white with fear.

Harry drove the three of them to the hospital, and helped Elena into the maternity unit, his arm around her shoulders. Once he'd got her seated and spoken to a member of staff, he drew Sonia aside and said something Elena couldn't hear. Sonia nodded, then strode back towards Elena.

'I'll be thinking of you,' she said, her hand squeezing Elena's arm. Then she walked away.

A pain gripped Elena's belly, stronger than anything she'd experienced before. A nurse helped her into an adjacent room, with Harry following.

'It hurts,' she gasped as she was taken to the maternity suite, but she hadn't a clue how bad it would get.

After what seemed like forever, she pushed out the first baby. Bone-weary, she dredged up sufficient energy for the second, then the afterbirth. From somewhere far away, she heard Harry's voice. Two bundles were laid in her arms, but she was too dazed to look at them. Exhausted, she slept.

Elena woke up to a world shrouded in cotton wool. She didn't try to move, content in her cocoon of post-birth stupor. Part of her wondered where Harry was, but she couldn't bring herself to care.

Her babies. Were they all right? But that concern also slipped away.

Sometime later, a nurse approached Elena's bed. Her name, according to the tag she wore, was Priya. She smiled at Elena. 'Good to have you back with us. How are you feeling?'

Elena pulled herself from the warmth of her mental cocoon. She managed a faint smile. 'Tired. Sore.'

'Well, you would be. You needed stitches, remember. Don't worry, we can increase your pain relief if necessary.'

'What about—' Elena sucked in a breath. 'The babies?' She couldn't bring herself to say 'my babies'. They weren't hers. They belonged to Sonia and Harry.

Priya smiled again. 'A healthy boy and girl. They're a little underweight, as you didn't go full term, so we've got them in incubators in the special babies' unit. Now you're not to worry,' she said, as Elena blanched in alarm. 'Both of them are fine, with an excellent set of lungs on them. They shouldn't need long in there.'

'Harry? My husband,' Elena managed, her mouth dry. 'Where is he?'

'Outside. I'll let him know you're awake.'

Seconds later, Harry rushed in. He dragged a chair towards Elena's bed and perched on it, pulling her left hand into a firm grasp. Tears hovered in his eyes. 'Thank you,' he said, his voice hoarse. 'For giving us two beautiful babies.'

'You've seen them?' Stupid question. Of course he had.

'Yes. They're gorgeous.'

'Can I…?'

'As soon as you feel up to it, we'll visit them together. With Sonia too.' He lowered his voice to a whisper. 'She's desperate to be here, but I persuaded her to wait a while longer. It'll look odd if she visits the twins on her own, or with me.'

Elena nodded. What Harry had said made sense.

Later, she'd recovered enough to walk around a little. Sonia had just arrived, and the plan was for Harry and her, along with Elena playing the ecstatic new mother, to visit the babies. It'll be fine, Elena persuaded herself. With Harry's arm around Elena, the three of them made their way to the special babies' unit.

'Mr and Mrs Harding?' a nurse said, her gaze flitting between Elena and Harry. Elena sensed the tension emanating from Sonia. The nurse waved her arm towards the far wall. 'Your babies are down the end. Last two units.'

Elena, Harry and Sonia made their way to where the nurse indicated. As they grew nearer, Elena fell back, conscious of Sonia. 'You go first,' she said, her voice a low whisper.

Elena sank into the nearest chair, while Harry and Sonia stared into the two incubators. 'Oh, my God,' Sonia said, awe in her voice. She burst into noisy sobs.

Sonia wept for a while before turning to face Elena. 'Thank you,' she said. 'I can't tell you how grateful I am.' She pulled Harry back to the incubators.

Elena listened to them rhapsodise about the babies, one thought hammering through her head:

Please God, let this be over soon. She'd felt oddly tearful before Sonia's arrival at the hospital, as though she yearned to cry and never stop. Post-baby hormones, she told herself, even though it seemed way too early. By the time she was discharged, she'd probably be fine.

'Don't you want to see the babies?' Harry's voice tore her from her thoughts. Elena nodded; it seemed the right thing to do. On seeing her struggle to get up, Harry rushed to assist her. His arm around Elena's shoulders, he steered her towards the incubators. 'Meet Olivia Rose and Cameron James Harding,' he said.

Elena stared into the nearest incubator. A gasp caught in her throat.

Inside lay the most perfect baby Elena had ever seen. Small, sure, but so beautiful. A blue knitted hat covered his head, but a wisp of dark hair poked out on one side. Cameron James Harding's eyes roved over her face, his tiny fists waving in the air. As she inched closer, a thin wail sounded from the adjacent incubator. Elena edged over to peer inside, and saw another perfect baby, this one wearing a pink hat. Her eyes flitted between the two of them, and a love so fierce, so intense, that she could hardly stand engulfed her. Elena sagged against Harry; were it not for his arm around her, she'd have crumpled to the floor. He steered her to the chair next to Sonia, who jumped up to admire the babies again.

'We need to get you back to bed, so you can rest. Can you give us a few minutes more with them?' Happiness filled his tone, and Elena nodded.

Nothing had prepared her for the visceral love she felt for the two tiny human beings in the incubators. This was what she'd dreaded, what she'd persuaded herself wouldn't happen, but it had. Olivia Rose and Cameron James Harding had claimed Elena's heart, and the enormity of what Harry and Sonia expected of her hit her like a sledgehammer. Her hands gripped her seat, their knuckles white. What on earth had she done?

Harry turned to Elena, and a frown crossed his face.

'You don't look well. Let's get you back to bed.' He helped Elena to her feet, Sonia supporting her other side, and the three of them left.

'We'll return tomorrow,' were Harry's last words.

Alone at last, Elena attempted to gather her thoughts. Had she been less sore, she'd have rushed off to marvel at her beautiful babies. Tears flooded her eyes and she fumbled for a tissue. At that moment, Priya entered the unit and spotted Elena's distress.

'What's the matter, Mrs Harding?' she said, concern in her tone.

'I don't know,' Elena managed, between sobs. How could she explain the jumble of thoughts in her head?

Priya smiled, a knowing look on her face. 'There's no need to worry. You've just got a touch of the baby blues, kicking in earlier than usual.' She explained further, but Elena was only half listening. This, she knew, was more than her hormones running riot. Terror gnawed at her guts; the idea of handing over Olivia and Cameron once she left hospital was unbearable.

Once Priya had gone, Elena tried to think. She'd made an agreement with Harry and Sonia, the facts of which hadn't changed. Elena might not have signed a contract, but she still had a moral obligation to keep her side of the bargain. Besides, she couldn't care for one child, let alone two.

For the next couple of hours Elena lay on her bed, picturing her beautiful twins. Knowing that she'd soon leave the hospital with them, like any normal mother, but the story would end when she handed them to Harry and Sonia. Her heart cracked into a thousand pieces at the thought.

Later, after Elena had eaten lunch, she made her way back to the special babies' unit. Guilt surrounded her as she walked towards the end of the room, her gaze on Olivia and Cameron's incubators. She shouldn't be doing this, not without Harry and Sonia. Sonia, in particular, wouldn't approve. To hell with her. A quick peek couldn't hurt.

Elena reached Cameron's incubator and placed a palm on one side. 'Hello, my darling.'

Her eyes travelled over his miniature fingers, those perfect nails, the pink of his mouth. However did she create this exquisite creature? So fragile, yet so beautiful, and Elena was entranced. She imagined his head nestled against her arm as she rocked him back and forth. Her baby, her Cameron, the little boy she'd always envisaged having. Elena's eyes filled with tears and she couldn't speak, so great was the emotion welling inside her. She hadn't realised such intense love was possible. At that moment, her son opened his eyes to stare at her as he stretched a finger in her direction. Elena's hand mimicked Cameron's, tapping the cool Plexiglas as his tiny nail clinked against it. They were connected, and she never wanted the moment to end.

A passing nurse smiled when she saw Elena. 'They'll be out of there before long,' she said. 'Both of them are fit and healthy, and they'll soon be able to maintain their body temperatures by themselves. You and your husband will be able to take them home in a day or two.'

Except that they wouldn't. But Elena couldn't say that aloud.

Instead, she stared at her son, and almost burst with love. Cameron was her soul, her everything. She'd give everything she owned to hold him for a few minutes.

A faint noise from the adjacent incubator roused her from her thoughts. She shuffled over to stand beside her daughter. As she did with Cameron, Elena placed her hands on the Plexiglas and stared at the scrap of life within its walls.

Like her brother, Olivia was gorgeous beyond measure. The same perfect mouth, identical miniature fingernails. Her daughter shifted in her sleep, snuffling sounds escaping her lips; Elena wondered what she was dreaming of.

'My beautiful girl,' she whispered, as mesmerised by Olivia as she was with Cameron. Although Elena had never imagined having a daughter, there she was, and she adored every inch of her little Olivia Rose.

How long Elena stayed with her babies, she didn't remember. She only knew that she was stiff and sore when she walked back to her bed, desperate for sleep, yet torn with the urge to remain with her children.

CHAPTER 16

The hours ticked by as Elena dozed on and off. Every waking moment was dominated by thoughts of Cameron and Olivia. Fantasies drifted through her mind. Their first steps and words. Herself, walking them to school each morning. Olivia's wedding dress.

None of that could happen, however. In a few short days she'd have to turn her beautiful babies over to Sonia; she cursed the day she made that damn agreement.

Logic battled with emotion inside Elena. She pictured herself in her tiny flat with her babies, two cots squeezed into her small bedroom. There was barely enough room for her, let alone her twins, and Elena's neighbours wouldn't appreciate screaming newborns keeping them awake at night. Neither would her landlord. Should he choose, he could make her homeless, and then what could she do? She'd end up with nowhere to live, Olivia and Cameron dependent on her, at the mercy of Social Services to house them. Her babies deserved better.

*****

Elena was woken the following morning by two nurses, each wheeling a tiny cot. She sat up in bed, ignoring the discomfort in her belly. Here were her babies, and it was too early for Harry and Sonia to visit. A glimmer of triumph flickered within her.

She'd be the first to hold those precious bundles now they'd left their incubators.

The nurses placed the cots on either side of Elena's bed. After they'd gone, she reached into Cameron's one. His feet and hands wriggled adorably as he opened sleepy eyes in Elena's direction. She was terrified to touch him, yet exhilarated too. With great care, she picked him up. A slick of drool escaped his mouth, and Elena had never seen anything so enchanting. Her son had a good head of hair, thick and dark, and she traced the fingers of her free hand over the silky strands. Then over his cheeks, his skin so soft and delicate. Elena could swear Cameron smiled at her, his tiny lips upturned at each end. She pressed a kiss on his forehead, marvelling at its petal softness. His eyes drifted shut again. Elena's own ones closed in bliss as she rocked him. Her son lay in her arms, and all was well with her world.

After ten minutes, he was fast asleep. Elena settled him back in his cot, relieved that he didn't wake up. Then she turned to marvel at her daughter.

Olivia was also asleep, and Elena wondered whether to risk waking her. The temptation proved too strong. Harry and Sonia would arrive before long, and she needed this precious time alone with her children. Elena picked up her daughter; Olivia didn't stir as she placed her where Cameron had lain a few moments before. She gazed at her child, unable to believe a plain Jane like her had produced something so beautiful. As she did with Cameron, Elena traced her fingers through Olivia's hair, also dark and plentiful. She rocked her daughter while she stared at her son, still asleep in his cot.

Elena checked the clock on the wall. The time was one minute to nine, and she knew Harry and Sonia would arrive the second visiting hours begin. With infinite care, she placed Olivia in her cot. Her arms already felt empty. Tears threatened to overwhelm Elena, but the door opened, and she choked them back.

'Oh, my God!' The words issued simultaneously from Harry and Sonia as they spotted the two cots. Sonia rushed towards Olivia, picking up Elena's daughter with the utmost gentleness before cradling her against her heart. Meanwhile Harry had headed to Cameron's cot and was holding his son. Jealousy roared through Elena as her gaze flitted between Harry and Sonia.

'Why don't you sit down?' Irritation edged into her voice. They shouldn't be standing, not with her beautiful babies in their arms. What if they dropped them?

Harry glanced at her as he took a seat, with Sonia doing the same. 'How are you feeling this morning?'

Elena shrugged. 'Sore. Tired. Like I've just had twins.' Inside, she was screaming. *I'm so stupid. Why did I ever agree to give up my babies?*

Harry and Sonia continued to fuss over Cameron and Olivia. Elena's mouth tightened with anger. She deflected their attempts at conversation, her gaze on her children. So perfect. So beautiful.

After half an hour, Sonia placed Olivia in her cot. 'Back in five minutes. I need the toilet.' With that, she was gone.

Harry also laid Cameron down. He glanced at Elena, his expression unreadable. From the messenger bag he'd brought, he extracted scissors and two envelopes. Elena stared at him, puzzled.

Harry positioned the scissors against his son's hair and snipped off a lock an inch long. From one envelope he produced a tiny blue ribbon, which he used to bind the hairs together before placing them in the envelope. Taking a pen from the bag, he wrote his son's name and date of birth on the outside. Then he turned his attention to Olivia's cot. Seconds later a lock of his daughter's hair lay inside the other envelope, bound by a pink ribbon. Harry wrote a similar inscription on the front.

'I want you to have these,' he said. 'As a memento. In a few days we'll take Cam and Liv home and I won't see you again. You'll never know how much happiness you've brought Sonia and me.' He opened her bedside cabinet and placed the two envelopes inside.

Before Elena could respond, Sonia returned. She gazed at Olivia, adoration in her face, and the sight pushed Elena's irritation into overdrive.

'I'm tired,' she announced, closing her eyes. 'It's time I rested.'

'Are you okay? Should I call a nurse?' Concern in Harry's voice.

'No. Just go, please.'

'But we've only just got here.' Sonia's mouth was pinched with annoyance.

'We'll return later,' Harry said, as he got up to leave. 'Come on, darling. Elena needs to sleep.'

Wrong, Elena thought. After they'd gone, she called for a nurse. To her relief, it was Priya who responded.

'Could you—?' Elena waved her hands towards her babies. 'I'd love to cuddle the two of them together. If you wouldn't mind helping?'

'Of course.' Priya placed the twins, one after the other, in Elena's arms.

'Thank you,' Elena managed, overwhelmed with emotion.

Priya smiled. 'I'll come back later and settle them down again. You need to rest, Mrs Harding.'

Love and fear battled within Elena as she cradled her children. How could she ever relinquish them?

Over the course of the next hour, she reached a decision. After Priya had placed Cameron and Olivia back in their cots, Elena got out of bed and shuffled down the corridor to a row of pay phones. Before she knew what she was doing, she'd called the landline at Harry's house, praying he'd answer rather than Sonia. To her relief, he did.

'Are you okay?' he asked.

'I'm fine. Listen, can you pop in this afternoon? Not with Sonia, though. I need to talk to you in private.' Elena held her breath.

'What is there to discuss?' Suspicion in Harry's voice.

She moistened her dry lips. 'I can't tell you over the phone. Please come. And don't tell Sonia.'

Harry continued to baulk, but caved in at last. 'I'll stop by at lunchtime. If you insist.'

Fifty minutes later he burst into her room, his face pale, his expression harried. He stared into Cameron and Olivia's cots, then pulled up a chair. 'What's this about? Why all the subterfuge?'

Elena dragged in a breath. This wouldn't be easy. 'I don't know if I can do it. Give them up for adoption, I mean.'

Harry's jaw tightened. His eyes became two chips of ice. Elena braced herself.

'You gave us your word,' he said. 'There might be nothing in writing, but you gave us—Sonia and me—your solemn promise. Doesn't that mean anything to you?'

'I didn't think I'd fall in love with them.' Elena couldn't look at him. 'I never meant this to happen.'

'You said it yourself. You'd never be able to cope with twins.'

She didn't know what to say. He was right.

Elena found the courage to glance at him. 'I'm begging you. Please. I'll go away, and you'll never hear from me again, I swear. Sonia—she might still get pregnant. Or she can have IVF or adopt. But don't take my children from me.'

Harry got up and sat on Elena's bed. He was so close his face was only a few inches from hers. Elena shrank against her pillows, scorched by the anger in his gaze.

'Like I said, you promised. We asked you repeatedly whether you were sure. You always said yes.' He leaned in further. 'I want to make something very clear. In two days' time, I expect to walk out of here with my children. Afterwards, I'll give you the rest of your money so you can leave Bristol. Then I never want to see you again. Got it?'

Elena nodded, incapable of speech.

'Let me make something else clear. Don't even think about telling people you're Cam and Liv's mother. A DNA test will prove they carry my genes as well as yours. Who do you reckon the courts will favour in a custody case? You, dependent on state benefits, living in that poky shit-hole? Or me, their father, with a stable income, job, house and wife?'

His eyes bored into her as Elena digested Harry's words. Should she remind him he and Sonia had broken the law in paying for a surrogate pregnancy? She lacked the strength to argue, however. Exhausted, she nodded her defeat.

'I'm bringing Sonia in later. You will not, under any circumstances, mention this conversation to her. She deserves those babies, will be a far better mother than you'll ever be.' He strode from the room, leaving Elena stunned.

*****

As promised, Harry returned with Sonia that evening. His eyes delivered a warning to Elena as he entered.

Sonia sat beside Elena, Olivia in her arms. Harry leaned into Cameron's cot, picked his son up and cradled him against his chest.

'Harry tells me he's spoken with the midwife, and the babies will leave hospital on Friday.' Sonia smiled, her face radiant. 'I can't wait to get Cameron and Olivia home.'

Harry shot Elena another warning glance. 'Sonia and I have agreed it's best I come alone to collect you. It'll look odd for her to be there if we're supposed to be husband and wife.'

'I'll be busy making sure everything's ready,' Sonia chipped in. Elena forced herself to make small talk with them, counting the minutes until they left.

At last Sonia stood up, reluctance in her face. 'It's time we got going.' She cleared her throat. 'Thank you again.'

'You're welcome,' Elena managed through dry lips. As Sonia turned away, busy with buttoning her coat, Harry caught Elena's eye. He extracted an envelope from his pocket and placed it on her bedside cabinet. His gaze never leaving Elena's, he crossed to Sonia and took her arm. 'We'll see you tomorrow,' he said, before the two of them left.

Elena tore open the envelope with trembling fingers. She pulled out the piece of paper inside and read what was written there.

Dear Elena,

What you said today disturbed me. I hope you understand that giving the babies to Sonia and me is the best way forward. The only one, in my opinion. We had an agreement, remember. You said it yourself—you can't look after one child, let alone two. Cameron and Olivia will have stability, security and love. They will want for nothing, I can promise you that.

You'll receive the rest of your money after the babies leave hospital. I wish you all the best, but what you asked of me earlier is impossible.

Yours, Harry

Elena stuffed the letter back in the envelope. Harry had made his position very clear. The problem was, she wasn't prepared to relinquish her babies so readily. A plan was forming in her mind. Elena couldn't look after two children, but one might be possible, right? Other women coped as single mothers. Why not Elena?

Resolve flooded through her. She'd honour her promise to Harry and leave Bristol. Elena would also keep her word to Sonia. Her former friend would be a mother, just not to twins. Both women would get what they wanted.

She knew Harry and Sonia couldn't say anything to the authorities once they discovered one of the twins gone. They'd committed a crime in paying Elena surrogacy money. Falsified information on the birth records, too. Elena was pretty sure Sonia would keep quiet.

But oh—the thought of abandoning one of her babies was torture. Elena gazed at Cameron in his cot and remembered how she'd always pictured herself with a son. Sonia, on the other hand, would adore a daughter. Elena loved Olivia so much it hurt. But it seemed best to allow Sonia and Harry to parent Olivia, while Elena made a new life with Cameron.

The more she thought about it, the more it appeared the perfect solution, even if it meant separating the twins. Babies needed love and stability more than siblings, right?

It wouldn't be easy. Paperwork and checks would be involved; she couldn't just walk out of hospital with Cameron in her arms.

She believed she knew a way, however.

CHAPTER 17

Elena awoke early on Friday morning, showered and got dressed, then managed a few mouthfuls of breakfast. Next she packed, filling her small holdall with her clothes and stuff for Cameron. The envelope containing her first instalment of cash went into a side pocket, along with Harry's letters.

'Today's the day,' Priya said as she watched Elena pack. 'When's your husband arriving?'

'Ten o'clock,' Elena replied, her gaze fixed on Cameron. 'Plenty of time yet.'

Once Priya had gone, Elena turned to Olivia's cot. Her baby girl was awake, all gurgles and wriggling limbs; Elena's love burned so fiercely she was scared she might faint. She pulled her daughter into her arms, inhaling her scent of baby shampoo and something uniquely Olivia. Elena held her child against her breasts, the soft warmth of her delicious beyond words. The world narrowed itself to her and Olivia. Elena knew if she didn't let go soon, she'd never be able to part with her gorgeous girl.

She pressed a kiss into Olivia's hair. 'I love you so much, my darling. You'll be in my heart until I die.' She laid her daughter back in her cot, then picked up Cameron. Elena couldn't look at Olivia again. If she did, her resolve would break.

Harry arrived on the dot of ten. Once they'd completed the discharge process, they headed towards his car, Harry carrying Olivia in a car seat with a handle, Elena with Cameron in another. The wind blew cold around them, a steady drizzle in the air. In her mind, Elena was married to Harry, and they were like any other couple leaving hospital with their newborns.

He caught her staring at him. 'What?'

Elena forced a smile. 'Nothing. Just relieved it's all over.'

They reached Harry's Volvo. He fastened Olivia's car seat in the back, then traced a finger over his daughter's cheek. 'So beautiful,' he said. Elena still couldn't bear to look.

'Cameron's turn.' Harry said. Elena handed her son to his father without a word.

Once his children were secure, Harry slipped into the driving seat, with Elena beside him, her holdall at her feet. Harry turned to Elena. 'I can't thank you enough,' he said.

Elena nodded, unable to meet his gaze. Harry handed her an envelope, fat with cash. Elena tucked the money inside her holdall, and they set off.

Elena needed to implement her plan before she lost her nerve. She feigned a retching sound while clutching her stomach. 'Could you stop the car, please? I'm going to be sick.'

'Oh, my God. Yes, of course. Take some deep breaths to see if that helps. Damn. There's nowhere to pull in.' Harry turned into a side road. It was lined with parked cars, but Harry bagged a spot close to the main road. He killed the engine, then scrutinised Elena, a frown on his face. 'Are you all right?'

'Better now the car's stopped. Could we go get a cold drink somewhere? Please?'

'Sure, provided we're quick. Sonia's waiting, remember.'

As if Elena could forget. She grabbed Cameron, one hand on his baby seat, the other grasping her holdall, then shut the car door. Harry followed suit, taking Olivia.

'I can lock your bag in the boot if you like,' he said. 'Or carry it for you.'

Elena shook her head. 'I'd prefer to keep it with me. All that money. What if your car gets stolen? And I'm not helpless.'

He shrugged. 'Fine.'

Harry set off, Elena trailing behind. Once they were back on the main road, Elena scanned the area for what she knew, from previous trips to the area, was around somewhere. Ah, there it was. A taxi rank, and one with cabs lined up.

'There's a cafe ahead,' Harry said over his shoulder.

'Sounds great,' Elena replied, keen to show she was still nearby. She hurried towards the taxi rank, her heart constricted with fear, Cameron wriggling in his baby seat. She wrenched open the door of the nearest cab, her holdall banging against the paintwork.

'Broadmead bus station, please,' she told the driver. After he set off, they passed Harry, his eyes scanning the pavement, his expression frantic. Alone with his panic, he took no notice of the taxi.

I've done it, Elena thought. Then she remembered. She'd never see her daughter again.

*****

Elena ditched Cameron's car seat at the bus station, preferring to hug him close to her instead. She pulled a woollen shawl from her bag to wind around herself and Cameron, then scrutinised the departures board. There was a coach leaving at half eleven for Newcastle-upon-Tyne. As good a destination as any, she supposed. It also had the advantage of being three hundred miles from Bristol. Newcastle it was, then.

Cameron was fractious during the first part of the journey, drawing disapproving glances from the couple across the aisle. Once the coach reached Leeds, however, he settled into a restless doze. At last the coach pulled to a halt in Newcastle's St James Boulevard. The journey had taken nine bone-shaking hours, and by now it was dark. Once Elena disembarked, she stood on the pavement, trying to get her bearings, the wind about her chilly.

'You lost, hen?' a woman said. 'If you want the nearest Metro, it's that way.'

Crowds of people jostled Elena as she headed towards the Metro station. Inside its warmth, she scrutinised the route map, a name catching her eye. Tynemouth. She'd seen pictures in holiday brochures of the beach, the castle. Decision made. Elena slumped on a seat, exhausted in both mind and body. A dull headache pounded at her temples, and Cameron chose that moment to awake. His face all screwed up, he emitted a series of loud wails. A pungent odour assaulted Elena's nostrils, and she realised his nappy needed changing. That would have to wait until she'd found somewhere to stay. A little bed-and-breakfast place; she'd rest, and tomorrow she'd rent the first available flat. She only had to make it through another twenty-four hours.

Cameron continued to wail. Elena wound the shawl tighter around him to keep him warm.

'Not long now, darling,' she murmured, but he still grizzled.

The train arrived, and Elena boarded it. Not long after, she disembarked in Tynemouth. After exiting the station, she walked through the village in search of a cheap hotel. Her legs were lead-heavy as she trudged past the castle, her holdall a dead weight at the end of her arm. Cameron still grizzled against her in his makeshift sling. At last she found a rundown guest house, a 'Vacancies' sign in the window. Elena walked up the path and rang the bell.

The woman who answered eyed Cameron with disfavour, but didn't refuse them. She even provided a cot for him. The room was shabby and not particularly clean, but Elena was past caring. She changed Cameron, fed him and settled him down. Although desperate for sleep, she needed a plan of action for tomorrow and beyond. First she'd register Cameron's birth, and afterwards—

Horror washed over her. Harry, of course, had the twins' paperwork from the hospital, without which Elena couldn't register Cameron as her son. And what about his infant health record, that red book that was also with Harry? Clearly she hadn't thought this through. Why did her brain feel like it was shrouded in fog? She climbed into bed, still clothed, and shut her eyes.

Right when Elena was drifting into a doze, Cameron awakened in a burst of angry howls.

Elena hurried to his cot to pick him up. She was so exhausted, so drained; why was he doing this? His stomach was full, his nappy clean, so what was the problem? She gritted her teeth as he continued to cry, his face red with fury, and she rocked him harder, the movement almost brutal, in an effort to soothe him. Two words pounded in her brain: *Shut up. Shut up. Shut up.*

At last Cameron's wails petered out, and he drifted off to sleep. Elena didn't dare put him back in his cot, too frightened of waking him. Her arm under his body grew numb, then painful. Tears streamed from under her lids, and Elena hated herself for her weakness. She stared at the ceiling, her mind a blank.

Cameron stirred and awakened amid more loud yells. His screams sliced through Elena's brain and obliterated any chance of rest. She glared at his red face, his eyes dark with fury, and anger surged within her. Was she to get no peace?

She struggled to a seated position and checked his nappy. It was soaked with urine. Damn. Elena shuffled to the edge of the bed, dragged her holdall towards her, and extracted wet wipes and a nappy. She changed him, her actions robotic, her son crying all the while. Once his nappy was clean Elena offered him her nipple, but Cameron turned his head away. Was he ill? She placed her hand on his forehead, but it was cool.

'What do you want?' The words emerged through clenched teeth. 'What the hell is wrong with you?'

A knock on the door. When she opened it, Cameron still in her arms, the landlady stood there.

She cast a sour look at the screaming child. 'I'm sure you're doing your best. But I hope you'll get him to settle through the night. My husband needs to get up early for work.'

Elena was too tired, too defeated, to reply. She nodded, then closed the door.

She laid Cameron, whose cries had subsided to an occasional whimper, in his cot. Once that was done, she climbed into bed again and shut her eyes.

Sleep didn't come. Elena was on edge, every nerve primed in case the howling recommenced. She'd been deluded to think she might be mother material. Why hadn't she given both her babies to Harry and Sonia instead? Stupid, so stupid of her.

When the night was at its darkest and coldest, and Elena's thoughts were at their bleakest, Cameron woke up. His screams started straightaway.

Elena forced herself to go to him. Her hands fingered the blue woollen blanket around her son. How easy it would be to wrap its length over that tiny mouth, seal it shut, hush the endless wails. To sink into blessed quiet, during which she'd sleep at last. Her grip tightened on the wool. Cameron fell silent, and Elena relaxed a little. She unwound the blanket and recoiled at the stench from his nappy.

Cameron continued to howl even after Elena had changed and fed him, and the tension in her belly became as hard as stone. Her rocking of her son grew furious, a harsh see-sawing that only distressed him more. His face was beet-red, his hands fists of fury. In an instant, he turned ugly beyond measure. Repulsed, she thrust him away, causing him to tumble into her lap; he shrieked even louder in protest. Elena's patience, stretched way too far, finally snapped.

'SHUT UP! SHUT UP! FOR GOD'S SAKE, WILL YOU SHUT THE HELL UP!'

That red, enraged face. His constant wailing. She hated him. Wished he were dead.

A door opened. Footsteps strode across the landing. A fist pounded on the door. A male voice. 'Keep the noise down, can't you? My wife and I are trying to sleep.'

Elena was incapable of a reply. She held her breath, her heart thudding in her chest.

'Is everything all right? Do we need to call Social Services? The police?'

'No,' Elena managed. 'I'm sorry. I'll settle him soon, I promise.' Her nerves were in tatters as she waited for a response. Instead she heard footsteps retreating, a door closing.

Elena stayed immobile, Cameron still in her lap. His cries were quieter now, as though he'd exhausted his rage. As had Elena. Drained, bone-weary, she was unable to process the meltdown she'd had.

Cameron's wails soon trailed into silence. Elena shuffled back to bed with him, drew the duvet over them and lay there sleepless. Thoughts floated into her mind of the North Sea, so close to her hotel. She pictured the ocean, dark and restless before her, and imagined walking into its depths, her child clasped to her breasts. The icy coldness that rose up her legs as she pressed forward. In her head, the sea covered her son's face, entered his tiny mouth, filled his lungs. Before long Elena was out of her depth. They drifted away into oblivion.

Cameron shifted against Elena, breaking the spell. Her eyes flew wide in horror. Had she really contemplated killing her son?

You did earlier too, her inner voice answered.

'No, no, no,' she whispered.

Elena knew her brain wasn't functioning as it should. The ecstasy she experienced on first seeing the twins seemed very far away. All she could remember was that, for a few moments, she'd hated Cameron. Only a monster would do that, surely?

Her son wasn't safe with her. Sonia should have been Cameron's mother, not Elena, but that was no longer an option. No way could she return to Bristol; the idea of facing Sonia's rage terrified Elena. She was so exhausted, though. Inside she was dead, and she didn't think she'd ever come alive again.

Cameron dozed off at last, but Elena stared at the ceiling, a solution edging into her consciousness.

Was she capable of it? When she could barely think or move?

The answer, when it came, proved a relief. She'd do it. It would be best all round.

*****

When morning arrived Elena peeled herself off the bed, her eyes scratchy from lack of sleep. She fed and changed Cameron, who was still dozing, on autopilot, then wrapped him in the shawl, secured him against her chest and grabbed her holdall. A little more awake now, she padded downstairs. Nobody was around. Elena opened the guest register and tore out the page she'd signed yesterday. The landlady hadn't glanced at it afterwards; didn't even ask her name. Elena crumpled the paper into a ball and stuffed it into the handbag she'd already taken from her holdall, along with the envelopes of cash and hair, and Harry's letters. She placed her key on the side table and walked out the door.

Elena headed towards the seafront, exhaustion dogging her every step. Against the skyline stood the ruins of Tynemouth Priory and Castle, the metal gate open due to resurfacing work on the access path. Rubbish bins awaiting collection lined the pavements. Few people were up so early: a homeless guy in a doorway, a man hurrying towards the Metro. Nobody paid Elena any attention. If anyone saw her, she doubted they could describe her. A woman, dressed in dark clothing, a holdall in one hand. Ordinary, forgettable. They wouldn't notice the baby she held against her breast, hidden under her coat.

Cameron stirred, let out a weak wail. Elena ignored her son as she stumbled past the homeless guy, towards the rubbish bins. Behind them stood the castle, the sound of the sea below a distant murmur.

Elena persuaded herself she was doing the right thing. For everyone.

Part Three

Elena - now

CHAPTER 18

Thirty years later Elena walked out of Bristol's Royal Infirmary hospital, having just been discharged following the attack on her at her flat. A mild concussion, she'd been told; plenty of rest, no driving, limited screen time. A persistent ache throbbed at the back of her head. All Elena wanted was to sleep for a week and then talk to Olivia. Her daughter needed to know who her biological mother was. That she had a twin brother. The timing hadn't been right before, what with Olivia's grief over Sonia. Now it was. Cameron—no, Connor, as he was now called—also deserved the truth.

Elena's guts twisted in revulsion at the ugly words her son had screamed at her the day before, prior to attacking her. *Dumped in a rubbish bin.* He must have meant them metaphorically, she decided. She couldn't forget the fury in his face, however. The force with which he shoved her to the floor.

The summer sun worsened the throb in her head. She'd pop a painkiller once she got home. A couple of hours' sleep, then she'd visit Olivia. Tell her everything.

'Hello, Elena.' The voice, so unexpected, startled her. Elena stared at the woman in front of her. Tall, slim, with greying hair swept into a messy topknot, blue eyes cold and distant. Her clothes proclaimed casual elegance: black trousers with a knife-edge crease, a cerise wool jacket. Shiny shoes, matching leather handbag. The accent, Elena realised, had a twang of Geordie in it. This woman hailed from the north-east.

Elena had never seen her before. 'I'm sorry. Do I know you?'

'We've never met.'

'Then how—'

'My son's told me all about you. Including your name.'

A chill stole over Elena, despite the sunshine. She stared at the woman, confused.

'What you look like. Where you live.' An icy hardness pervaded every word.

Elena took a step backward. 'I don't understand.'

'No. But you will.'

To Elena's relief, a taxi drew up. She moved towards it, eager to escape the unhinged stranger. A hand on her arm stopped her.

'I wouldn't do that if I were you,' the woman said.

*****

Elena shrank back against the car window. She was in the passenger seat of the woman's Nissan, those cold blue eyes pinning her in place.

'I don't understand,' she repeated. Words echoed in her head. *We need to talk. About the letter you wrote to Connor Brady.* The reason she was here with this person who made her every nerve in her body shudder. What connection did she have with Elena's son?

'My name is Rebecca Brady. I'm Connor's adoptive mother.'

Elena almost heard the click in her brain as understanding slotted into place. Rebecca Brady must regard her as a rival. Hence the hostility.

'His proper mother, I should say,' Rebecca continued. 'Not like you. What kind of woman abandons her baby?'

She didn't wait for an answer, and Elena had none to give. Fear had dried her mouth, stilled her tongue.

'He's suffered hell, thanks to you. Years of mental illness, weeks in psychiatric wards, unable to work or even function sometimes. His father and I—well, we've done our best, but he's damaged.'

Ice formed in Elena's belly. She'd feared as much, having seeing her son for the first time in three decades after he came to her flat yesterday. The stench of him. His matted hair. The fury in his face as he pushed her, his hands hard and angry, causing her head to slam against the coffee table. Spit flying from his mouth as he ranted, while she lay on the floor, bleeding and confused. The dreadful accusations he'd made.

'So you'll understand my anger when he told me you'd tracked him down. Written him a letter, trying to worm your way back into my son's life.' Rebecca's knuckles were white against the black steering wheel. 'I warned him. Begged him to ignore you. But he was adamant. Said he needed to know.'

Elena found her voice. Only one word, the sound strangled. 'Know what?'

'The reason you abandoned him. The shame of it—it's messed up his head. Do you have any idea how badly you've hurt him?'

Elena shrank back further. She'd give everything she owned to turn back time. Reverse the terrible decision she made decades before. But she couldn't.

'How do you think it feels to discover you were thrown in the trash? Tossed away like you were garbage?' Rebecca jabbed a furious finger into Elena's arm.

The words echoed those of Connor before he attacked her. They swirled in her head, but made no sense.

'I didn't,' Elena whispered. 'I would never—
'

'But you did. Don't try to deny it.'

'You're wrong.'

'No, *you* are. You're vile, disgusting, abhorrent. The bag was on top of a pile of potato peelings. Not only did you abandon your baby, but you didn't even bother to leave him somewhere safe. Didn't you realise why the bin was on the pavement? Because it was collection day, you rotten bitch.' Spit flew from Rebecca Brady's lips. 'If he hadn't been found, he'd have ended up crushed to death in the bin lorry.'

'That's not what happened. I—'

'You even zipped the bag shut. He could have suffocated.' Hatred laced Rebecca's every word.

Elena's mouth was so dry she struggled to speak. 'I left him at the castle. Under shelter, where the staff would find him when they arrived later. I made sure the bag was open so he could breathe. I'd never—'

'Don't lie, you cold-hearted cow. However many times you say it, repetition doesn't make it true.'

Memories washed over Elena. Sleep deprivation. Shredded nerves. Herself, exhausted, unable to cope. Her fantasy of walking with Cameron into the sea, never to return.

Above all, Elena recalled a baby's incessant screams, matched by her own. '*SHUT UP! SHUT UP! FOR GOD'S SAKE, WILL YOU SHUT THE HELL UP!*'

Elena understood she'd most likely suffered post-natal depression, or even psychosis, thirty years ago. She recalled the love—pure, intense, like nothing she'd ever imagined—that had overwhelmed her as she gazed at her babies. Once she left hospital, however, darkness had descended, until everything else disappeared.

'I left him by the castle,' she repeated. But did she? Right now, her brain still foggy after the concussion, Elena was certain of nothing.

'Zach and I gave him a home, warmth, love, everything you didn't,' Rebecca said. 'So you'll understand why I'm not exactly thrilled you've resurfaced. Why I can't allow my son any contact with you. He's way too fragile.'

Because of me, Elena thought. The pain in her heart doubled, grew even harder to bear.

'Why track him down after so long? Why write him that letter? Don't pretend it's because you care. That you're sorry.'

Elena wetted her lips, but the words wouldn't come. I had my reasons, she thought.

'He hates you. Says he never wants to see you again. But he's weak, and you're a manipulative bitch. And now there's Olivia.'

Elena's heart pounded at the mention of her daughter. 'What about her?'

'Connor's still in Bristol. He wants to meet his sister.'

'She doesn't know,' Elena managed. 'I haven't told her. About any of this.'

'She soon will. I intend to pay her a visit.'

Goose bumps rose on Elena's arms at the thought of this woman talking to Olivia.

'I've been keeping an eye on her. On both of you.' Fresh fear shot through Elena.

'I want you gone,' Rebecca said. 'From my son's life. For good.'

'No.' Impossible, now Elena was this close to him.

'It's not a request.'

'I can't. He means too much to me.'

'You'll do as I say. That includes leaving Bristol.'

Anger sparked in Elena. This woman was acting like she was some gunslinger try to run Elena out of Dodge City. 'Why would I do that? Olivia's here.'

'Like I said, I'll be paying her a visit. I might need to bend the truth at times, and I can't risk you putting her straight.'

'You can't force me to—'

'I can and I will. Because if you don't—' Rebecca leaned closer. Her breath smelled of garlic and something sour. Her next words drove ice into Elena's heart.

*****

A short while later they were at Elena's flat. 'You have ten minutes,' Rebecca told her. 'Don't dawdle.'

Elena walked into her bedroom and pulled a suitcase from under her bed. In it she stuffed clothes, underwear, toiletries. On top went a folder containing essential documents: passport, driving licence, etc. It was there less than a second before Rebecca grabbed it, flicked through the contents. When they met with her approval, she tossed the folder back in the suitcase. 'Five minutes,' she said.

Elena's eyes drifted to the boxes inside her wardrobe. They contained items to counteract whatever verbal poison Rebecca Brady had fed Olivia. Her gaze travelled to the painting of Tynemouth Castle that hung on the wall. Impossible to take it with her, of course. And perhaps, like the box of sketches, it might help reveal the truth to Olivia.

As would the envelopes of baby hair she held in her hand. It was vital Rebecca didn't see those and imperative Olivia did. Elena was tempted to leave them in her bedside cabinet, but Rebecca might check its contents. Her palm grew sweaty around the envelopes, before an idea struck her. She bent down and, under pretence of opening the box of sketches inside her wardrobe, she attempted to slide the envelopes underneath. The one on top snagged on the duct tape across the bottom of the box. Elena was about to try again, when—

'What are you up to?' Rebecca's voice made Elena jump.

She straightened up, the remaining envelope scrunched in her hand, but held out of sight.

'Nothing. I just need to check up there.' Elena gestured towards the top of the wardrobe. She grabbed a chair, then stood on it to retrieve one of two shoeboxes. With her back to Rebecca, she stuffed the envelope—Cameron's, she noted—inside. She climbed off the chair, smacking dust off her palms.

'You done?' Rebecca asked.

'Yes.' Elena extracted her mobile from her handbag. 'Let me say goodbye to Olivia. Please.'

When Rebecca didn't answer, she continued, 'You can check the text before I send it.'

'Hand the phone to me once you've finished. Remember what I'll do if you mess me around.'

Elena nodded. She opened her list of contacts, then tapped out a text to her daughter.

Hi, Olivia. This will come as a surprise, but I'm returning to London, so we won't see each other again. I know this leaves Barry in the lurch, so could you do me a favour, please? I've taken what I need, so can you pack up the stuff I've left? Keep anything you want and give the rest to a charity shop. All the best. X

That should work. Nothing to alarm Rebecca, but Olivia would find the envelope of her hair, along with the paintings. Cameron's envelope, too. She handed her mobile to the other woman, who read the text. Satisfied, Rebecca nodded, then pressed the 'send' button. To Elena's surprise, her fingers continued to tap the screen.

'What are you doing?' Elena asked.

Rebecca grinned. 'A quick text to Connor. Saying it's best if the two of you don't meet again. How you can't forgive his anger.' She tapped a few more times, then returned the phone to Elena.

'We're done here,' she announced. 'I'll drive you to Temple Meads. You'll be on the next train out of Bristol. Don't come back.'

The two of them left Elena's flat. Once they were at Bristol's main train station, Elena bought a ticket to Paddington, in London. Rebecca waited beside her on the platform. Neither woman spoke.

The 14.25 London train pulled in. Rebecca broke her silence. 'Don't forget what I'll do if you ever contact Connor again.'

Elena nodded, keen to appear defeated. She needed Rebecca to believe her threats had hit home. They had, but Rebecca had underestimated Elena. Very much so.

It wasn't that Elena didn't realise there was a scorpion coiled inside Rebecca Brady. She refused to be cowed, though. Memories of the way Sonia had bullied her forced themselves into her head. She couldn't, she *wouldn't*, be that timid person anymore.

Once the Bristol passengers had alighted, a guard motioned the London travellers on board. Elena entered the nearest carriage and found a seat. From the corner of her eye she saw Rebecca, still standing on the platform. Ten minutes afterwards, the train pulled out of the station.

Three hours later, Elena boarded a train back to Bristol.

*****

Later, she stared at the rain pattering against the window. It was almost dark, but she hadn't moved from her armchair since she arrived. The dull ache from her concussion still lingered at the back of her skull. She should have taken a painkiller, but couldn't be bothered.

What Elena yearned to do was call Olivia. She would, but not yet. As for Cameron—no, he was Connor now; she needed to remember that—her son had made it very plain he hated her. The words he screamed at her bounced around in her head. *How could you do that? Throw me away like I was garbage?*

He was wrong, of course. But if she tried to see him, to convince him he was mistaken, he'd hate her even more. Rebecca Brady would make sure of that. The consequences for Olivia would be much worse.

Elena shuddered. Around her the room had grown cold, but she didn't bother putting on warmer clothes. Her new home was temporary, rented on a week-by-week basis via a website that offered short-term accommodation. The place was shabby, sparsely furnished, but its chief advantage was its location, a five-minute walk from Olivia's flat.

Elena hadn't yet worked out how to outsmart Rebecca Brady, but she would. To do that, she needed to stay close to Olivia.

As for Connor—that was more difficult. Maybe Olivia would know what to do, once she'd re-established contact with her daughter.

Baby steps, Elena reminded herself.

Her memories of that awful time after her son's birth remained fuzzy, but Elena was certain of one thing. She hadn't tossed her baby in a rubbish bin.

Part Four

CHAPTER 19

Connor Brady learned when he was eight that his parents had adopted him as a baby. It was a Saturday, the first weekend of the summer holidays, the weather wet and windy. After breakfast, Connor settled down to enjoy his favourite cartoons. His parents were talking in the kitchen, but his attention remained fixed on the screen. With animated creatures running rampant before his eyes, he didn't hear Zach and Rebecca Brady enter.

'Connor, can you turn off the television, please? You can watch that later.'

'But, Mammy—'

'Now, Connor.' His mother's tone sent him scrambling for the remote. He wasn't bothered, though. She never raised her voice to him, and he knew he'd been a good boy.

Rebecca sat beside him on the sofa, Zach on the other side. Connor glanced between them, unsure what was going on. Their smiles seemed forced.

'Connor, darling,' Rebecca said. 'You know we love you very much, right?'

Fear prickled in Connor's stomach. Were his parents divorcing? He'd not seen this coming. They'd always seemed so happy together.

Tears flooded his eyes. 'I don't want Daddy to leave,' he wailed. Then he launched himself into Zach's arms.

His father pushed Connor away, confusion in his face. 'What do you mean, son? I'm not going anywhere.'

'You and Mammy aren't getting divorced?'

'Oh, sweetheart.' Rebecca pulled her son in close. 'No, of course not. Whatever gave you that idea?'

Connor stayed silent, unsure what to say.

'Daddy and I love each other very much. I'm afraid you're stuck with us, darling.' Rebecca laughed. 'Nobody is going anywhere. But we have something to tell you.'

'What's that?'

His father cleared his throat. 'We think you're old enough to handle the truth.' His gaze edged away towards his wife.

Rebecca took over. 'When Daddy and I got married,' she said, 'we were sure of one thing. That we wanted children. A little boy, just like you.'

Connor stared at his mother. Why was she telling him this?

'But Mammy found out she couldn't have babies.' Rebecca's voice wobbled. 'So another lady helped us. You grew in her tummy—remember when we talked about that?—and she gave birth to you.'

Her words roared in Connor's ears. He had no idea what she meant. Except that he did.

His father took up the narrative. 'Connor, not everyone can care for a baby. The woman we're talking about—she couldn't. Your mammy and I agreed with her you'd be our son instead. So she gave you to us, and you've been our special boy ever since. We love you so much, kiddo.'

'To the moon and back,' Rebecca said.

Connor remained silent. 'Do you understand what we're telling you, son?' his father said.

Connor nodded. Then: 'Can I watch television now?'

His parents exchanged a glance. 'Do you want to ask us anything? About what we've told you?' Rebecca said.

Connor shook his head, his fingers reaching for the remote. Zach patted his son's hair. 'Okay, then.'

Later, Connor found he did have questions. Over the family's evening meal, he paused, a piece of chicken speared on his fork. 'What's her name? The lady who gave birth to me?' He was proud of himself for not mentioning tummies he once grew in. That sort of thing was for babies.

Rebecca shot a look at her husband. Zach cleared his throat. 'Sorry, son. We've no idea.'

'What about my daddy?'

'We don't know his name either.'

'So who called me Connor?'

'We did,' Rebecca said. 'Your daddy and I chose it especially for you.'

'I hate it.' His feet drummed against the table leg. 'Connor's a stupid name.'

The smile on his mother's face faltered. 'Eat your meal, darling. That way you'll grow up big and strong.'

Connor didn't think, just reacted. He seized his plate of food and hurled it at the wall. Chunks of chicken, roast potatoes and gravy slid down the paintwork towards the shattered china below.

'Don't talk to me like that! I'm not a baby!' he yelled, before running upstairs to his bedroom.

Later, he tiptoed onto the landing. The door to the kitchen was open. His parents' voices floated up the stairs.

'Should we tell him everything? Even though we agreed we wouldn't?' his mother said.

'He's not old enough. How the hell do you tell a kid something so awful, anyway?' Anger filled his father's voice.

'We have to, Zach. Imagine if we don't, and he discovers himself what happened. Because he will one day, and then he'll be seriously messed up.'

'In a few years, maybe. But not yet. At least he knows now he's adopted.'

'I love him so much. I'd give my life for him.'

'We both would, Becca. And he needs all the love we have right now.'

'It's late. We should go to bed.' Connor heard his mother's chair being scraped back. He scuttled into his room, scooted under his duvet and pulled it over his head. A minute later, his door was pushed open. Connor held his breath.

'He's asleep,' Rebecca said. 'Poor darling.' His door closed. Not long after, silence descended on the house.

*****

Connor glared at Rebecca in the kitchen after breakfast the next day. 'I want to know my real mammy's name. And why she gave me away.'

'We've explained all that, darling. We can't tell you what we don't know.'

Connor clenched his fists. 'Liar! You're a liar! I hate both of you!'

Rebecca stepped in front of her son, then pulled him into a hug. Connor tried to break free, but couldn't. His nose pressed against her blouse, the scent of her perfume strong in his nostrils. Her fingers stroked his hair, and Connor squirmed. He could *feel* the weight of her love, pressing on him, and it was yucky and uncomfortable.

Rebecca dropped to her knees, her hands cupping Connor's face. The tenderness in her eyes was so immense he couldn't bear it.

'I adore you,' his mother said. 'I loved you from the moment I first held you. That will never change, Connor. Never. I would fight for you. Die for you. I may not have given birth to you, but I'm your mammy, in every way that counts.'

Connor struggled, eager to pull away, but Rebecca tightened her hold. Her gaze burned so hot Connor was scared it might kill him.

'Nobody will ever love you as much as I do,' his mother said. 'Nobody, darling. Remember that.'

*****

From then on, Connor retreated inside himself, refusing to discuss his adoption with his parents. They either couldn't or wouldn't reveal any more details, so what was the point? A sense of rejection took root in him. Over the next few years, his feelings of abandonment grew, became ever more twisted.

The world turned worse for Connor after his twelfth birthday. Dark moods descended on him without warning, heavy and malevolent, disconnecting him from everyone and everything. Except for the shame. In his bleaker moments,

Connor realised he was, most likely, rejected by his biological mother. What else could explain his parents' refusal to tell him anything? Even her name?

If she'd cared enough about him, she'd never have given him away. He must, therefore, be unlovable.

He became surly around Zach, downright rude to Rebecca, who bore the brunt of his fury because she was female. Connor sometimes thought he hated all women.

Some days hurt more than others. Christmas was tough, given the emphasis on family. Worst of all was Mother's Day, which turned his stomach sour.

'She's not my mam,' he shouted when Zach reprimanded him for his refusal to give Rebecca Brady a card or buy her flowers.

'Don't ever say that again! She's your mother, of course she is!' Zach yelled.

'No! She's defective, remember? She can't have kids!'

His father clenched his fists, fury in his face. For the first time in his life, Connor thought Zach might hit him. He ran to his room and slammed the door so hard the frame shook. A small part of him realised he was testing Zach and Rebecca. If he pushed them far enough, would they reject him too?

*****

Not long after he turned thirteen, Connor summoned the courage to enter his parents' home office while they were out of the house. In one corner stood a three-drawer cabinet. Connor rifled through the contents, arranged in suspended file holders. Bills, bank statements, insurance policies. Nothing of any interest. At the bottom of the third drawer, however, hidden under the files hanging above, was a blue document folder. Connor pulled it out. His name was on the front, the handwriting that of Zach Brady.

His adoption papers were inside. Connor's eyes danced over the words, three in particular punching him in the gut. *Mother's name: unknown.* So his parents hadn't lied about that.

Also in the blue folder was a newspaper cutting, dated not long after his birthday. Connor extracted it, oblivious to the horror that awaited him.

NEWBORN BABY ABANDONED IN TYNEMOUTH

A local woman told yesterday how she found a baby boy abandoned in a rubbish bin during a morning walk in Tynemouth village.

Police began a search for the baby's mother...

Blood rushed from Connor's brain. Before he could help himself, he vomited his breakfast onto the carpet. Behind him, the filing cabinet was still open, his adoption file on the floor.

Words battled in his head. *Amy Sutcliffe's discovery of the child... thought she heard a cat crying... clearly distressed... found before the bins were collected...*

Connor ran from the room. He wrenched open the front door and sprinted down the path. He didn't stop running until his heart threatened to pound out of his chest and his body dripped with sweat. He stared around him with wild eyes. He was on the seafront, Tynemouth Castle and Priory outlined in the distance against a stormy sky. Without thinking what he was doing, he trudged towards the ruined buildings.

Connor rounded the road by the castle into Front Street. Shops, bars and cafes lined its length, but he spotted some houses too, along with flats above the commercial properties. Rubbish bins stood outside some of them. Connor opened the lid of the nearest one. It was empty, but a lingering whiff of rotten food assaulted his nostrils. A slice of carrot, black with mould, clung to the bottom. Connor imagined himself zipped into a holdall and thrown into its depths. How could anyone do something so vile?

Connor kicked the bin repeatedly until it hit the wall of a building. His trainers continued to pummel the hard plastic. The world around Connor had vanished, leaving only his fury and the bin.

At last the pain in his toes grew too great. Connor shoved the bin away, then staggered in the direction of the castle. Exhausted, he slumped on a bench close to the boundary wall. Hours passed, and the light faded from the sky. Midnight came, bringing with it an icy wind. Too cold to remain where he was, he trudged home.

*****

The Bradys' front door slammed shut behind Connor. Zach's expression was furious, but anguish filled Rebecca's eyes.

'What the hell were you thinking? We were worried sick!' Connor didn't even flinch at the anger in Zach's voice.

'I was so concerned about you, darling,' Rebecca said, her words shaky. She reached out to hug him.

'Don't touch me! Leave me alone!' Connor yelled. Zach and Rebecca would have realised why he went missing; they'd have found the newspaper cutting, his adoption file, the puddle of vomit. He had no desire to discuss any of it.

*****

Connor's sleep became erratic after that day, his memory poor. His moods could swing up and down within minutes. He often skipped school and spent hours wandering the streets. Concerned, his head teacher met with Zach and Rebecca, but nothing changed. Connor's behaviour worsened until, at fifteen, a marked deterioration occurred. He often wore his clothes until they reeked of sweat, didn't brush his teeth or hair. All he wanted was to doze or watch television.

'You need to see a doctor, son. Get counselling, medication, whatever will work,' Zach said, more than once. 'And for God's sake, take a shower. You stink.'

'Go to hell,' Connor always replied. The pain he carried couldn't be helped by pills.

By the time he left home at eighteen, he was barely speaking to his father. His mother, not at all.

CHAPTER 20

Twelve years later, Connor Brady stared at the envelope his father had just handed to him. Now aged thirty, he was back in his childhood home; he'd tried rooming with other guys, even rented a scruffy bedsit for a while. Connor either forgot to pay his rent or else played music at full volume to stifle the constant chatter in his head. Eventually he'd be asked to leave; when that happened he knew his old bedroom, its walls still covered with posters of sports cars, was available.

'You'll always have a home here, son,' Zach Brady had told him many times.

The envelope had been handwritten, the loops and swirls unfamiliar to him. Who wrote letters these days, anyway? He tore open the flap, then pulled out the contents. A single sheet of paper, covered in the same flowery script, along with an address in Bristol. A phone number.

Connor settled himself against his pillows. He took a swig from the nearby bottle of cider, although it was only ten o'clock in the morning. Then he read the letter.

My darling son,

Your name is Connor now, but I can't help calling you Cameron in my head. I hope you've been happy, that your adoptive parents treated you well. Please forgive this intrusion into your life, but I felt compelled to contact you. I've wondered many times about finding you, but didn't know if I could. In the end, I used a tracing agency to locate you. You're still in the north-east, which made it easier. Connor, I gave birth to you, but wasn't able to keep you. I would love the chance to explain, darling.

There's another reason I want us to meet. I have something important to tell you. Please call, or write, to me. Or text if you prefer. I don't trust emails and I'm not good with technology.

With love,

Elena Munro.

Connor's fingers reached for the bottle of cider. A minute later he slammed it on his bedside table, the contents drained dry.

Elena Munro. He turned the syllables of her name over in his mind. What was she like, this Elena Munro? Tall, short, dark, fair? Slim, fat, kind, cruel? The tone of the letter was warm, loving. How did that fit with its sender chucking him in a rubbish bin?

It didn't. This made no sense.

Connor screwed the letter into a ball and hurled it across the room. Next he seized the cider bottle and threw it against the mirror, shattering his reflection into a jagged mess. He ripped his bedside lamp from its socket and smashed it against the wall. He swept books from their shelves, kicking them around the carpet, ripping pages from spines. His fingers tore down his Maserati poster and ripped it to shreds. A demon possessed him, and he was unable to stop.

Connor's bedroom door was yanked open, and Zach Brady strode into the room. Within seconds, Connor found his arms pinned against his body. His father, two inches taller and far more muscled, had always been able to subdue his son when the rages struck. Connor both loved and hated him for such power.

'Fuck off! Let me go!' he screamed.

'I've got you, son. It'll be all right.' Zach's palm rubbed Connor's back. Once Connor was drained, silent, Zach steered him towards his bed. He sat his son down, then seated himself beside Connor.

'What caused it this time?' he said.

Connor couldn't bring himself to reveal what provoked his meltdown. 'Nothing. Just a bit depressed, you know?'

'You been taking your medication?'

'Yes.' Well, on and off. That counted, right?

'Do you want me to call your doctor?'

Connor shook his head. 'Nah. I'm okay.'

Zach fixed his son with a steely gaze. 'That letter. It upset you, didn't it?'

The lie came automatically. 'No.'

Zach looked unconvinced. 'Here's what's going to happen,' he said. Connor knew what was coming; he'd heard it often enough. 'I'll give you time to chill out, then you'll clear this mess up. I'll see you downstairs soon.' He walked from his son's bedroom and closed the door behind him.

At least, Connor thought, his adoptive mother didn't witness his meltdown. Rebecca Brady would have been so hurt, so distressed.

Across the bedroom, the crumpled letter mocked Connor. He retrieved it and sat on his bed again, smoothing out the paper against his thigh. The words still made no sense.

She threw me in a rubbish bin, he thought. Now she says she loves me.

But did she? She'd ended the letter 'with love', but lots of people signed off that way. It meant nothing.

Or it might mean everything.

He should burn the letter.

Or text her.

A phone call was beyond Connor; he wasn't ready for that yet. To hear her voice might destroy him if she said the wrong things. A letter was too risky. He wasn't good with words. Besides, what if it got lost in the post? If he didn't receive a reply, it would trigger all his fears of abandonment. His first rejection had scarred him for life. A second—he might not survive.

A text, however—that was possible.

Footsteps on the landing, followed by a knock on his door. 'Connor? We agreed you'd clear up the mess you made. Get downstairs and grab yourself a bin bag. Now, son.'

Connor complied. As expected, his father badgered him throughout the morning—what caused the meltdown, was he sure he'd taken his medication, etc. Connor said the bare minimum, his mind on the letter. He had no intention of mentioning he was considering contacting Elena Munro. What if Zach accused him of disloyalty to Rebecca?

After they'd eaten lunch, Zach placed his knife and fork on his plate, then cleared his throat. 'I'll ask you again. Did that letter set you off?'

Connor shook his head. He couldn't meet his father's eyes. If he did, Zach would know he was lying.

'Didn't recognise the handwriting,' Zach continued.

'Some girl I went to school with,' Connor mumbled.

'Son—'

'Dad! Drop it, will you? She doesn't matter. Neither does the letter.'

Except it was all he could think of. *There's another reason I want us to meet. I have something important to tell you.* Connor had no idea what Elena Munro meant.

By the time he went to bed, Connor knew he'd contact his biological mother. It was a question of when, not if.

*****

The letter nagged at Connor's mind when he awoke. He withdrew the crumpled sheet of paper from beneath his pillow to read it again. Was he really going to do this?

It seemed so. Connor picked up his mobile and entered Elena's number. He tapped out a message.

Why did you do it?

He backspaced and started again. *What do you want with me?*

That was no good. She'd already told him she wanted to meet. He tried again. *I got your letter. Why wait until now?*

Yeah, that would do. His finger hovered over the 'send' button.

There. The deed was done.

Ten minutes later, Connor's mobile beeped. His heart hammering, he opened Elena's text.

I can explain once we meet. Remember I have something important to tell you. I'd rather not do it in a text.

Did he dare risk it? Connor chewed his lower lip, uncertain. But he knew what he'd do. The die was cast the instant he first read the letter.

Another text. *An hour of your time. That's all I ask.*

Bristol. A few days looking around, meeting his mother. He'd sleep in his car. Showers—who needed them?

Deep inside, Connor believed himself unworthy of being clean. Who would, after starting life in a rubbish bin? He knew he looked haggard, his beard bushy and unkempt. Grease matted his hair. His skin was pasty and unhealthy. A cluster of cold sores nestled on his upper lip. Elena Munro wouldn't, he realised, be proud of the person her son had become.

Another beep sounded from his bedroom. When Connor retrieved his mobile, he'd received a further text from Elena. *Please. I'm begging you.*

Satisfaction stole over him. She was begging, was she? The balance of power had swung in his favour.

Connor typed out a text. *I'll meet you in Bristol. Next Thurs, 2 p.m., your place.*

*****

Now here he was, about to reunite with Elena Munro the following day. Connor shifted around in the rear seat of his tatty Toyota, unable to sleep. He had no money for hotels or a bed at a hostel. He'd been in Bristol a couple of nights now, and had parked somewhere different each time, wary of being moved on by the police.

Maybe he should have checked out that derelict house he spotted yesterday. Boarded up, set back from the road and on Bristol's outskirts. Away from prying eyes. It was too late tonight, though.

His father was no longer in the dark about the letter, which was good. Connor already felt disloyal to Zach, and doubly so to Rebecca. In his head, he imagined her voice. 'Oh, darling. I wish you'd take better care of yourself. Can't you at least try? For me?'

If only he could.

'I've always loved you,' Rebecca Brady continued. 'Let me help you. Please.'

'Go away,' Connor shouted.

He'd been warned against coming here. *She doesn't deserve you, darling. Remember how she threw you away like you were garbage? Whereas me—I've adored you from the moment I first held you in my arms.*

Then: *I wish you'd reconsider. Stay here, where you're loved and wanted. But if you're determined to go to Bristol, if your heart's set on meeting this woman, I'm coming with you.*

Connor had demurred. 'I don't need you there.'

Useless to protest, of course. *I may not have given birth to you, but I've tried to be a mother to you. Don't shut me out. Please.*

'I'd rather go alone.' Not that she'd listened. She'd followed him to Bristol anyway.

I won't get in the way, I promise. You'll need me when she hurts you again. As she will; she's done it once, and she'll do it again. She's that type.

The worst thing was—Connor suspected she was right.

CHAPTER 21

Connor's finger hovered over the doorbell. In his head, he'd waited for this moment forever, yet in reality it had only been a few days since he'd received Elena's letter. He pulled his mobile from his pocket to flick through the texts they'd swapped. *I have something important to tell you. Please. I'm begging you.*

He leaned against the wall, his eyes closed. Perhaps he should leave, drive back to Newcastle, burn the letter. Avoid more hurt.

He knew he wouldn't, though.

Eight minutes past two. His phone lit up with an incoming message. *Where are you? Please tell me you're still coming.*

All he had to do was reach out and ring Elena's bell. When he finally did so, the sound seemed unnaturally loud.

The door was wrenched open. His mother stood in the gap.

Connor's first impression was that she looked older than he'd expected, the lines around her mouth carved deep, her skin sallow. Greying hair that had once been dark, worn in a wash-and-wear style, eyes pale blue beneath her fringe. Like her hair, her clothes had clearly been chosen for comfort: navy trousers, a loose white shirt.

'Oh, my God.' Elena's hand flew to her mouth. A huge smile broke across her face, and one of Rebecca Brady's favourite sayings came into Connor's head. Elena Munro looked, he decided, like all her Christmases had come at once. 'You're here. I always hoped…' Her words trailed away as she stared at him. Dismay flashed across her face, and her nostrils wrinkled; Connor remembered he'd not washed his hair or showered for several days. Why bother? This woman might not be worth the effort.

He was unable to speak. The seconds ticked by, and neither of them moved.

Until Elena broke the spell. 'My beautiful son. My precious boy. I can't believe you've come.' Tears swam in her eyes. She stepped forward, and Connor found himself in her arms. Too stunned to respond, he stood still while Elena squeezed him tight, her head against his chest. The moment he'd craved, yet he was unable to return the embrace. All he could remember was that damn rubbish bin.

Elena released him to wipe her eyes on her sleeve. She stepped back, cleared her throat. 'Come in, please. Make yourself comfortable.' She gestured behind her, and Connor followed. He found himself in Elena's living room, which was cramped, the furniture old-fashioned, yet neat and clean. His chest tightened, as if all the air had been sucked from the room.

'The kettle's boiled,' Elena said. 'Would you like tea? Coffee?'

Connor's mouth was drier than the Sahara, but he shook his head. His stomach was too knotted for coffee.

Elena plumped herself in an armchair and gestured to another. 'Sit down, please. I can't believe you're here,' she repeated. Connor sat in the other chair, mere inches from Elena's. She reached out as if to stroke his face, then withdrew her hand, her expression guarded. Connor had no idea whether he was relieved or hurt.

For a few seconds neither of them spoke. 'Why did you contact me?' Connor asked at last.

Elena bit her lip. 'It wasn't the right time before,' she said. 'I wanted to, for so long. Peter—my late husband—never knew about you. I couldn't search for you while he was alive.'

Pain twisted inside Connor, although he wasn't surprised. Who on earth confessed to their spouse that they'd chucked a baby in a rubbish bin?

'He guessed I'd once been pregnant, of course,' Elena continued. 'I told him I'd had a child, but that it died.'

Anger replaced pain. She admitted to being a liar, then.

'Then Peter got colon cancer. I nursed him through three rounds of chemo, but he didn't make it. I ended up a widow, alone in London, a city I'd long since tired of. Desperate to return to Bristol, where I was born. Once I was settled, I dared to hope I might find you.'

'Through a tracing agency, right?'

'Yes. They located you for me.'

Connor failed to repress his bitterness. 'Sure they did. Can't be many abandoned babies, right?'

Elena paled. 'I can explain that. If you'll listen—'

Connor wasn't certain he could handle whatever bullshit she might throw at him. Not yet, anyway. 'Never mind all that. What did you want to tell me?'

Elena's expression turned stricken. She didn't reply.

'Spit it out.' Connor steeled himself for what he was about to hear. He couldn't claim he wasn't warned. *You'll need me when she hurts you again. As she will…*

Words issued from Elena's mouth, and for a second Connor thought he'd misheard. 'What did you say?' His tone was brusque, but he didn't care.

Elena shrank away, her face chalk-white. 'I had twins.'

'What?'

'You have a sister, my love. She's bright, beautiful—'

'Shut up. Shut the hell up.' Connor leapt from his seat to pace the room, his fists clenched.

'Please, darling—'

'Don't you dare.' Connor's voice was a growl. 'You don't get to call me that.'

'I'm sorry. But Connor, please hear me out—'

Connor stopped his restless to-and-fro across the carpet. He stared at his biological mother. Her expression was tense, drained. Right now he hated her.

'I have a twin sister?' Connor's voice held disbelief. Whatever he'd imagined he'd discover by coming to Elena's flat, it wasn't a sibling.

'You didn't know. Well, of course not. You had nobody to tell you.' Elena's hands twisted around themselves.

'What happened to her?' Connor wasn't sure he could bear to find out Elena kept his sister. Why do that, but throw him away?

'She was adopted. By a friend of mine.'

Fury boiled within Connor. 'Why only her? Why not me as well?'

'I can explain. My head was all muddled. I couldn't cope with one baby, let alone two. And—'

'Let's get this straight.' Connor's voice was deceptively calm, given the rage he was struggling to control. 'You found a home for your daughter, but not your son? Instead, you zipped me into a bag, without access to air, and tossed me in a rubbish bin. How could you do that? Throw me away like I was garbage?' All the colour had drained from Elena's face, but Connor ploughed on. 'On collection day, no less. I could have been crushed to death by the bin lorry.' He gripped her arm, hard enough to make her gasp. 'Explain that to me.'

When Elena didn't respond, Connor grabbed her other arm, gave both a shake. Her skin was a sickly white, her mouth open. He grasped her harder, and she moaned in pain.

'A rubbish bin, for fuck's sake.' He was shouting, not caring who heard.

'I didn't, I swear. It wasn't like that.'

Her denial stoked the fury higher in Connor. 'Yeah, it was.'

'I can explain—'

'What's her name?' He shook Elena again. 'My sister. Tell me.'

'Olivia.'

'Where is she? Do you know?'

Elena's skin paled even further. 'She's here. In Bristol.'

'You found her first. Well, that figures. She always did take priority with you, didn't she? She got adopted, whereas I—' Connor screwed up his lips in disgust. 'Where in Bristol, exactly?'

'Oh, my love. Please don't get angry. She was easier to track down, you see. Because of my friend and her husband. The ones who adopted her. I found them first, then Olivia.'

'Stop messing me around. Tell me where my sister lives.'

Elena's gaze slipped away. She mumbled something, so low Connor couldn't catch it. 'What did you say?'

'Upstairs. She's in the flat above this one.'

Connor couldn't believe what he was hearing. 'You moved in below her? When?'

Tears shone in Elena's eyes. 'You're angry. I get that. But—'

'When?' Connor was shouting again.

'A couple of months ago. I discovered her address, and afterwards found this flat was available to rent. I'd not long arrived from London and needed somewhere to live. It seemed like fate.'

'How cosy.' Connor thrust Elena away, disgust sour within him. He spotted her mobile on the coffee table and grabbed it, bringing up her contacts list. Seconds later he'd located an Olivia Gilchrist, the only person listed with Olivia as a first name. He shoved the phone towards Elena. 'Is this her? Is she my sister?'

Elena nodded. Connor sent Olivia's number to his mobile, then tossed Elena's across the room. It hit the floor with a thud. He pulled Elena to her feet. 'You vile, pathetic excuse for a woman. I hate you. I never want to see you again.' With that, he pushed her away with all his strength, so that Elena staggered, her head clouting the coffee table as she fell. She cried out in pain, but Connor was already halfway to the door.

*****

Back in his car, Connor leaned against the headrest, weary to the bone. For most of his life he'd sought the truth. Now he had it, he wished he hadn't bothered, because he had no idea how to process his pain.

He replayed the meeting with Elena on a continuous loop in his head. Maybe he'd dodged a maternal bullet by that whore dumping him at birth.

Or perhaps not. Despite his righteous anger, Connor's misery prevailed. He was trash, worthless. Amy Sutcliffe, the woman who rescued him, should have left him in that damn bin.

He muttered a curse. With everything that had happened, he'd forgotten to ask Elena Munro who his father was. The bitch might not even know. His paternal genes probably came from some faceless fuck, long forgotten. Anger surged in him, hot and heavy.

Still, he'd discovered something he didn't before: he had a sister, Olivia Gilchrist. He knew where she lived, too. Maybe he'd pay her a visit sometime. Or not.

To contact her or let it slide? Risk further hurt, or return to Newcastle? It could, Connor reflected, go either way.

Half of him loathed his sister for her better start in life. The other part wondered. What was she like, this bright, beautiful Olivia, the daughter his biological mother favoured over him?

For a second, guilt stabbed him when he remembered Rebecca Brady's passionate devotion to him. He loved her; he always would, but nature trumped nurture, at least for Connor.

His mobile buzzed with an incoming call. 'You were right,' he said as soon as he answered. 'Elena Munro hurt me. Just like you predicted.'

After the call ended, Connor decided he was done with his biological mother. His sister, however, this Olivia Gilchrist—she was a different story.

Part Five

CHAPTER 22

Eager to distract herself one evening, Olivia set to work on the photo album for her father. She'd bought the largest she could find, and it was already half-full with the pictures she'd retrieved from her childhood home. Her fingers stroked over a picture of Sonia and Harry, taken by a teenage Olivia on a family holiday in Cornwall. Happy times, she thought.

A text pinged through from David. *Can I call you?*

Olivia typed a reply, her mood having soured. *Wouldn't you rather call Tiffany?*

Told you before. We're just friends.

Don't lie. You had lunch in town with her the other day.

I can explain that. You've got this all wrong.

Olivia didn't agree. Kirsten had sounded very sure about seeing David outside the Llandoger Trow with Tiffany. She trusted her friend more than her husband.

Her phone rang, David's name on the screen. Olivia swiped to accept the call, her mouth tight with anger. 'What do you want, David?'

'Tiffany's a colleague. A friend, even. She means nothing else to me.'

Olivia didn't respond. Hadn't they said all this already?

'And she has a boyfriend. One she's crazy about.'

Olivia snorted. Did her husband take her for a fool?

'She might prove useful, though,' David continued.

That snagged Olivia's attention. 'How so?'

'Her brother's an investigative journalist. He's skilled at tracking down people.'

Anger stirred in Olivia. 'I don't care. I don't want you anywhere near that woman.'

'Her brother can help you find Elena. Maybe Cameron too.'

'So can a tracing agency. Without sleeping with my husband.'

'Oh, for God's sake, Livvy. Must we do this? Again?'

Olivia didn't reply. He had a point. They couldn't keep on fighting this battle.

'There's more,' she said. She filled him in on Rebecca Brady's visit, her subsequent rejection. The letters from Harry, the baby found abandoned in Tynemouth. David sounded shocked, asked the occasional question, but mostly he listened.

'Shit,' David said once Olivia slowed to a halt.

'Yup. Shit sums it up, all right.'

'Livvy, this is even more reason to get Tiff involved. Her brother can help.'

'Her name is Tiffany, for God's sake. Not *Tiff*.' Olivia spat out the abbreviation like it was poison. 'And don't assume I want to find Elena or Rebecca, because you'd be wrong. Both of them can rot in hell.'

'What about getting answers? Like why Elena dumped Cameron?'

'No. What possible reason could she give, other than that she's a vile excuse for a human being?' Olivia clenched the hand that wasn't holding her phone into a fist. 'As for Tiffany bloody Cook, let me spell it out for you. No more talking to her about my personal life. Is that clear?'

*****

Eight o'clock the following evening. A headache pounded in Olivia's skull, but she ignored it. Scribbled on a scrap of paper beside her laptop were names of tracing agencies, organisations who claimed to find missing people. Her brother would have a new name, of course, and might live anywhere, but Olivia had high hopes of success; she could provide his date of birth and the likely location in which he was adopted. She'd drawn up a list of six possible companies, based on length of time in business and customer reviews. Olivia was determined to have engaged the services of one of them by lunchtime tomorrow, .

She pinched the bridge of her nose, closed her laptop, released a breath. She was done here. A bath, followed by bed, was beckoning.

Her mobile beeped with a text. David's name appeared on the screen. For a second, Olivia considered not reading it. She wasn't sure she could deal with him right now.

She couldn't resist a peek. *I have information.*

Olivia bristled. He'd better not have got Tiffany Cook's brother involved, or there'd be trouble. While she was deciding her response, her phone rang. David, of course.

'What about?' She was too irritated to bother being polite.

'Elena Munro.'

'And how did you get this information?' Olivia's voice almost froze the air.

Her husband's silence confirmed her suspicion. 'You bastard,' she spat out.

A sigh sounded in her ear. 'Listen to me, Livvy, please. I spent one lunchtime with Tiffany. An hour, tops. In the cafeteria at work, in full view of everyone. She said she's already got her brother on the case. Tom's the best investigative journalist there is, according to her.'

She'd say anything to lure you into bed, Olivia thought. 'Has he got a lead on Cameron?' Hope rose within her. Perhaps this Tom guy had found him. She was angry with David about Tiffany, but her annoyance wasn't relevant right now. If the woman's brother had ferreted out useful information, she'd take it and run, thank you very much.

'I'm getting to that. Bear with me, Livvy. First, he's uncovered something interesting. About Elena.'

'What?'

'Elena Munro was an only child. No siblings.'

Shock rendered Olivia silent. She hadn't expected that.

'Which begs the question,' David continued. 'Who is Rebecca Brady?'

'And why did she claim to be my mother?'

'I reckon I know the answer.'

'Which is?'

'Tom did some digging into the baby abandoned in Tynemouth. Turns out a local couple adopted him. Zach and Rebecca Brady.'

Everything clicked into place in Olivia's head. Rebecca's preference for Cameron's lock of hair over hers, her refusal of further contact with Olivia—all signs of a woman with a hidden motive. Cameron's adoptive mother wouldn't have wanted her son's biological parent sniffing around. Or, if she was that possessive, any of his blood family. Hence her insistence that Cameron was dead.

A chill settled over Olivia. To be that calculating—Rebecca Brady clearly possessed a dark side that concerned her. But didn't Cameron deserve the chance to connect with his birth mother? His sister? And was it mere coincidence that Elena moved out and cut contact with her daughter at the same time that Rebecca Brady put in an appearance? Or a sign of something more sinister?

She was forgetting Cameron. 'Tell me my brother's still alive. That this Tom guy has found him.'

An awkward pause. 'Yes and no. He's not dead. Not as far as anyone knows.'

'What do you mean?'

'Zach Brady reported his son missing a while ago. Nobody's seen or heard from him recently.'

Olivia's burgeoning hope shrivelled. 'The police haven't been able to find him?'

'They said he left voluntarily.'

'How come?'

'Because the evidence showed that Connor—that's Cameron's post-adoption name—had packed a bag and taken his car. The police said that meant he was capable of rational decisions. Knew what he was doing.'

'So he's not missing? He went off somewhere?'

'It would seem so. Zach Brady disagreed. He told the police Connor's emotional state rendered him vulnerable. He has a history of mental health problems, Livvy. From what Tom can gather, Connor was particularly unstable when he left.'

Olivia's heart clenched. Cameron—no, Connor—might be hurting and alone, God only knew where. 'Any idea why he took off?'

'Elena Munro. Seems she tracked him down, wrote a letter saying she was his birth mother. How she wanted to meet. Zach only found out when Connor blurted out the truth not long before he drove off.'

Olivia sucked in a breath. She could see how Connor's world had been thrown into disarray.

'Zach Brady says his son was headed towards Bristol. He's not staying at any of the local hotels, however. Or using his bank cards.'

That concerned Olivia. How was her brother living?

With an effort, she pulled her attention back to what David was saying. She realised she'd missed a bit. The name Tiffany had come through loud and clear, though.

'Could you repeat that?' Her voice took on a distinct edge.

'I said I'm meeting Tiffany for lunch again tomorrow. To discuss Connor, that's all. Nothing you need worry about, Livvy.' He drew in a breath. 'She said Tom reckons he can dig deeper, perhaps even find where Connor is.'

Rage seared through Olivia, so strong she was afraid she'd combust. 'Whose idea was that? Yours or hers?'

'Hers. So she can update her brother for me.'

Olivia snorted. 'You're not that naïve and neither am I. Are you sleeping with her?'

'God no.' Anger bloomed in his tone. 'I've told you already—we're colleagues who get on well, that's all. Her brother can help you, Livvy. Don't throw away this chance because you've got the wrong end of the stick.'

Right when Olivia thought her fury couldn't burn any hotter, David had thrown fresh fuel on the flames. 'You bastard. You meet that tramp again and we're history.'

'Wait, Livvy. Listen to me, please—'

'I mean it, David. Stop thinking with your dick and more with your head.'

'There's something I haven't told you. It's really important—'

'And our marriage isn't?' Olivia had reached the point of no return. 'I'm warning you, David. If I find out you've seen her again, I'll start divorce proceedings.' She stabbed at her mobile to end the call, then threw it on the sofa. Screw David.

Sadness engulfed her. Once they'd been so solid. She opened the list of recent calls on her phone and blocked his number. It's for the best, she told herself. She had more important stuff to sort.

Olivia couldn't deny her husband had been useful, however. Cameron—no, Connor—was probably in Bristol, and Elena Munro most likely knew where. The only snag? Olivia was clueless as to the whereabouts of her biological mother. Desperate, she typed a text to Elena. *Is my brother with you? Call me. I need to know.*

Her phone remained silent. Olivia hadn't really expected a reply.

With a sigh, she headed for the bathroom. A quick soak, then bed. She'd contact a tracing agency first thing in the morning. She now had Cameron's new name and the likelihood he was in Bristol. Things were looking up. Before long, she might meet her brother. Elena, though—she was a different kettle of fish. Olivia wanted nothing to do with a woman capable of treating a baby like garbage.

She wondered what David was so eager to say. *There's something I haven't told you. It's really important.* Whatever it was, it didn't matter now.

Olivia slid into her bath, allowing the scalding water to soothe away her mental exhaustion. A fresh start awaited her once she'd tracked down Connor.

'Wherever you are, I'll find you,' she told her brother, the words disappearing into rose-scented steam. 'We've been apart for too long. Time to put that right.'

*****

Olivia found herself unable to relax once in bed. Her fingers stabbed at her phone. *I know you're Connor's adoptive mum. You lied to me. He's not dead, is he?* She pressed 'send'.

Rebecca wouldn't reply, of course. Olivia wasn't that naïve. It gave her a certain satisfaction, however, to shove her discovery of the other woman's duplicity in her smug face.

She fired off another text. *You can't stop me finding him. I will, and soon.*

CHAPTER 23

Olivia's mood remained upbeat throughout the following day. She'd chosen one of the tracing agencies, told them everything she knew, and had her fingers firmly crossed. Her texts to Rebecca had, as Olivia expected, gone unanswered.

Two days later, worry crept in. She'd received no news as yet about Connor but the tracing agency had assured her most missing people were eventually found alive and well. Olivia refused to give up hope.

Her resolve began to crumble on the third day. Her search for Connor was proving harder than she imagined; her brother appeared to have dropped off the grid. The tracing agency had drawn a blank so far, which concerned Olivia. She recalled Kirsten's advice from when they'd chatted earlier. 'Don't think that way. You'll find him, even if it takes a while. And if I can help, I will.'

Thank God for her best friend. Without her, Olivia wasn't sure she'd be even halfway sane. Kirsten was right. Positive mental attitude, and all that. The tracing agency would locate Connor before long.

Kirsten's recommended cure was a boozy pub night, although that had never been Olivia's thing. *I know a great bar in town. You need to chill out*, she texted. Olivia agreed, but how could she when her nerves were strung tighter than piano wire? Made worse by the envelope on her doormat when she got home. The handwriting was David's. Well, he certainly scored points for persistence, given that she'd blocked his number. At least he hadn't called round to the flat while she was there. Not yet, anyway. The letter got shredded and shoved in her waste bin.

Olivia ate a pre-packaged lasagne without tasting it, then poured herself a glass of Merlot. The moment she picked up her TV remote, her mobile trilled. An incoming call, the caller's number unrecognised.

Olivia frowned at the screen. She almost didn't pick up, but what if it was the tracing agency? Suppose they'd found Connor? Seven o'clock in the evening seemed a strange time to phone, but such companies might not keep regular office hours. She put her mobile in speaker mode and pressed the 'accept call' icon.

'Hello?' Her voice rose high with anticipation.

For a second she was met with silence. Then: 'Is that Olivia Gilchrist?' The voice was male.

'Yes. Who is this, please?'

Another pregnant pause. 'Oh, my God. I can't believe I'm speaking with you. This is so weird.'

Olivia's patience, already stretched thin, snapped. 'I'll ask you again. Who are you? What do you want?'

A sharp intake of breath. 'My name is Connor Brady. I'm your brother.'

Olivia gasped. Her world shrank to three things: her shock, the mobile phone, and the two sentences she'd heard a second ago. Never, in all her fantasises about Connor, had she imagined this. She replayed his words, savouring them. *My name is Connor Brady. I'm your brother.*

'Olivia? You still there?'

'Sorry. You took me by surprise, that's all.' Olivia wiped tears from her eyes. 'Where are you? How did you get my number?'

'I'm in Bristol. Drove down from Newcastle—that's where I live—a while ago. Some stupid notion about meeting my—sorry, our—birth mother. That didn't go well.' He snorted, and the anger in his voice was so palpable Olivia could almost taste it.

'She's gone,' she said. 'Disappeared. Any idea where she might be?'

Another snort. 'No. And I don't care. As for your number, I got it from her phone.' He blew out a breath. 'I saw the texts you sent to my mam.'

Thank God. Her messages to Rebecca weren't pointless after all. Olivia breathed a sigh of relief. Her luck was changing at last.

'Can we meet up?' she said.

When her brother didn't reply, she continued, 'Are you free now? You could come here—'

'No.' The sharpness of his tone shocked her. 'I don't think that's a good idea.'

Olivia sucked in a deep breath, tried to understand. This must be weird for Connor; he needed time to process the fact he had a sister. Once he'd done that, he'd agree the two of them should get together. She'd pushed him too far; how stupid of her.

'Maybe in a while,' she said, her voice artificially bright. 'Whenever you're ready.'

'I'll never be ready. That's not why I called.'

Shock thumped Olivia in the chest, rendering her mute. Why was his tone so cold, so hard?

'I should explain. My adoptive mother doesn't realise I snooped through her phone. She'd hate me calling you. But I felt I needed to.'

'Why?' Olivia managed.

'To ask you to leave her—us—alone.'

Olivia stared at her mobile, too numb to cry. 'I don't understand.'

'Let me spell it out for you. My mam's fiercely jealous; she always has been where I'm concerned. I was desperate to find out who my birth mother was, though. Why she dumped me in a rubbish bin.' Pain echoed in his voice, matching the hurt in Olivia's heart.

Connor cleared his throat. 'The bitch wrote me a letter. Said she wanted to meet. That she had something to tell me. Like a fool, I agreed.'

Olivia remained silent.

'Mam wasn't happy. Told me to let sleeping dogs lie. That nothing good could come of meeting my biological mother. I yelled at her, screamed that she was a jealous hag who had no business keeping us apart. I wish now I'd listened to her.'

'Why?'

'Because Mam was right. Elena Munro is a bitch. I went to her flat, and we argued. She pretended to care about me, but that's a lie.'

'What makes you say that?'

'Because actions speak louder than words. I can't get past her throwing me in a bin. Did you know about that?'

'I read the newspaper report. Connor, I've been looking for you—'

'Can't say the same. I hadn't a clue you existed until recently.'

'Really?'

'Yes. Came as a huge shock. The bitch mentioned in her letter she had something to tell me. I had no idea it would be that I have a sister.'

Realisation swept over Olivia. 'It was you I heard arguing with her that day.'

'That figures. She told me you lived upstairs. I never meant to hurt her. I got angry, and shoved her, and she fell.'

'She suffered a nasty head wound.' Despite Olivia's best efforts, judgement crept into her voice. 'I had to ring for an ambulance. You shouldn't have left her.'

'I need to explain something.' Connor's voice was contrite. 'My mental health isn't good, and I don't always take my medication. That day—it messed with my head. Big time.'

Olivia's annoyance softened. 'Why did you get so angry?'

'I hated the fact she'd moved in below you, had established a relationship with you. Plus you weren't shoved in a bag and thrown away, like I was. Right from birth, she's favoured you.' Resentment spilled from his voice. 'Do you have any idea how shitty that makes me feel?'

'I'm sorry.' Olivia didn't know how else to respond.

'Then later—that text she sent me. That vile, cruel text.'

So Elena had rejected Connor too. A sense of solidarity with him stole over Olivia. 'What did she say?'

'How she'd decided it was best we didn't meet again. Something about how she couldn't forgive my anger. Can you believe that? She says *she* can't forgive *me*. After the God-awful way she behaved.'

Elena, it seemed, was a woman of two halves. One side warm, caring, concerned, the Elena with whom Olivia had shared numerous bottles of wine. The other cold, rigid, lacking in empathy. Capable of abandoning a helpless baby.

'I've been a fool,' Connor said. 'Stupid, as well as unfair to my other mother. The one who's loved me unconditionally, despite all the hurt I've caused.'

Olivia stayed silent. Rebecca's love had a dark side, it seemed. Possessive, controlling. Capable of lies to keep her son from his own sister. Connor's next words confirmed Olivia's thoughts.

'She can be a bit of a control freak. Hated the idea of me reconnecting with Elena. We argued, and I insisted I was going to Bristol. Next things I knew, she'd also driven down.' He exhaled a long breath. 'I was mad at her at first. Now I'm glad she came.'

'She's been supportive? About Elena?'

'Like you wouldn't believe. Even persuaded me to take my medication again. I've hurt her so badly. Not anymore, though.'

'Did she talk you into making this call? Convince you not to meet me?'

'Pretty much. We discussed everything—you, Elena—and she told me no contact is the best option.'

Olivia stared at the magnolia walls, her potted plant on the windowsill, the blue curtains covering the windows. Everything was so normal, so ordinary. How was that possible? When her world had shattered yet again?

'We're both driving back to Newcastle in the morning,' Connor said.

His words came as a shock, even though he'd stressed he didn't want to meet her. Olivia had hoped for more time to persuade him otherwise, however. She understood Rebecca's reluctance for Connor to connect with Elena. To deny him contact with his sister, though? How was that a threat to Rebecca? Just how possessive was this woman?

'She loves me,' Connor said. 'Despite my mental health problems, my bad attitude—I've not been the best son, I admit, but I'm going to make it up to her. To my father as well.'

'Can't we get together before you leave?' Olivia hated the pleading tone in her voice, but she was desperate. 'You could come here one evening. I've always wanted a brother—'

'No.' His tone was flat, almost bored. 'Like I said, it's not a good idea.'

'What about you? Don't you want to reconnect with your own sister?'

'I can't hurt Mam again. She wouldn't be happy if we met.'

'Then don't tell her. Please, Connor. I need to see you.'

'Not going to happen.'

Why was he being so cruel? 'Can I call you? Once you're back in Newcastle?'

'No. That's the reason I got in touch. Don't phone me, or text. You won't be able to, anyway. Once this conversation is over, I'm blocking your number, like Mam's done.'

His casual cruelty drove daggers into Olivia's heart. Before she could unleash her anger, Connor spoke again. 'I need to go. Goodbye.' With that, he ended the call.

Olivia stared at her phone in shock. She poured herself another glass of Merlot and drained it in two gulps. Then she picked up her mobile to text Kirsten. *Can you come over? Please?*

Kirsten arrived fifteen minutes later, took one look at Olivia, and drew her into a fierce hug. She listened while Olivia relayed what Connor had said. After Olivia sobbed to a halt, Kirsten didn't hold back. 'Sod 'em all, babe. You're worth more than any of these morons. In time, you'll realise that.'

CHAPTER 24

Two days later, Olivia was seated opposite Kirsten in Club Coffee, a busy bistro in the Horfield area of Bristol. They were sitting next to the window, against which a steady drizzle pattered, matching Olivia's mood. They'd taken the last table, meant for four people, so there were two empty chairs. The glass was wet inside with condensation, the air heavy with the aroma of Colombian roast and freshly baked scones. Around them conversations buzzed, women chattered, men laughed. Olivia sipped her latte, grateful for the caffeine boost.

'How are you feeling, babe?' Kirsten asked, setting her mug of coffee on the table. Olivia spotted concern in her eyes. 'About David, for example?'

'I've not had time to think about him,' Olivia admitted. She knew she'd have to face the train wreck that was her marriage sometime. But not right then.

'You've not heard from Elena Munro again? Or Connor?'

'No. And I doubt I will.' Despite herself, Olivia couldn't keep pain from her voice. She wasn't that bothered about Elena, although her biological mother's rejection hurt. Until recently she'd always believed Sonia was her mum, so losing Elena wasn't that great a grief. Connor, though—her casual dismissal by the brother she'd always wanted still stung.

Kirsten snorted. 'Screw the pair of them. Remember what I told you. You're better off without those idiots.'

'You're right.' Determination coursed through Olivia. She'd concentrate on work, visit Harry more often, spend time with Kirsten. Sort out her marriage once and for all, even if that meant divorce. But Connor and Elena—they were out of her life. For good.

Kirsten seemed distracted, her eyes looking past Olivia towards the door. Olivia glanced round to see a man hovering by the counter. He was staring right at them.

'Not bad,' she said. 'If you like the rugged, mountain-man type. Which you do.'

Kirsten laughed. 'Am I that transparent?'

'Yes. But only to me.'

'I noticed him the second he walked through the door. His beard needs a cut, and that hair could use a wash, but I wouldn't kick him out of bed. Oh God. Don't look, but he's heading this way.'

Seconds later, the man stood beside their table. 'Sorry to bother you,' he said, in a northern accent. 'All the other tables are full, and I'm desperate for a coffee. Do you mind if I take one of these seats?' He gestured at the two empty chairs.

Kirsten shook her head. Her smile turned flirtatious. 'Be my guest.'

'Thanks. Won't be a minute.' He headed back to the counter, and Kirsten leaned towards Olivia, her grin triumphant.

'I think I've pulled.' A frown crossed her face. 'Not sure I want to, though. He smells like he needs a shower. And a change of clothes.'

Olivia had noticed that as well. 'He seems harmless enough. And if it turns out he's a weirdo, we can leave.' She glanced around. The man was returning with his coffee.

He pulled out the chair next to Kirsten and sat down, his gaze on Olivia. She saw Kirsten edge away, observed how her friend's nose wrinkled. The smell was more pronounced now the guy was closer to them. His sweatshirt was spattered with food stains, the collar and cuffs frayed and grimy. He wore his greasy hair pulled back in a ponytail. Dark circles underscored his eyes. Olivia guessed he was the same age as them, perhaps a little older. She wondered what his story had been.

The man took a gulp of coffee, his eyes still fixed on Olivia. She found his stare unnerving, along with the way his hands trembled. He didn't speak.

'Do you live near here?' Olivia said. Anything to break the tension.

He shook his head. 'Just visiting. I'm down here to meet a relative. As you can probably tell from my accent, I'm from the north-east. Newcastle, to be exact.'

'Are you staying long?'

'Depends.' He didn't elaborate, although he continued to stare at her. Olivia drained her coffee, then set her mug back on the table. She fiddled with her bracelet, counting the seconds until she could suggest to Kirsten that they leave.

'That's pretty. Silver, is it?'

Startled, Olivia glanced up. 'You mean this? Yes.'

'That's the one your mum gave you, isn't it?' Kirsten said.

'Yes.' The bracelet was a birthday present last year from Sonia. It was engraved with roses on one side and 'To my darling daughter, with love' on the other. Since Sonia's death, it had never left Olivia's wrist.

'Your mam gave it to you?' Olivia noted his use of the northern 'mam' instead of 'mum'.

Olivia nodded. She tried, but failed, to catch Kirsten's eye.

'Did I mention that I'm in Bristol to visit relatives?' the man continued.

'Yes. You did.' Olivia's tone was curt. She hadn't a clue what this guy's problem was, but he was annoying the hell out of her.

He didn't get the hint. 'What about you? Do you have brothers or sisters?'

Not for the first time, Olivia cursed Sonia's insistence on good manners. Unable to tell him to stop his intrusive questions, she bit out a clipped, 'No.' Why didn't Kirsten finish her coffee, so they could leave?

Anger crossed the man's expression. 'Really?'

Politeness be damned. 'I said no, didn't I?'

The strange guy flushed. Olivia couldn't tell whether his reaction was through temper or embarrassment. 'Are you sure?' he said. His voice sounded constricted, like he was forcing it through jam.

'What kind of dumb question is that?' Kirsten was also getting annoyed, it seemed.

Olivia's patience snapped. 'Yes, I've got a brother. Never met him, and I don't want to.' The memory of Connor's phone call was still raw in her mind. How ironic that this man was also a northerner and visiting relatives in Bristol.

'Olivia.' Kirsten's voice was calm, yet contained an underlying urgency. 'We should get going. You've a three o'clock session at the hairdressers, remember?'

Olivia, who had no such appointment, gave silent thanks for her friend's intervention. She shoved back her chair and stood up; Kirsten did likewise. Meanwhile, the guy was still staring at her.

'Why don't you want to meet your brother?' he said.

Olivia shrugged on her jacket. 'I just don't. He means nothing to me.' Not true, of course, but she wouldn't admit that to some random guy. She switched her gaze to Kirsten. 'Let's go.' She strode towards the door, Kirsten close behind.

Outside the bistro, Olivia hurried into the nearby alley, where she waited for her friend. 'What a weirdo,' she said, after Kirsten joined her.

'Yeah. We'll hang around here until we see him leave. That way he can't follow us.'

The sound of the bistro's door opening, then closing, reached Olivia's ears. From her vantage point she watched the strange guy cross the road, where a battered Toyota, its bodywork patched with rust, was parked. The man got in and drove off amid a screech of tyres.

'That's a relief,' Kirsten said.

*****

Connor stared through the windscreen of his car once he'd parked up, his eyes unseeing. His ears still functioned, although he didn't hear the rain hammer against the Toyota's glass or the howling wind. Only the voices in his head. The ones he should have listened to.

I tried, darling. I met with your sister, like I promised, but she wouldn't listen. Barely gave me the time of day. I told her you wanted to meet her, be a brother to her. She just shrugged and said she couldn't care less.

No, Connor had shouted. I don't believe you.

I wouldn't lie to you. She's not a pleasant person, Connor. But you'll be fine without her. You don't need anyone except your father and me. We both love you so much.

He should have stuck to his promise not to contact his sister. At the time, he'd meant it. Curiosity soon got the better of him, however, hence his snap decision to follow Olivia, find an opportunity to approach her. Clearly, he shouldn't have bothered. *Yes, I've got a brother. Never met him, and I don't want to. He means nothing to me.*

Anger flared in him over Olivia's indifference, along with jealousy over how their biological mother favoured her. His mind skated over the silver bracelet his sister wore. Given to her by her mam, she'd said. Connor didn't know whether she meant her adoptive mother, or Elena, but he suspected the latter. Even now, Olivia was the chosen one.

She didn't want him in her life? Well, two could play at that game. Olivia Gilchrist could go to hell.

His phone rang, jolting him from his thoughts. When he saw who the caller was, he sighed. She was persistent, he'd grant her that.

'Connor! Where are you? We need to meet, so we can discuss driving back to Newcastle tomorrow.'

'I need another couple of days before I can face Dad.' He wouldn't let slip he wasn't going back to Newcastle. Better to beg forgiveness than ask permission, right?

Silence for a second. Then: 'That's fine. Whatever you prefer. We should still chat, though. Can you come to my hotel? Now?'

'Sure. If you want.'

'And, darling? Have you taken your medication?'

'Yes.' A lie.

'That's my good boy. I'll see you soon.'

After he ended the call, Connor rested his head on the steering wheel. He was weary, right down to the marrow, of being rejected. Olivia didn't matter so much, given that for most of his life he hadn't known she existed, but his biological mother? She wasn't so easily ignored.

He'd told her he hated her. Never wanted to see her again. The first was true. The second, not so much.

Loathing thrummed through his veins. Pack your bags, Elena Munro, he thought. Before long, you're going on a guilt trip.

CHAPTER 25

'I just want a quiet evening in, Kirst. I'm not up to going to a pub.' Olivia closed her eyes in frustration, aware she sounded older than thirty. Much as she loved her friend, Kirsten's boundless energy could be exhausting. Conscious of the silence coming from her phone, she continued, 'Perhaps at the weekend. But not tonight.'

'Okay. But I'm worried about you, babe. You sure you're all right?'

'Positive.' Olivia was reluctant to tell Kirsten the real reason she needed space, which was Elena Munro.

Kirsten ended the call soon after. Olivia sank against the cushions on her sofa, replaying in her mind what she'd seen earlier.

She'd been driving home from work when a woman caught her attention. Walking along the pavement a few streets from Olivia's flat, her head bowed. Olivia didn't get a good look at her face, but the greying hair and blue coat screamed Elena at her. But didn't she say she was leaving Bristol?

Olivia realised she shouldn't let it bother her. Elena meant nothing to her, and vice versa; hadn't the woman made that clear? Upset Olivia it did, however. Her mother's rejection was a wound a boozy night at the pub couldn't fix.

With a sigh, Olivia trudged into the kitchen where she reheated a pasta bake. Once she'd eaten, she settled back on the sofa and reached for the TV remote. At that moment, her doorbell buzzed. A fist pounded against the door, followed by David's voice. 'Olivia! We need to talk.'

She hauled herself to her feet, then stood still. With any luck, he'd assume she wasn't home.

'I know you're there. Your car's outside.' So much for that idea.

'Don't do this, Livvy. You can't avoid me for ever. Open the door, will you?'

When she didn't respond, he exhaled a noisy breath. 'Have it your way. But we need to talk. Sooner rather than later.' Olivia heard his footsteps descend the stairs.

She'd been a coward, of course. Olivia wasn't proud of how she'd behaved, but she couldn't face her husband right then. Not with everything else going on, and given her certainty he was cheating on her.

Her phone rang with an incoming call. Elena Munro's name was on the screen.

Olivia caught her breath. To answer or not? Perhaps she *did* see Elena earlier. Shouldn't she find out what game the other woman was playing?

Or would it be best to ignore Elena? Block her number, even?

Curiosity won over caution. She accepted the call.

'Olivia?' Elena sounded terse, as if afraid Olivia would hang up on her. 'Can we meet up and talk? Please?'

'What about?'

'We need to discuss why I left Bristol so suddenly. Or seemed to, anyway. I'd rather not do it over the phone.'

Olivia didn't respond straightaway, wondering whether 'no' was an option. That awful newspaper report sneaked into her head. Did she really want to meet a woman capable of throwing a baby in a rubbish bin?

Oh, who was she trying to kid? Despite her doubts, Olivia knew the answer was yes. In order to heal, she needed closure with Elena.

She kept her voice neutral. 'If you want.'

'There's so much you don't know. Things I need to tell you.'

'I've worked out most of it already.'

Silence for a second. 'You have?' Uncertainty in Elena's tone.

'Yes.'

'Some of it you won't be aware of. That's why we should talk.'

'Okay. If you have stuff to say, I'm ready to listen.'

'Oh, my God. I can't tell you how much that means to me.'

'Text me tomorrow with when and where. Don't disappear again. Please.' Olivia ended the call before Elena could respond.

She turned on her television, tried to watch a film, but she was too wired to concentrate. A mug of coffee in hand, she retreated to her bed and arrived at a decision. If Elena failed to text the following day, Olivia was done with her. No third chances.

'Don't let me down,' she warned Elena in her head.

*****

Olivia's eyes strayed to her mobile every few minutes the next morning, willing it to beep. At five past eleven her patience was rewarded. A text, and it was from Elena.

Hope you still want to meet? Can you come to my place? I'll send you the address.

Olivia frowned. Elena had a place? So she'd not moved out of Bristol? The woman was an enigma.

Only one way to solve it. She sent a text. *Sure. When and where?*

Elena responded with an address, along with: *As soon as possible. I'll be here all day.*

'Here' was two streets away in a residential area. No coffee shops or restaurants, which was where Olivia had envisioned they'd meet. In addition, Elena's comment about being there all day hinted at residency. She tapped out a text. *You live there?*

Yes.

But you said you were leaving Bristol.

I'll explain everything, if you'll just come. Please.

Olivia dragged in a frustrated breath. An enigma didn't begin to describe Elena. *Fine. Will be there in 5 minutes.*

Outside, the sun was shining. Olivia thrust her hands deep in her jacket pockets as she walked the short distance. She arrived at the address she'd been given, a large Victorian house divided into four flats, as evidenced by the multiple doorbells. Elena had told her to press the top one; there was no intercom. Olivia rang the bell and waited.

A minute later Elena tugged open the door. At first she didn't speak, just stared at Olivia, in whose belly anticipation fluttered. Elena looked tired, pale, yet happy to see her.

'Come in,' Elena said, a smile on her face.

Olivia stepped forward. An odour of cooked cabbage, along with a whiff of damp, hit her nostrils. She followed Elena up the communal staircase to the top floor, where Elena pushed open another door. 'It's a bit small,' she said, as she waved Olivia inside. 'But it'll do for now. I won't be staying here long.'

Disappointment pierced Olivia. 'So you *are* leaving Bristol?'

'No! That's not what I meant.' Elena huffed out a sigh. She gestured towards a threadbare sofa. 'Sit down, and I'll make us some coffee. Then I'll tell you everything.'

Olivia complied. She watched the other woman grab mugs and spoons, before glancing around. The combined living and kitchen area was shabby, devoid of personal touches. From where she was sitting Olivia could see into the bedroom, which also looked down at heel. Elena was right. It wasn't a place anyone would stay long.

Elena walked towards Olivia, setting two mugs of coffee on the table. The ancient sofa groaned under her weight as she sat beside Olivia. Elena took a gulp of coffee, then looked Olivia square in the eye. 'Did you find the locks of hair? The letters from your father?'

Olivia nodded. So Harry *was* her dad. Thank God.

'I'm your mother,' Elena said.

'I guessed as much.'

'You have a twin brother too.'

'I know. I've been doing some digging.'

'I'd so love you to meet him.' Elena wiped a tear from her eye. 'He hates me, though. It was he who put me in the hospital. Yelled terrible things at me. Stuff I don't understand.'

Olivia couldn't hold back her anger. 'Why act so surprised? You dumped him. Chucked him away like he meant nothing.'

Elena's eyes grew wide with horror. 'No,' she whispered.

'Yes. He was found in a rubbish bin, in distress, barely able to breathe. Because you tossed him in there.' Olivia pursed her mouth in disgust. 'How could you do that?'

'I didn't.'

'Don't try to deny it.' A mental health problem must have been the reason, surely? With that in mind, she softened her tone. 'Were you suffering from postnatal depression? Or some form of psychosis?'

'Yes. I was exhausted. At the end of my tether. I was all alone, and Connor wouldn't stop screaming—'

'Why shove a newborn baby in a rubbish bin? Why not leave him somewhere safe, where he'd be found?'

'But I did.' Confusion filled Elena's face. 'Why are you saying I threw him in a bin? Left him struggling to breathe? As if I didn't love him, like he didn't own half my heart, even though I was so exhausted, unable to cope. I realise now I had post-natal depression. But I'm not a monster.'

'I'm saying it because that's what happened. I read the report in the newspaper.'

'That's not how it was.' Elena's face was ashen.

Anger swelled inside Olivia. 'A rubbish bin. God, what kind of woman are you?'

'Cameron—sorry, Connor—said the same thing. But you're wrong. All of you, the newspapers included. I don't have a clue what lies they printed. Afterwards, I went to London. Avoided the news.'

'You're lying.'

'I'm not.' Elena sat up straight, her mouth a determined line. 'Yes, I abandoned my son. But I left him at Tynemouth Castle, safe and warm, able to breathe, where he'd be found.' She glared at her daughter, her expression resolute.

Olivia refused to let it drop. 'So how did he end up in that bin?'

Elena wiped away a tear. 'I don't know. Let me tell you what happened. At least, as I understand it.'

So she did. Olivia heard how Elena and Sonia were once best friends. About Elena's one-night stand with Harry. She learned about the deal Sonia and Elena struck. Elena sobbed as she told Olivia how she adored her twins the second she laid eyes on them. Why she left her baby girl with Harry in Bristol, despite the pain that crushed her heart.

'Your mum was desperate for a daughter. And I'd promised her a child. You do see, don't you, darling? I was unwell, not able to cope, and I'd not been a true friend to Sonia. But I could at least give her the little girl she yearned for.'

Elena went on to tell Olivia how she ended up in Newcastle. Olivia listened, and tried to picture herself alone with a fractious baby, in a strange city, exhausted and suffering post-natal depression. She didn't get why Elena abandoned Connor, though. Why not contact Social Services?

'I wasn't thinking straight. Plus I was afraid,' Elena explained, after Olivia voiced the question. She reminded Olivia that Sonia and Harry had paid her for the pregnancy. The fear they could all have faced police enquiries.

'I loved you so much, darling,' Elena said. 'But I was sure Sonia would give you a good life. And I was right.'

'Yes. You were.' There were still things Olivia didn't understand. 'How did you find me? Once you decided to, I mean.'

'That wasn't too difficult. I had no idea if you'd married and taken your husband's name, so I hired a tracing agency to locate Sonia and Harry. I hung around their house and one day I got lucky. You visited, and I followed you home.'

'That text you sent after leaving hospital. You said—' Olivia cleared her throat. 'That you didn't want any further contact. Why not?'

Distress filled Elena's eyes. 'Oh, darling. I never sent that text. Well, I did, but not by choice.'

Olivia stared at her, unable to speak. What on earth did Elena mean?

'I need to tell you about Connor's adoptive mother,' Elena said.

Olivia heard about Rebecca Brady's threats towards Elena. How Elena boarded a train to London but returned to Bristol, refusing to be coerced into leaving. Her short-term rental of this flat, chosen to be close to Olivia.

'The woman's unhinged,' Elena said. Olivia realised her mother was afraid of Rebecca. 'Neither of us is safe around her. She only cares about Connor.'

'She paid me a visit. Told a load of lies about you two being sisters. How Connor was dead.' No wonder Connor was screwed up with Rebecca for a mother.

'We need to find him,' Elena said.

Olivia needed to be sure of something. 'You definitely didn't dump him in a bin?'

Elena sat up straight again, steel in her gaze. 'No. I did not.'

In her gut, Olivia was certain Elena was telling the truth. About everything. It was obvious from the plea in her tone, the paintings found in her bedroom. Ones that screamed pain, loss and anguish. They portrayed a baby, abandoned, alone, yet sheltered, close to being found. She'd misjudged Elena. This woman hadn't left her baby to die.

'We have to find him,' Elena repeated.

'He called me.' Hurt seeped into Olivia's voice. 'Told me his loyalty was to Rebecca. Said he wanted no further contact with me.'

'Oh, darling.' Elena squeezed Olivia's hand. 'He's jealous. He thinks I favoured you over him. And he still believes—' A sigh. 'That I threw him away. He's mentally ill, Olivia. That much is clear.'

'Do you—' Olivia swallowed hard. 'Have any idea where he is?'

Elena shook her head. 'All I can do is hope he returns to Newcastle. I have his address there. Maybe we could visit him? We'd just need to avoid Rebecca.'

The woman wouldn't share her son without a fight, Olivia thought. 'Tell me about the rest of your life. What happened once you got to London?'

Olivia learned how Elena struggled with depression for years after the birth. How guilt plagued her, leading to a suicide attempt. Followed by counselling and medication. The long haul back to health, including losing the weight she'd gained. How art proved therapeutic, with Elena using her full name, Madelena Baxter, to initial her work. She told Olivia about meeting and marrying Peter Munro. Her later life sounded happy to Olivia, for which she was glad. After all the heartbreak, Elena deserved joy. Perhaps, Olivia thought, she could be part of that.

She remembered something else. 'I found one of Mum's earrings in your carpet. You two met up again, then?'

'We did. Sonia dropped by your place one day when you were out. She had no idea I lived in the flat below. We ran into each other in the hallway, and she was shocked, as you'd expect. So I invited her in for a coffee. We chatted, and I told her I wanted to get to know my daughter.'

Olivia couldn't imagine her mother accepting Elena's return so readily. 'What did she say?'

'She wasn't thrilled, of course. She'd assumed she'd never see me again. But we talked, and I persuaded Sonia you should know the truth. That, at thirty years old, you could handle the shock. We agreed we'd tell you together, once you'd resolved your marriage problems.'

'That's why you didn't reveal who you were?'

'Yes. I also couldn't bear the thought of rejection, my love. You adored Sonia, whereas you hadn't a clue who I was. Or even that you'd been adopted. I had no idea how you'd react to the news. So I waited, became your friend, and all the while I loved you more and more. As long as I didn't tell you, I was safe. Didn't have to risk you hating me.'

'I wouldn't have hated you. We were friends, remember?'

'Yes. I wanted so much more, though.' Elena sat up straighter, her gaze fixed on Olivia. 'Can we try, darling? To build a relationship, even if it's thirty years too late?'

Olivia would always think of Sonia as her mother. Elena, though—in time she could love her too, now she knew she didn't dump her son in a rubbish bin.

'Darling?' Elena's voice shook a little. 'Please?'

Olivia didn't hesitate. 'I'd like that.'

CHAPTER 26

Connor stared at the dilapidated house he'd spotted before while driving around Bristol. It looked perfect for his purposes. Remote, abandoned, yet not so derelict he couldn't make it his base for a while. It had a roof that was only missing a handful of tiles; anything else he judged a bonus.

He'd parked his Toyota around the back, out of sight from the road. He stepped onto the gravel path that was thick with grass and walked to the boot of his car. From it he took a crowbar and hammer. He stood for a moment, surveying his new home.

The house was in a sorry state. Every window and door was boarded over; the place must have stood empty for years. It was old, probably Victorian, set back a hundred yards from the road. No neighbouring properties within sight, which suited Connor just fine. The brickwork needed re-pointing, and damp had stamped an ugly tide-mark a few feet from the ground. Connor's eyes drifted upwards, taking in the once-proud balcony that slumped from the upper floor. The rusty drainpipe, no longer attached to the sagging gutter. The rotten window frames. None of that mattered. For his purposes, it was perfect.

Connor strode to the back door, tools in hand. Plywood boarding sat around a padlock fastened to an old-fashioned bolt. He hacked at the plywood with his crowbar and hammer, intent on exposing the door underneath. Before long he'd accomplished his task; he prised the bolt loose, but the door remained locked. Connor returned to his car and took a chisel from the boot. A few minutes later, the latch yielded to his efforts, and he stepped inside.

Connor's nostrils flared as he breathed in the musty air, a stagnant blend of decay, rot and mould. The kitchen was large, twice the size of the one at his childhood home. What few appliances that remained—a cooker, toaster and fridge-freezer—were ancient, thick with grime and dust. The worktops were filthy and chipped. Two of the drawers underneath were missing. A gap yawned where Connor judged a washing machine once stood. If he had to guess, he'd say nobody had lived there since the nineteen eighties.

He pulled open a cupboard door. A stack of plates were inside. He tried another. In that one was an elderly saucepan, black with age. In a drawer a few items of cutlery languished, along with several rusty keys. Connor extracted them, his gaze on the back door. It was thick, windowless, perfect for what he had in mind.

The first key he tried fitted the lock. Now he needed to check out the rest of the house.

Connor strode across the cracked tiles and into the hallway. It was narrow and dark, although some light entered from the glass above the door. He peered into the large room next to the kitchen. It was completely empty, right down to the bare floorboards. A cursory glance showed Connor the front room was the same.

He swung back into the hallway, heading for the staircase. The steps were rotten in places, and they creaked under Connor's feet; he took care to tread towards the edges rather than the centre. A wide landing greeted him at the top of the stairs. Almost no light reached this part of the house, and Connor fumbled in his pocket for his phone to locate its torch function. Several doors opened off the landing, the nearest being the bathroom. The toilet seat was missing, revealing the filth within. There was no bath or shower, although the scarred floor revealed their former locations. A chipped sink sagged from the wall.

The other four rooms were all spacious. The two front ones were empty, but those at the back contained wardrobes, along with mattresses on the floor. Connor paced to and fro in the larger room, thinking. Boards ran from ceiling to floor, covering the windows. He eyed them, wondering.

To remove them was risky, but less so at the rear of the house. The property stood next to thick woodland, and the possibility anyone would notice their absence seemed remote. Connor set to work. Within minutes the plywood lay on the floor and light filled the room for the first time in decades. French doors led onto a narrow balcony; most of the glass was missing and the wood was rotten, the paint flaked and peeling. He pulled on the handle, and it yielded. Connor didn't step onto the balcony. It looked in poor condition, the iron flaking and rusty, the bolts that secured it to the wall loose and eroded.

Should he bother removing the plywood in the other back bedroom? The answer was no. Better to keep its windows boarded up.

Connor headed downstairs to fetch the rest of his stuff from the car. Several carrier bags, along with a camping stove and gas canister, ended up in the kitchen; he took everything else upstairs to the larger bedroom at the back of the house. By then it was late afternoon, but the sun was still strong as it streamed through the French doors. The house was, he thought, already becoming a home.

Connor spread his sleeping bag on the stained mattress and opened a packet of crisps, his thoughts on Elena Munro. Once he'd finished eating, he pulled out his mobile.

*****

Elena stared at her phone, her delight so fierce she thought she might faint. Connor's name was on the screen. Scenarios flashed through her head. He was going to tell her he didn't mean the terrible things he said. How he'd love to get to know her better.

Her fingers shook as she opened the text. Tears blurred her vision as she read Connor's message. *I'm sorry I got so angry. Can we meet and talk?*

Elena typed a reply, long and gushing, then deleted it. Too much, too soon. Besides, she'd rather say those words to his face. *When and where?*

Connor replied with a complicated set of directions. He didn't have the postcode for where he was staying, which came as a relief to Elena. She had no idea how to work the sat nav on her phone. He told her to come to the rear of the house rather than the front entrance.

Elena sucked in a deep breath. She'd make things right with Connor, then Olivia. At the thought of the second meeting she'd arranged with her daughter for the following day at a local coffee shop, joy flooded her once more. Her luck was turning, it seemed.

Don't mess this up, she warned herself in her head. She knew she wouldn't get a second chance.

Another text pinged through. *Can you come now?*

Elena didn't hesitate. *Yes*, she typed.

She grabbed her coat, keys and handbag, then headed out of her flat, towards her car. The sun on her face was strong, despite it being almost six o'clock. A perfect summer evening. Elena smiled as she unlocked her Fiat and slid into the driving seat. Life couldn't be better, apart from her lingering fear of Rebecca Brady. The woman's words, mouthed into Elena's ear in Rebecca's car and again at Temple Meads station, boomed through Elena's head. She straightened her shoulders. She couldn't, she *wouldn't*, allow that awful woman to intimidate her.

Elena read her scribbled directions, then started the car and headed across the city, the sun behind her all the way. Twenty minutes and a couple of wrong turns later, she slowed the car to a crawl, her eyes on the dilapidated house set some distance from the road. This couldn't be where Connor was staying, surely? The place looked deserted, as evidenced by the boards over the windows. She checked the directions. No mistake. Elena recalled Connor's unkempt appearance when he'd arrived at her flat, and her heart contracted with love. Her poor boy must have been squatting here, without access to a shower or laundry facilities. What kind of mother was Rebecca Brady, if she was okay with her adopted son living in such squalor?

Elena drove down the side access and parked at the back alongside Connor's car. She stared at the house, noticing the sagging balcony, the rusted drainpipe. A plan formed in her head. As soon as possible, she'd rent a two-bedroomed flat so she could care for Connor, provided he agreed. Be a mother to him at last.

As if he had sensed her, the back door opened to reveal her son. Elena stared at him, drinking in the sight, knowing she'd never get enough of Connor. Sure, he was dirty, dishevelled, his expression guarded, but oh, how beautiful. Elena stepped out of her car to walk, then run, towards him, his attack on her forgotten. Love, warm and wonderful, filled her as she hugged her son. His body was stiff, unyielding, but Elena didn't care. Connor was in her arms again, and Elena couldn't be happier.

Connor shoved her away, breaking the magic. 'Don't touch me,' he said, his voice rough. 'You lost that right thirty years ago.'

Elena's mouth went dry with shock. This wasn't the tender reunion she'd hoped for.

'Get in here. Now.' Connor's tone warned Elena he wouldn't tolerate a refusal.

Once they were both in the kitchen, Connor locked the back door. 'Give me your handbag.'

Elena was too stunned to reply. Connor huffed out an impatient breath, then grabbed it from her. 'You won't be needing this.'

'I don't understand.' Elena managed.

'No. But you will.' Connor's eyes were made of stone.

'Is there somewhere we can sit?' Elena's voice was tight with fear, but she ploughed on. 'So we can talk. You said that's what you wanted. I need to explain—'

Connor snorted, his expression one of contempt. 'Do you? I don't think so.'

His terrible accusations from before crowded into Elena's brain. 'Yes. Please. You must listen to me.'

'Wrong.' Connor dragged Elena towards him, his other hand still clutching her bag. His stale breath flooded her face. Bloodshot eyes drilled into hers.

'You're going to stay here. With me.' A fleck of spittle landed on Elena; she drew away, but Connor yanked her closer. 'It's time for you to be a mother at last.'

'What… what do you mean?' Inside Elena's head, thoughts swirled. *He's angry, but you can fix that. Reason with him. Once he's calm, persuade him to let you leave.* Once she was out of here, she'd call Social Services, talk to someone experienced in psychiatric problems, get help for Connor.

'Yeah, right. You need to ask, because you're clueless about being a mother. But you'll learn.' His hand still clamped on her arm, Connor pulled her into the hallway. He pushed her towards the stairs. Elena almost lost her balance, but he didn't relax his hold on her, not for an instant.

'Get up there. Turn left at the top. Second door on the right.' With a last shove, Connor let go of her. He was close behind, leaving Elena no option but to comply. She stumbled upwards over the creaking boards. As she rounded the top of the stairs onto the landing, Connor delivered a vicious jab to the small of her back. 'Move faster, can't you?'

Seconds later Elena found herself in one of the bedrooms. Thick boards hid the windows; in the half-light from the landing, she managed to make out the contents. An ancient mattress stained and torn, was on the floor, along with an old wardrobe lined up against the opposite wall. The air was stale, chilly. Elena shivered, drawing her coat closer around her. Fear tickled her spine with icy fingers. Her beloved baby had grown into a man she didn't recognise. One who frightened her.

Connor pushed her towards the mattress, her handbag still in his grasp. Elena didn't dare move. Instead she stared at his face, which was pinched with fury, and waited for him to speak.

'Welcome to your new life,' Connor said.

Elena moistened her dry lips. 'I don't understand.'

He rolled his eyes. 'Let me make it crystal clear, then. This is where you'll sleep. You'll stay here unless I decide otherwise. I expect you to cook my meals, wash my clothes, keep the house decent. Like a proper mother would do for her son. Not that you were ever that. Far from it.' He snorted again, the sound angry and dismissive.

Elena's gaze scanned the shabby room: the thick dust on the floor, the tired furnishings. *This room is where you'll sleep... keep the house decent...*

She still didn't understand. Well, she did, but couldn't admit the truth.

His words from before slithered into her head. *It's time for you to be a mother at last.* Everything she'd yearned for, but not like this. Never like this.

'Please,' she whispered. 'Let me explain. If you'll just listen—'

A sneer twisted Connor's face before he strode from the room. A key turned in the lock. Elena realised her son was deranged, and she was his prisoner.

CHAPTER 27

To Elena's relief, Connor made no attempt to interact with her after he'd locked her in her room. She heard sounds from the kitchen after he went downstairs, then his footsteps coming upstairs again. She called out, pleading that they should talk, all to no avail. Too frightened to do more, she judged it wiser to stay silent.

Later, once snores sounded from Connor's room next to hers, Elena checked out her surroundings. The door was thick, the lock sturdy, offering no chance of escape. She crossed to the window, running her fingers over the wooden boards, feeling for a gap. There wasn't one big enough to be of use. Besides, even if she pried the boards loose, could she open the windows? They might have been locked or painted shut. And what about the balcony? Elena recalled how rickety it had appeared, how the drainpipe had pulled away from the wall. She doubted either would support her weight.

After a few hours, the pressure in her bladder became hard to ignore. Humiliated, her only choice was to urinate in the ancient wardrobe.

Elena stared at a sliver of moonlight that pierced a crack in the window boards. What time was it? She'd barely slept, just a shallow doze here and there. Without bedding, Elena was cold, and the mattress was lumpy and uncomfortable. She huddled in a ball and waited for morning.

*****

Elena's worry increased once the sliver of moonlight changed to sunshine. She was locked in a derelict house at the mercy of a man who hated her, with no clue what time it was. She thought a couple of hours had passed since dawn, but couldn't be sure. Perhaps it had been longer. Olivia might be at the coffee shop this very second, wondering where Elena was. Her poor darling probably believed her mother had let her down again. Elena had to escape from this house, and soon, for everyone's sake.

She heard Connor's bedroom door open. His footsteps strode across the landing, then came the unmistakable sound of piss against porcelain. Then they returned, and a key rattled in the lock.

Connor threw open the door. 'Get up. I want my breakfast.'

Hunger gnawed at Elena's stomach; she hadn't eaten since lunchtime the day before. She was thirsty, too. Might Connor allow her some food? A cup of coffee?

Aware he was waiting for a response, she scrambled off the mattress, her body stiff and sore. 'Can we talk? Please?'

Connor's face became a mask. 'There's nothing to say. Get downstairs.'

Best to do what he said, Elena decided. If she did, his attitude might soften. He wanted her to mother him, right? Well, she could do that. Meanwhile, she'd assess her chances of escape.

'Move,' Connor ordered. Elena complied. As she crossed the landing, she cast a quick glance into

Connor's bedroom. Unlike hers, this one didn't have boards at the windows, meaning it was flooded with light. Her handbag was on the floor beside his mattress. Good to know.

'I need the toilet,' Elena said.

'Two minutes. That's all you've got. Don't try pulling any stunts. I'll be waiting outside.'

Elena opened the bathroom door, her nostrils closing over at the stench. The toilet lacked a seat, and to her horror Elena saw it was full of piss and shit. A rubbish bag sat on the floor, together with a roll of paper. Of course it did; the house was derelict, minus a water supply. There was no way to flush the toilet, hence the bag for the used paper.

She turned to Connor, her mouth open in mute appeal. The thought of using that cesspit repulsed her.

'Please,' she said. 'I can't—'

A sneer crossed his face. 'Not good enough for you? Use it or go without. Your choice.'

Defeated, Elena closed the door, plunging the room into darkness. Like her bedroom, the window had been boarded over. She used the toilet as quickly as possible, and rubbed a sheet of paper over her hands to try to clean them, all the while yearning for water, soap and a towel.

After she emerged Connor gestured towards the stairs. 'Breakfast. Now.'

Elena glanced around her once in the kitchen. Like the bathroom, the old units and appliances wouldn't be functional. On a worktop sat a camping stove and gas canister, along with several carrier bags. Connor pushed past her and pulled one open.

'Cleaning stuff's in here,' he said. 'Toilet paper and kitchen roll too. Everything else is food and drink. Make a start on my breakfast.'

Keep him sweet, Elena reminded herself. The sooner she worked out how to escape this place, the quicker she'd get help for her boy. Without thinking she moved towards him, her arms outstretched.

'Back off! Don't touch me!' Connor's furious words burst Elena's bubble. She stepped back, keen to appease him.

'I'm sorry,' she said. 'I didn't mean to upset you. What would you like for breakfast?'

He shrugged. 'Don't care.'

Elena rummaged in the carrier bag Connor said held cleaning supplies. She extracted a bottle of antibacterial fluid and sprayed her hands, which she then wiped with kitchen roll. Next she opened one of the food bags. Bread, peanut butter, a packet of sliced ham, another of sausages. Bottled water, a jar of coffee and powdered milk were in a different bag. Elena eyed the camping stove, then pulled open cupboards and drawers, finding mugs, plates, an ancient pan and some cutlery. Her stomach growled all the while.

She set water to boil on the stove while she slapped together a ham and peanut butter sandwich. Her mind was focused on her handbag, upstairs by Connor's mattress. Her phone was in there. If she could just grab it, under the guise of cleaning his room—

'Get a move on,' Connor said. His patience was wearing thin, it seemed.

Elena made the coffee and set it before him, along with his food. She watched him eat, love battling fear inside her. She didn't dare speak.

Connor banged his empty mug on his plate. 'You can get yourself something now.'

Elena fixed herself a sandwich and coffee, desperate to fill the void in her belly. Once she'd finished eating, Connor gestured towards the cleaning supplies. 'Get to work.'

Elena did her best. She wiped everything down with disinfectant and kitchen roll, Connor's gaze on her all the while. Then she moved into the hallway. 'I'll make a start on upstairs,' she said, injecting false cheer into her voice. Connor didn't reply, just nodded.

Elena hurried up the stairs, willing to bet Connor had forgotten about her handbag. She walked into the bathroom, depositing a bottle of cleaning fluid on the floor with a loud thud, keen to convince Connor she was at work in there. Instead, she tiptoed towards his bedroom.

As she'd hoped, her mobile was inside her bag. Elena extracted her phone, then paused. Her plan was to call 999, but now she had the opportunity, she was reluctant. Her son wasn't a monster, despite keeping her a prisoner. He needed psychiatric care, not a criminal conviction. Would the justice system do what was right by him?

Her fingers hovered over the '9'. Lost in her thoughts, she was oblivious to the sound of Connor's footsteps on the stairs. Too late, Elena thrust her phone back in her bag, but Connor was already in the doorway.

'You bitch,' he spat out. 'This was a test to check if I could trust you. Turns out I can't.' He grabbed Elena's arm, then tossed her handbag onto his mattress. 'Get in your room. Now.' Without waiting for a response, he dragged her towards the door. Terrified, she tried to pull away, but his grip was inexorable. She was too frightened to speak.

Seconds later Elena found herself locked inside her bedroom. She huddled on the mattress, her mind a blank, too numb to cry.

Connor's feet stomped down the stairs. A door banged, then there was silence.

*****

Olivia stared out of the window of the coffee shop where she'd arranged to meet Elena, but her eyes didn't register the street outside. Her thoughts were with her biological mother, and how Elena had let her down. Again.

It was now eleven twenty-five, and Elena had been due there at eleven. Olivia reached for her phone, worried she'd missed a text amid the din of the coffee shop, but no notifications showed on the screen. She grabbed her coat and handbag, ready to leave. To hell with Elena Munro and her mind games.

At that moment, a ping sounded from her mobile. Olivia seized it, expectation coursing through her. Elena, surely. She'd overslept, perhaps, or her car had a flat tyre. Kirsten, however, not Elena, had texted her. *Hiya! Hope all is going OK with Elena. You up for a Chinese sometime?*

Misery washed over Olivia. Right then she needed a sympathetic voice.

Her friend sounded surprised when she answered Olivia's call. 'Hey, babe. I didn't expect to hear from you so soon. Weren't you meeting Elena at eleven?'

'She never turned up.' Olivia's eyes swam with tears. Oh God. She was losing it in public, all over a woman who'd proved she wasn't worth the effort. How stupid of her.

'Did she get in touch? Give a reason?'

'Nope.'

'What a bitch. You're better off without her. I know it's hard, but—'

'You're right.' Olivia's tone was firm. 'She's messed me around once too often. I'm done with her.'

'Listen, babe. I need to tell you something.' Kirsten's voice sounded strained. 'About David.'

Ice formed in Olivia's stomach. 'Have you seen him with Tiffany Cook again?'

'Yes. But not the way you think.' Kirsten explained she'd spotted David in the Llandoger Trow the day before, lunching with his colleague. Two guys were also at their table. One, according to Kirsten, was Tiffany's brother, the investigative journalist. The other was Tiffany's fiancé.

'David accosted me while I was at the bar,' Kirsten said. 'Gave me a right ear-bashing for jumping to conclusions. He said Tiffany's madly in love with her boyfriend.'

'Really?'

'Yes. I saw the way Little Miss Perfect looked at the guy. The ring on her finger. David's telling the truth.'

Thank God. The knot of tension inside Olivia relaxed somewhat. Shame washed over her. Like Kirsten, she had leapt to conclusions. Treated her husband unfairly, all because of her jealousy. Sonia had been right about David, it seemed.

'Maybe you should call him,' Kirsten said.

'You're right. One thing's for sure. I won't be contacting Elena bloody Munro again.'

CHAPTER 28

Two hours later, Olivia stared at her mobile, shock surging through her. A message from Connor was on the screen. He wanted to meet her. Said he was sorry he'd blanked her before. How he'd like the chance to connect before he returned to Newcastle.

Her brother had been so determined to break off contact. What had changed? Because something clearly had.

Olivia leaned back in her chair, her phone still clutched in her hand. She had a client due in five minutes, and little time in which to think. Should she ignore Connor?

That's not what you want, her intuition whispered. Olivia agreed. Her brother had got in touch, and she couldn't—*wouldn't*—miss the opportunity to meet up. Hadn't she always yearned for a sibling? Perhaps, as twins, they'd stayed connected subconsciously, despite being separated as babies. Now here he was, wanting to see her. She needed to guard against further hurt, though. Hadn't Connor wounded her enough already?

Why the change of heart? she typed, and pressed 'send'.

A reply came back almost immediately. *Been doing a lot of thinking. Realised I'll always regret it if I don't meet you. Give me another chance. Please?*

Hope bloomed in Olivia. He'd been reflecting on things, had he? Well, that was good. Elena Munro might be a lost cause, but Connor Brady wasn't. This could be the fresh start Olivia needed, one in which she'd have the brother she'd always wanted. How could she say no?

In her mind, she formulated a plan. They'd meet, she'd weigh up what kind of man he was, and take it from there. She tapped out a message. *When and where?*

Another instant reply. He'd given directions rather than a postcode. Olivia wasn't familiar with that part of Bristol—the address was on the outskirts of the city—but she didn't care. She was free that evening, and she had every intention of meeting Connor.

I'll be there, she typed into her phone. *So glad you got in touch.*

The afternoon couldn't pass quickly enough. Olivia counted down the hours until it was time to go home, shower and change. Back at her flat, her microwaved curry lay heavy on her stomach, and she abandoned it after a few mouthfuls, too wired to manage more.

Six-thirty arrived, which meant it was time to go. Olivia grabbed her coat, keys and bag, hope bright in her heart. She arrived at the address Connor had given a minute before seven, having driven past it once, certain that somewhere so ramshackle couldn't be where he was staying. Was it a squat, perhaps? Olivia pulled up opposite, her gaze on the boarded windows, the air of neglect that hung over the place, and checked her phone. No mistake. She drove down the side of the house, convinced only when she spotted a battered Toyota. Something about it looked familiar, but she couldn't think what.

Next to it was a blue Fiat. Olivia's mood deflated. The car was Elena's. What was *she* doing there?

Well, no matter. Olivia resolved to ignore her mother and concentrate on Connor. She'd hoped for a private talk with her brother, but that wasn't to be. Still, tonight was a start.

'Don't screw this up,' she told herself as she switched off her engine.

The back door was ajar a fraction. Olivia pulled it open and stepped inside.

What a dump, was her first impression. Someone had attempted to clean the kitchen worktops, but dishes sat piled in the sink, and the stink of burnt food hung in the air. 'Hello?' she called out, her voice echoing through the empty room. 'Connor? Where are you?'

She didn't get a reply, but she heard someone clumping around upstairs. Male, from the heaviness of the footsteps. There was no sign of Elena.

Olivia started up the stairs, hesitating when she reached the landing. She froze when a man exited one of the bedrooms, a scowl on his face. She recognised him straightaway as the strange guy she and Kirsten met at the coffee shop.

Shock pounded through Olivia. This man was her *brother*?

'Connor?' Olivia's voice trembled a little. 'It's nice to meet you at last.' He didn't reply. Instead he stared at her, his expression hostile.

Olivia studied him. God, he looked rough, even worse than before. His hair was more matted, the stench of sweat more pronounced. Anger suffused his face, a flush creeping from his cheeks towards the tense line of his jaw.

'What the hell are *you* doing here?' Connor demanded. He pushed past her to head downstairs, leaving Olivia speechless.

Elena appeared in the doorway of another bedroom. Her cheeks were pale, her eyes set amid dark circles. It'd been a while since her hair had seen a brush or her clothes an iron. 'Olivia,' she said, her voice a strained whisper.

'What's going on? Why are you here?' Olivia was aware her tone was brusque, but didn't care.

Olivia listened as Elena told her how Connor had lured her to the house. His fantasy that she'd be a mother to him, in this decrepit place where nothing worked. 'He unlocked my door just now so I can make him some food. I'm frightened, Olivia. Connor needs psychiatric help.'

'I think you're right. He's not acting rationally. He sent me a text suggesting we meet up. Just now, though, he yelled at me, demanded to know why I was here. As if he'd forgotten all about the text.' Olivia took Elena's arm and guided her to the filthy mattress, on which they both sat.

Seconds later, she heard a car pulling up, followed by the back door to the house opening. Voices, one Connor's, the other too low to distinguish, but recognisable as female. Rebecca Brady, of course. Who else could it be? Olivia glanced at her mother, whose expression showed she'd also noticed the car's arrival.

The thud of footsteps sounded from the stairs. Both women scrambled off the mattress. Feet strode across the landing, and the door flew open. Connor stood in the doorway.

Olivia peered past her brother towards the landing, but couldn't see Rebecca Brady. She could hear someone moving around below, however. Connor's gaze was fixed on Elena, his expression furious. Olivia laid a hand on her mother's arm, causing her to start. She guided her back onto the mattress, then patted its grubby surface. 'Join us, Connor. Please.' Right now she needed to defuse his anger.

Connor ignored her. Instead, he paced back and forth, one hand raking through his hair. His hands were balled into fists. For a second Olivia wondered if she was in over her head. Might he turn violent? She glanced around, unable to spot anything Connor—or she—could use as a weapon. Right when Olivia was about to plead with him again, he sat beside her. The stench of sweat and unwashed clothes was overpowering.

She chose her words with care. 'I didn't know you were my brother when you showed up at the coffee shop. I shouldn't have said those things.'

'You told me I meant nothing to you. That you didn't want to meet me.' Connor's voice held a world of pain. He jerked his head towards Elena. 'Mother and daughter, both dyed-in-the-wool bitches.'

'Oh, my love. Please let me explain.' Elena's voice trembled, yet her gaze remained resolute. 'You've got it all wrong. What you said before, about me throwing you away—none of that is true.'

'Don't lie!' Connor's roar caused both Elena and Olivia to jump. 'I read the newspaper report. My head's a mess because of you.' His fists clenched tighter, their knuckles white.

'Connor.' Elena's voice was gentle. 'I admit I abandoned you. But not the way you think.'

Connor snorted. 'Yeah, whatever. It was different for *her*, wasn't it?' He gestured towards Olivia. 'You weren't so depressed that you couldn't find *her* a decent home.' He paused, and his expression grew more thunderous. 'Or did you keep her, even though you threw *me* away?'

'No,' Olivia interjected, her tone firm. 'Elena's told me the full story. I was adopted, just like you.'

'I don't believe you. You were living in the same block of flats.' Before Olivia could stop him, Connor's fingers wrenched her mother's gift off her wrist, causing her to gasp with pain. 'She gave you this. You get jewellery, whereas I got a garbage bin.' He hurled the silver bracelet across the room. It thudded against the ancient wardrobe, then clattered against the floorboards.

'You're wrong.' Olivia's gaze never left Connor's face. 'The bracelet was a present from my adoptive mother. I only met Elena a while ago.'

'It doesn't change the basic facts. You ended up with a cushy life, whereas I got dumped in a bin.' He pushed himself to his feet to tower over Elena, his face inches from his mother's. 'Explain that to me. Can't wait to hear what lies you come up with.'

Elena's hands twisted around each other in her lap. 'I don't know what happened. Wait—' she said, as Connor sneered in contempt. 'I believe I was suffering severe postnatal depression. The woman who adopted Olivia was my best friend, and desperate for a daughter. I never doubted she'd give your sister everything I couldn't. You, though—I persuaded myself I could care for one baby, even if two were impossible. Turns out I was wrong.'

Another snort from Connor. 'Am I supposed to feel sorry for you? There's no excuse for throwing me in that bin. None.'

'But I didn't.' Elena's voice rose high, her desperation obvious to Olivia. 'That's what I can't understand. I changed your nappy, fed you, wrapped you up nice and warm. I left you at Tynemouth Castle, in a sheltered area, somewhere I knew you'd be found. It's the hardest thing I've ever done. Leaving you broke my heart, yet I believed it was for the best.'

'So how did I end up in that bin?'

Elena sucked in a breath. Her face was very pale. 'I've racked my brains about that. All I can think of is this. Earlier that morning I noticed a homeless guy hanging around. At the time, I didn't pay him any attention. I suspect he saw me leave the bag with you in it at the castle and came to check the contents after I'd gone. He must've been pretty spooked when he found what was inside and ditched the bag.'

Connor looked sceptical, but didn't comment. 'I'm not lying, I swear,' Elena said.

'She's telling the truth.' Olivia made sure her voice stayed calm, but firm.

Connor switched his attention to his sister. 'How do you know?'

'Elena's an accomplished artist. I've seen her paintings of you as a baby at Tynemouth Castle. I can show them to you if you want. They're at my flat.'

Connor pursed his lips in a sneer. How could she convince him, Olivia wondered.

'If you saw them you'd be in no doubt. The castle is where she left you.'

'I don't believe you.' Connor's tone, however, betrayed uncertainty.

'Why would I lie?' Olivia risked a question. 'That day you turned up at Club Coffee. You'd not long before told me you wanted nothing to do with me. Why, Connor? I don't understand.'

Confusion crossed Connor's face before anger took over. 'Pot, kettle, black? *You* were the one who said you didn't want any contact with *me*.'

'At the cafe, yes. I was hurting, didn't know you were my brother. You told me during our phone call you didn't wish to meet me, or pursue a relationship.'

'What the hell are you talking about? We've never spoken on the phone.'

Olivia strove to calm herself, despite her growing disquiet. 'You called me the other night. We spoke for quite a while. You said your first loyalty was to your adoptive family. In particular, Rebecca Brady.'

Connor's fists clenched once more. 'You lying bitch,' he spat out. 'How dare you even speak her name? I'll say it again. I've never called you, not once.'

He sounded so sure, so rational. His shaky mental health must have meant he'd forgotten their conversation. Tread carefully, Olivia warned herself.

'You spoke about your adoptive mother,' she said. 'How Rebecca loves you, despite everything you've put her through. Her jealousy, her tendency to control.'

'I've no idea what you're talking about. And I certainly wouldn't have said—' Connor swallowed, and Olivia spotted tears in his eyes, before he blinked them away. He dragged in a deep breath. 'What you claim I did. About my adoptive mother.'

'But—'

'Shut the fuck up. I told you—don't mention her. Don't talk about her as if she's still alive.'

Olivia stared at him, open-mouthed. 'I don't understand.'

'Rebecca Brady died fifteen years ago,' Connor said.

CHAPTER 29

Rebecca Brady died fifteen years ago. Elena stared at her son. From the corner of one eye she saw Olivia had frozen, shock on her face. Elena imagined hers was probably the same.

A shiver ran through her. If the woman who'd threatened her and lied to Olivia wasn't Connor's adoptive mother, then who the hell was she?

'That's impossible,' she said, aware her voice sounded thin, reedy. 'She came to meet me after I left hospital. She—' Elena stopped, reluctant to divulge the threats Connor's adoptive mother had made.

'I've met her too,' Olivia said. 'She visited me at my flat. Told me a pack of lies about Elena. About you too. She said you died soon after birth.'

Connor's gaze switched between his mother and sister, anger still predominant in his face. Until understanding replaced it. 'This woman. What did she look like?'

Elena cleared her throat. 'Tall. Slim. Smartly dressed, about my age. Greying hair in a messy bun.'

'That describes who I met as well,' Olivia said. 'She had the same accent as you.'

Connor shook his head. 'Holy shit. I knew she was weird, obsessive even, but I never expected this.' His hands trembled, and Elena suppressed the urge to clasp them in hers. Soon, she promised herself. Right then wasn't the time.

'Who's *she*?' Olivia burst forth.

Connor didn't appear to register the question. 'That bitch. She's downstairs right now. She was here earlier too, nosing around, claiming to be worried about me.' He turned to Elena. 'When she discovered I'd come to Bristol to find you, she insisted on driving down as well. Said I needed her, that she'd help me deal with whatever happened. All crap, of course. She's obsessed with me. Always has been.'

'Why, though?' Olivia shifted forward on the mattress. 'I'll ask you again. Who is this woman?'

Connor turned his gaze towards his sister. 'Her name's Amy Sutcliffe. She's the one who found me in that rubbish bin thirty years ago.'

Amy Sutcliffe. The name meant nothing to Elena.

'I remember her from the newspaper report,' Olivia said. 'She kept in touch with your new family, then?'

'Yeah. God knows how, but she managed to discover who'd adopted me. It always struck me as creepy the way she behaved like she was a Brady. Then I found the newspaper article and understood why Mam and Dad tolerated her. She has nothing else but me in her life, you see. Never married or had kids.' His mouth twisted with scorn. 'She always tried to hug me a bit too long, you know?' He blew out a breath. 'Like I was *her* son, not anyone else's. It got worse after Mam died. She tried to get Dad to marry her, but he had more sense.'

'Wow. She's obsessed all right,' Elena said. 'She must see me as competition. That's why she warned me off.'

Shock flooded Connor's face. 'I had no idea she'd go that far.'

Elena nodded. 'Yes. She insisted I leave Bristol.' Again, she elected not to elaborate on the threats Amy had made. 'I came back, however. Whatever you might think of me, my love, I couldn't leave, not now I've found you both again.'

A hard look sneaked into Connor's eyes. 'Yeah, right. You abandoned me once. Why not a second time?'

'Because that was thirty years ago. I was a different person.' Elena reached inside the neckline of her sweater and brought out a silver locket. Her fingers rubbed over the cool metal, a smile of love on her face. 'I wear this every day to feel close to my babies.' She held the locket out in her palm. Olivia leaned in, but Connor appeared suspicious.

'It's beautiful,' Olivia said.

She was right. The locket was a four-leafed clover suspended from a heavy chain. Elena flicked open the clasp to reveal a name engraved inside three leaves of the clover: Elena, Olivia, Cameron. Along with a date, the twins' birthday, on the other one.

Elena proffered the locket to Connor. 'See the inscription, right here? I know you're Connor now, but you were Cameron then.'

For a second Elena saw her son's expression soften. 'Cameron,' he said. 'Not bad. What made you choose that name?'

Now wasn't the time to lie. 'I didn't,' Elena said. 'Sonia and Harry, the couple who adopted Olivia—they chose your names. The original plan was that they'd adopt both of you.'

Too late, she realised she'd said the wrong thing. Connor's expression hardened again. 'You should have let them,' he spat out, eyes dark with anger. 'That way I'd have grown up with a sister. Never had to discover I got dumped in a bin.' Elena shrank at the hatred in his tone. 'You're a liar and a manipulative bitch. That homeless guy never existed, did he? Amy Sutcliffe might be a fruitcake, but at least she cares about me.' Connor buried his head in his hands, his fingers tugging at his hair. He rocked back and forth, unintelligible sounds issuing from his mouth. Elena realised her son was damaged, very much so, and she'd played a part in that.

The compulsive rocking stopped. So did the noises. Connor struggled to his feet, his movements like those of a drunken man. Tears hovered in his eyes, and his skin was pallid. His gaze was unfocused, glassy.

The door opened. Amy Sutcliffe, a.k.a Rebecca Brady, stood in the doorway. Elena wondered how long she'd been there.

Amy ignored Elena and Olivia, her focus on Connor.

'Could you do me a favour, darling?' she said, as though she was his mother. 'We're almost out of bread. Milk, too. Can you go and buy some, please?'

When Connor didn't respond, Amy crossed to where he was standing. Her hands roamed over his matted hair, bliss etched on her features. Connor shifted position, clearly uncomfortable, but didn't pull away.

'Please, darling,' Amy said. 'Besides, I want to talk to Olivia and Elena. You can trust me. Neither of them will leave this house.'

'Yeah, whatever. I'm done with them.' Connor strode from the room.

Amy pushed the door shut. Elena stared at the woman she suspected was a rattlesnake in human form. Amy appeared calm, composed, but malevolence glinted in her eyes. Elena had been foolish to hope she could outsmart her.

'I did warn you, Elena.' Amy's tone, like her expression, was mild.

Yes, thought Elena, you did. She should have taken heed. Amy, in her role of Rebecca, had been very explicit.

'I made a promise, and I always keep my word.' Amy skewered Elena with her gaze. 'You remember, right? What I said I'd do if you returned to Bristol?'

The words were engraved on Elena's memory. *If you ever come back, or if you don't stop sniffing around my son, I'll kill Olivia. Then you.*

'Connor will be gone a while,' Amy said. 'The nearest shop's miles away.'

Before Elena could speak, Olivia did. 'It was you who texted me earlier, wasn't it? Not Connor. What did you do? Grab his phone when he wasn't around?'

'Got it in one.' Amy folded her arms, a smirk on her face.

'Why? What was the point?'

'To lure you here. So I could kick you meddling bitches out of his life for good.'

Elena stared at the woman. Amy Sutcliffe was, she realised, quite mad. Her obsession with the man she regarded as her son made her dangerous, too. Elena shivered, unsure what to do. A similar uncertainty emanated from Olivia. Elena shifted closer to her daughter, eager for any crumb of comfort.

'I followed him last night,' Amy said. 'Connor thought he could give me the slip, but he's wrong. Nowadays it's easy to track someone via their mobile. I'll always know where my boy is.' She laughed, and Elena itched to slap the woman's face. 'I saw you arrive a while later. Heard what he said to you. After all this time, everything you've done, he still wants you as a mother, not me.' She spat out the words.

'But you're not his mother,' Olivia said. 'Not even close.'

'Shut the hell up.' Fury filled Amy's face. 'He's mine in every way that matters. I've adored that boy since the moment I rescued him, and I've only loved him more as the years have passed. Oh, I saw the homeless guy you mentioned, running away from that rubbish bin. Maybe he dumped Connor there, maybe you did. It doesn't matter anymore.'

'You've no business interfering.' Olivia sounded angry. 'You've lied to us, and probably to Connor too. Why keep him from his own mother? His sister?'

A sneer crossed Amy's face. 'I'm all the family he'll ever need. Me and Zach, that is.'

Elena found her voice at last. 'You needn't make a contest out of it. If Connor wants to see you, then I won't object. There's room in his life for us all.'

Amy snorted. 'Not in mine, though. You two—you're superfluous to requirements.' She edged closer to the door.

'He doesn't want you here,' Olivia said. 'Doesn't that tell you something?'

'Shut up.' Anger sounded in Amy's voice, and Elena shivered. Don't provoke her, she warned Olivia in her head.

Olivia ploughed on regardless. 'Who'd you get to make that phone call?

Amy smirked. 'Don't know what you mean.'

'Oh, yes, you do. Some guy claimed to be Connor, said he wanted nothing to do with me. That was *your* doing, right?'

Amy shrugged. 'I found an out-of-work actor who'd sell his soul for a coke fix. Didn't even cost me that much.'

'You bitch,' Olivia spat out.

'Here's what's going to happen. A tragic accident. One which neither of you will survive.'

Elena gasped. Amy laughed, the sound a harsh guffaw. 'Connor's taken his wallet, phone and keys with him. All my stuff, apart from my handbag, is in the boot of my car. There's nothing here that can identify him. Or me.'

Fear closed around Elena's heart. Olivia must have felt it too, because she reached over to grasp her mother's hand. Her skin was warm and Elena derived solace from her touch.

'Why is that relevant?' she asked. The words 'tragic accident' pounded in her head.

Amy retreated to the doorway. 'I'll tell you the rest from outside.' With that, she stepped onto the landing and locked the door behind her.

'This place is old,' Amy's disembodied voice said. 'Wooden floorboards, ancient furniture. A terrible fire risk. So is that camping stove Connor's been using. You understand what I'm saying, right?'

A gasp of horror escaped Elena. Beside her, Olivia went rigid.

'No,' Elena managed through dry lips. 'You wouldn't.' Yet Amy was more than capable of carrying out her threat. Escape was more imperative than ever. Elena cast a glance at the boards covering the windows. Alone, she couldn't manage them, but with Olivia's help—

'Neither Connor nor I have any connection to this dump,' Amy said. 'The roads around here don't have traffic cameras. There are no neighbours, and the cars parked around the back can't be seen from the road. Once Connor and I are heading towards Newcastle, we'll be in the clear.'

'Don't do this. Please.' Olivia's voice was hoarse. 'We'll leave Connor alone, I swear. You'll be in a different city, hundreds of miles away. Elena and I have each other. You'll never hear from us again, I promise.'

A laugh sounded from the landing. 'Do you really expect me to believe that?'

Thoughts tumbled through Elena's head. Persuade her to unlock the door, lure her into the room. Wrestle her to the ground, grab the key, shut her in here instead of them—

'You're wrong,' she said. She held her breath amid the silence that followed.

'About what?' Suspicion in Amy's voice.

'I have something of Cameron's that can identify him. Link him to this place.'

'You're lying. I don't believe you.'

'You should.' Elena's mind scrambled for ideas. Think, she told herself. What could she pretend to have?

An answer came to her. The entire premise was shaky, but all she needed to do was create doubt in Amy's head. Enough to make her unlock the door.

'Ever noticed that thick gold bracelet he has?' She held her breath again.

'Cameron doesn't wear jewellery.'

'I gave it to him that day he came to my flat. Connor must have not wanted you to see it. He got angry last night. Flung it back at me. It's under my mattress.' She remembered her locket, tucked inside her sweater, and an idea surfaced. 'It has his name engraved on the inside, along with mine and Olivia's. Their date of birth, too. It's clearly a man's bracelet, not a woman's. The police will find it and ask questions. Ones that might break Connor, given how fragile he is.' She hated using her precious boy's mental illness as a weapon, but what choice did she have?

'Bullshit,' Amy said. 'It'll melt. If it even exists, which I doubt.'

'You're wrong,' Elena replied. 'Most house fires don't get hot enough to melt gold. I married a jeweller, so I know these things.' She was willing to bet Amy didn't.

Silence held sway for several seconds. Then the door unlocked. Amy pushed it open, her hand on the latch, clearly ready to retreat should either of the two women try anything.

'Show me,' Amy said.

Elena got ready to charge towards the woman, shove her out of the way, when faint sounds reached her from below. Car tyres on gravel. The back door opening. Connor had returned early, it seemed.

'Let's talk about this,' Elena said. 'I'll return the bracelet to Connor once you've persuaded him to let me and Olivia go, and we're safely out of the house. But first we discuss the situation, like adults.' Inside she was shaking, although her tone was firm.

'You're bluffing.' Amy spat the words from behind thin, angry lips. 'You think I'd fall for your pathetic lies? There is no bracelet, is there?'

The sound of footsteps below became loud enough to alert Amy. 'Is that you, darling?' she called out.

'Yeah. The car's making weird noises. Decided it was best to turn around.'

'Drive mine. I'll throw you down the keys.'

'No need. I'm coming up for a piss.' Connor's feet thudded up the stairs, then the bathroom door banged shut.

'We're wasting time here,' Amy said. 'Once Connor's gone, I'll lock you both back up, then burn down this dump.'

'No,' Elena's throat was closed over with terror. 'You can't. You wouldn't.'

'I can. And I will.'

'Please. Just let us go.'

'Not going to happen. I've killed for Connor before. I won't hesitate to do it again.'

Elena froze. 'What do you mean?'

'I got rid of that bitch Rebecca Brady fifteen years ago. Now history's about to repeat itself with you two.' Amy's lips twisted into a sneer.

A gasp from Olivia. Elena heard the bathroom door open and footsteps cross the landing. She didn't think Amy had noticed. The woman was lost in her own world, Elena realised, one in which only her warped version of reality mattered. So much so that Amy didn't register Connor's presence behind her.

Time hung still. Elena stared at the woman, unable to comprehend what she'd heard.

'You killed Connor's adoptive mother?' Olivia said, her voice high with horror.

Amy smirked. 'Hit and run accident, according to the police. Not so accidental, though. Yeah, I killed the bitch.' She clearly had no idea Connor was mere inches away.

His roar of fury caused them all to jump. 'You murdered my mam?' He shoved Amy against the door-frame, his face a mask of hurt. 'She might not have given birth to me, and I didn't treat her the way she deserved, but I loved her. I've never liked you, however. Always thought you were weird.'

Amy stared at Connor, her eyes wide with fear. 'I did it so we could be together. You, me and your father. I was so patient, darling, hoping Zach would notice me, divorce her. But he didn't, and then you discovered you'd been dumped at birth. I couldn't bear to see you so depressed, so miserable. I decided I could take better care of you than Rebecca did, and if Zach gave me a chance, we could be happy.'

Connor's face was sickly pale. Without a word he bolted into his bedroom. Tormented footsteps sounded from its floorboards, a rhythmic pacing back and forth. Amy seemed to hesitate, then followed him.

Elena realised the woman had left the door open. She pulled Olivia off the mattress, and the two of them ran into Connor's room. Her son's hands raked through his hair, over and over, the movements frenzied. His face was flushed, his eyes wide and staring. A vein pulsed in his forehead. 'Get away from me! All of you!' he yelled.

Shock must have caused the abrupt change in Connor's mood, Elena reasoned. If only he'd let her help him.

Olivia stepped forward. 'I understand you feel betrayed. Elena and me, though—we're not the bad guys here.' Her daughter jabbed an accusing finger in Amy's direction. 'She was going to burn us alive. She's already admitted killing the woman who raised you. Let's leave this place and talk things through at my flat. Please, Connor.'

'No.' Connor shrank away, his arms crossed over his body as he edged closer to the French doors. 'You're liars, the three of you.'

He eyed Olivia with disgust. 'You told me you wanted nothing to do with me.' One arm swung in Elena's direction. 'And you're a heartless cow.'

Amy took a step forward. 'You can trust me, darling. I only want what's best for you.'

'You're a murdering bitch. My life sucks. I don't want to live anymore.'

In a second he was at the French doors, pulling them open, and horror filled Elena at the realisation of what her son was about to do.

From what she'd seen from the outside, the balcony was old and rickety. They were only one floor up from the ground, however; Connor obviously hadn't considered that. Elena doubted a suicide attempt would kill him, unless he hit his head, but what if he ended up horribly injured? Paralysed?

Connor was too quick, though. The French doors were open before any of them can reach him, and he was astride the guard rail of the balcony, swinging his legs over to perch on top of it. His hands, their knuckles white, gripped the metal.

'Get down, darling! Don't do this to me!' Amy's voice was a strangled wail.

'None of you gives a damn about me,' Connor said. 'Nobody does.'

'That's not true.' Elena didn't dare touch him for fear he'd jump. 'I love you. I always have, despite what happened when you were a baby. As for Olivia—she's desperate to know her brother. Please, my love, get off the balcony.'

Connor shook his head. His face had grown even paler, and dots of sweat lined his brow. 'I've nothing to live for. Never have done.'

The balcony shifted under Connor's weight. A groan issued from the tortured metal. From her peripheral vision, Elena saw the bolts that held the structure to the wall slide a few millimetres from their holes. The balcony couldn't support Connor much longer. Elena had to persuade her son to climb off it. Had to, or else—

'Get down, Connor,' Amy pleaded. 'We'll drive back to Newcastle, just the two of us, and I'll explain everything. I didn't kill Rebecca, I swear.'

Connor turned his gaze her way. 'Yes,' he said. 'You did.' He shifted his weight further forward.

Elena tried again. 'You have so much to live for, darling. Me and Olivia, for example. Both of us love you, need to be part of your life.' Connor didn't reply, so she ploughed on. 'Besides, what about your father? Zach Brady?'

A tear slipped down Connor's cheek. 'Dad's better off without me. Everyone is.'

'Don't say that. He's raised you from a baby. He'd hate to lose you this way.'

Connor snorted. 'Yeah, he's been wonderful to me. Whereas I'm just a deadbeat. Time to spare him more disappointment.' He slid his buttocks a few millimetres forward on the guard rail, still clinging to it with both hands. An anguished squeal sounded as one of the bolts slipped further from its hole, the entire balcony now at a perilous angle.

Amy rushed towards Connor. 'You're not thinking straight, darling. Let me help you down.'

What happened next was a blur in Elena's head. Connor's panicked arm rising to fend off Amy. A wrenching sound as the balcony broke free from the wall. Olivia seizing Connor's right arm at the same time as Elena grabbed his left one. It wasn't enough. Connor weighed too much, they couldn't hold him—

She was wrong. Elena and Olivia retained their grip on him as the balcony crashed to the ground. Amy, still intent on saving Connor, became the casualty instead. As the other two women attempted to drag Connor to safety, a desperate shriek tore from her as she lost her footing, plummeting through the gap where the balcony once was. A second later, a thud, wet and sickening, sounded from below.

'Get the fuck off me! Leave me alone!' Connor struggled in their grasp, and for one terrifying second Elena was convinced he was about to plunge, like Amy, onto the unforgiving concrete. Despite his skinny frame, he was strong, and Elena couldn't risk another scuffle. She mouthed words—*pull him back, hard, now*—at Olivia, who nodded.

They hauled Connor out of danger, dumping him on the mattress. Taken by surprise, he didn't resist. Elena relinquished her hold on him, desperate to slam the French doors shut. Keep her boy safe.

Connor was doubled up, his breathing harsh and heavy. 'You should have let me jump,' he managed between gasps.

'Never.' Elena's voice was firm. She knelt beside her son, her arms around his shaking body. 'No matter what you think, I love you. Always have. Always will.'

Connor shoved her away. He staggered to his feet, then headed for the bedroom door and onto the landing. Elena grabbed his sleeve, desperate to stop him doing anything rash. Connor pushed her so hard she crashed into Olivia. Then, without a word, he was gone, his footsteps clattering down the staircase.

Elena and Olivia followed him. Outside, Connor was huddled in a foetal ball next to Amy. Her legs lay on top of the wrecked balcony at an unnatural angle, as if twisted by a giant hand, and blood stained the concrete around her head. Her eyes were open, but dull. Strangled sounds issued from her lips. 'Con… Con…'

Olivia rushed back into the house. Seconds later she appeared, talking into her mobile. *Ambulance. Hurry.*

CHAPTER 30

It was the morning after, and Olivia and Elena were in Olivia's flat. Mugs of coffee sat untouched on the table, the two women perched on the sofa. Olivia, for the first time in ages, felt a surge of happiness. The search for her birth mother was over, and Olivia liked the woman she'd found. Affection might one day turn to love. Different from that which she gave to Sonia, but still love.

Elena shifted in her seat. 'I'm worried about Connor. Zach Brady promised me he'll call after he's visited him at the psychiatric ward. His flight landed in Bristol early this morning. Must have been awful for him to hear his son's being held in a secure facility.'

'Don't worry. Connor will get the support he needs now. Thank goodness he was admitted voluntarily. He must have known he needed help.'

'But suppose the police prosecute him? He lured me to that house, remember. Kept me a prisoner. I've been honest with them about all that, because what else could I say?'

'You did the right thing.' Olivia knew her brother needed professional care, and he was in the best place to get it. 'The police won't bring charges, not considering his mental instability. Or if they do, he'll be treated leniently.'

Elena's phone trilled with an incoming call. 'Zach Brady,' she mouthed at Olivia. The ensuing conversation was lengthy.

'He's just said goodbye to Connor,' she told Olivia once the call ended. 'Says he's stable and responding to medication. If all goes well, his doctors hope to discharge him soon. Zach's assured them Connor has the support of his family, a safe place to stay. He asked if I could care for Connor once they release him, just for the first couple of weeks. So I can monitor his tablet regimen, etc.'

'How come?'

'Zach's scheduled for hernia repair surgery tomorrow. He's flying back to Newcastle tonight, and he'll phone me again then. The timing's lousy, but he's waited months for the operation, apparently.'

'He must have been devastated to learn his wife was murdered.'

Elena nodded. 'Of course. Once he's recovered from the surgery, he's insistent Connor should go home to Newcastle.'

'You agreed, I take it?'

'Yes. Although Zach told me Connor took some convincing.' Elena wiped her eyes. 'He wanted me to be a mother to him. Now I will be.'

*****

A week later, Olivia was at Elena's flat, helping her prepare for Connor's discharge. A duvet and pillow lay folded on the sofa. Elena had stocked the kitchen cupboards with her son's favourite foods. Olivia had taped a list detailing his medication regime to the fridge door. They were almost ready.

'I can't help feeling it's too soon,' Elena said, a frown on her face. 'He should have spent longer in hospital. Seven nights isn't enough.'

'That's how it is with the National Health Service. Too many patients, insufficient resources. He seemed okay when we last visited, though.'

At that moment Elena's doorbell sounded. When Olivia opened it, Connor stood on the mat, an older man behind him. The latter stepped forward, offering his hand to Olivia. 'Zach Brady,' he said in a strong Geordie accent. 'You must be Olivia.' He eyed her with a penetrating gaze. 'It's a pleasure to meet you. I'm sorry it's not under different circumstances.'

Elena came to the doorway. 'Hi, Zach. I'm Elena Munro.'

Zach nodded at her, his expression guarded. Olivia could understand his reserve, given the awkward situation. He looked like he'd not slept for several nights. Understandable, now he knew Amy Sutcliffe had murdered his beloved wife. Not to mention his recent surgery.

Zach cleared his throat, breaking her train of thought.

'Come in, both of you.' Olivia said. She stepped aside, but neither Connor nor his father moved.

Zach shook his head. 'Can't, I'm afraid. I need to fly back to Newcastle today.' He pulled his son into a hug. 'I'll call you later. And I'll come and collect you as soon as I'm fully recovered. Make sure you take your medication, you hear?'

'Yes, Dad.' Zach, clearly reluctant, released Connor. With a brief goodbye to the two women, he headed downstairs to the exit.

Connor nodded his head to Olivia, then strode inside, two steps behind Elena. At first Olivia couldn't pinpoint what was different about him, until she realised. His hair and beard were still long and shaggy, but they were clean. Her brother didn't smell bad, either. A faint scent of lemons clung to him and his clothes sported neat creases. He wasn't the agitated, distraught man from the abandoned house. Her brother looked tired, though.

Connor's gaze was on Elena. 'You okay?' His voice was gruff, like he was reluctant to show he cared.

Elena smiled. 'I am now.' She reached for his hand, then stopped herself. 'May I?'

Connor hesitated, then nodded. Mother and son held hands before Connor pulled away. He dropped into an armchair. Olivia sensed he wasn't up for any emotional discussions, but that was okay. They'd get to that later.

Most of the time Olivia was there, Connor dozed; she chatted to Elena over his soft snores. After Elena went into the kitchen to brew fresh coffee, Connor awakened to stare at Olivia, his eyes bleary.

'There's something I want you to see,' Olivia told him. 'It's at my place. If you feel up to it, we could walk there. I only live a couple of streets away.'

He nodded. 'It'd be good to chat alone, just the two of us.' To Olivia's relief, he didn't ask what the 'something' was. She wasn't ready to reveal her hidden agenda just yet.

'I meant what I said to Dad,' Connor said. 'About taking my medication. I'll be seeing a shrink every week, too. Gonna get well in my head at last.'

'That's great.' Olivia smiled at her brother. She'd be cheering him on every step of the way.

Elena returned, and the moment was lost. Later, however, when Olivia rose to leave, so did Connor. 'Shall I go with you now?' he asked, with a glance at Elena.

'Connor's coming to my place for a while,' Olivia told Elena.

'Fine. But hurry back here afterwards, okay, Connor? Please, darling.'

He nodded. 'I will.'

Outside, the sun shone brightly, forcing Olivia to shield her eyes. A few minutes later they reached her block of flats. Once they'd reached her floor, she fumbled in her bag for her keys, then unlocked the door. 'Come in. I'll make us some coffee.'

When Olivia returned from the kitchen, Connor was seated on her sofa. She placed his mug on the side table, then smiled at him. 'Give me a minute, will you?'

Olivia went into her bedroom to retrieve the sketches and paintings of Tynemouth Castle. Something else, too.

'Check this out,' Olivia said, once seated beside him. She grabbed the top painting and pointed at the bleeding heart, the baby sheltered by the castle entrance. 'That's you. She didn't dump you in a bin.

The homeless guy must have done that. Instead she put you somewhere safe, where you'd be found. And left her heart behind with you.'

Connor's fingers traced over the painting. He didn't speak, but Olivia could tell the picture's raw emotion had pierced his defences. When he raised his gaze to meet his sister's, tears glistened in his eyes.

'She didn't throw me away,' he said, wonder in his tone.

'No. Instead, she cherished your memory. Mine, too. See these?' Olivia placed two envelopes on top of the painting. 'These contain our baby hair. I found them when clearing out Elena's flat. Amy Sutcliffe tricked me into giving her yours, but I spotted it in her handbag after I called the ambulance. Elena loved us, Connor, so much. She just didn't know how to care for us.'

Connor picked up the two envelopes. 'She has neat handwriting,' he said, before frowning. 'That's odd. It's different to the letter she wrote me.'

Olivia drew in a breath. This would be tough for her brother to hear. 'That's not her writing.'

'So whose is it?'

'Our father's.'

Shock filled Connor's face. 'I assumed—' He swallowed hard. 'That whoever fathered us didn't stick around. A one-night stand, maybe, or a failed relationship. She said she was alone, had nobody to help her.'

Time to set her brother straight. Her voice gentle, Olivia told Connor how Elena's fling with Harry ruined her friendship with Sonia. The surrogacy arrangement, how Elena feared prosecution. How Olivia grew up believing Sonia was her mother. What a wonderful father Harry Harding had always been.

'He's still alive?' Connor asked. 'Here, in Bristol?'

Olivia's heart grew sad as she told Connor about the accident. 'Dad remembers you, though. He tried to say your baby name, Cameron, once I started digging into my adoption. His memory is shot, but he's never forgotten his son.'

'Wow.' Connor's face was pale, but hope filled his expression. 'I can't believe this. Suddenly I have a new mam, a sister, another dad.' He scrubbed a hand over his jaw. 'It's a lot to take in.'

Olivia pictured Harry and Connor, reunited. She hoped her father would understand that this man with the world-weary eyes was his son.

'You need to meet him,' she said. 'In the meantime, I have lots of photos to show you.'

*****

Olivia laid the photo album she'd put together on her father's lap. Inside were decades of cherished memories: Harry and Sonia's wedding, Olivia as a baby, toddler, teenager. Towards the back was a plastic folder. In it Olivia had placed the envelopes containing the locks of hair.

Elena had granted with a smile her request to include them. 'I have my babies back, and Harry's lost so much. He needs those locks of hair more than I do.'

Also in the album were recent photos of Connor, both alone and with Olivia. Her brother was waiting outside Harry's room. Elena had already told Olivia she wouldn't be there.

'It's inappropriate,' she'd said the previous day. 'Harry and I had a moment together, nothing more. It would be disrespectful to Sonia's memory.'

Olivia agreed. She didn't believe in an afterlife, but she liked to think Sonia was with them in spirit, overjoyed that the son she almost raised was about to meet his father.

'Dad,' she said. 'I've put together a photo album for you. Would you like to see it?'

Together, they flipped through the photos. Olivia spotted tears in her father's eyes, but they were happy ones, judging by his expression. He might not remember the exact circumstances, but he knew he was looking at the people—his wife and daughter—that he'd adored the most. They'd not yet reached the photos of Connor.

Olivia turned the page, revealing the two envelopes in their plastic pouch. She drew out the one containing her brother's hair.

Olivia placed the tiny curl in her father's palm. Harry's fingers stroked the blue ribbon. His eyes filled with tears again. He remembers, Olivia thought, her heart thumping with joy.

'Cam,' Harry said, his voice thick with emotion. 'Cam.'

'I've found him, Dad.' Olivia got to her feet. 'And he wants to meet you. So much.' She walked to the door and opened it. 'Come in,' she said to her brother.

Connor walked into the room, his movements hesitant. He was nervous, Olivia realised. Well, of course he was. This was a monumental moment.

'Dad, this is Cameron.' Best not to confuse her father over names. 'Your son.'

She watched Harry as he stared at the man before him. Connor was clean-shaven now, his hair shorter and neater, his clothes washed and pressed. His time staying with Elena had wrought a marked change in his appearance and personal hygiene. He bore a distinct likeness to Olivia: the shape of his nose, his chin, the same eyes. Olivia prayed her father would notice and understand. If not that particular day, then soon.

It seemed he did. Tears trickled down Harry's face. He opened his arms. 'Cam,' he repeated.

Connor stepped into his father's embrace, his body stiff at first. They hugged for several seconds before Connor disengaged himself. He dragged up a chair to sit beside Harry.

Olivia wiped a tear from her cheek, before snapping a photo of them. She'd promised Elena that much.

*****

Later, back at her flat, Olivia was in her bedroom. It was late, but she was too hyped up to sleep. Instead, she took out her mobile to call Kirsten. Her friend was due an update. She'd been a rock to Olivia once she'd heard what happened with Amy Sutcliffe.

'Lunch tomorrow?' Olivia enquired, once Kirsten answered.

'You bet, babe. Been way too long since we last caught up.'

Now for the more difficult call. Earlier, she'd arrived at a decision about her marriage.

Olivia navigated to the list of blocked contacts on her mobile and found her husband's number to unblock it.

David answered on the first ring. 'Hey, Livvy,' he said. Olivia detected no trace of resentment in his tone, which was a good start.

'Can we talk?' she said. 'Maybe get together soon?'

For a second, David didn't reply, and fear gripped Olivia. Had she left it too long? Then: 'Sure. I'd like that.'

They decided to meet tomorrow after work. 'I'll come to you,' Olivia said, a flutter in her belly at the thought of setting foot in their marital home again.

David pulled her in his arms the second she arrived the next day. Olivia rested her head on his shoulder, drinking in his strength. She could only pray it wasn't too late to mend their marriage.

'I've got so much to tell you,' she said, her voice muffled by his shirt. 'You won't believe everything that's happened.'

Over mugs of coffee, seated in their kitchen, she told him. David listened, shock in his face. 'That Amy Sutcliffe sounds like a psychopath,' he said.

'I was so scared, David. The thought of being burned alive—' Olivia shuddered. 'Will you hold me? Please?'

David got up and came round her side of the table. His arms wrapped around her in a fierce hug. Their embrace lasted a long time, during which neither of them spoke.

He eventually released her to walk back to his side of the table. 'I hate the thought of what you went through,' he said, once seated again. 'I'll say it again. We shouldn't be apart. Not at a time like this.'

Olivia glanced around. Everything was so familiar, so evocative of home, of love, that tears stung her eyes. She'd missed this. Not half as much as she'd missed her husband, however.

Time to repair her marriage. 'I want to be with you David. I really do. It's just that the whole baby thing, along with Tiffany Cook—'

Anger sparked in his eyes. 'For God's sake, how many times must I say it? I'm not having an affair with Tiffany. She's only ever been a colleague, I swear. Anything else is all in your head.'

'I believe you.' Kirsten's words sounded in Olivia's brain. *I saw the way Little Miss Perfect looked at the guy. The ring on her finger. David's telling the truth.*

David looked surprised. 'You do? What changed your mind?'

'Kirsten made me see sense.'

'Thank God for that. You blocked me. That hurt, Livvy.'

'I'm sorry.'

'I tried to tell you. But you wouldn't listen. About how Rebecca Brady died fifteen years ago, I mean.'

Shame filled Olivia. Guilt, too. If only she'd not been so pig-headed. So much hurt could have been avoided.

'I even wrote you a letter. You didn't read it, did you?'

'No. I'm sorry—'

'I came to your flat. Begged you to open the door. But you wouldn't.'

I was angry. Confused, too.'

'Oh, Livvy.' David shook his head. 'I love you so much. You know that, don't you?'

She reached across the table to clasp his hand. 'Yes.' For a few seconds there was silence.

'If our marriage is to work, you have to trust me,' David said. 'I realise you're bruised by what happened with your ex. But not all men are cheating bastards.'

'I get that.'

'Do you? Really? Because I won't stand for you walking out on me again. Not when I've done nothing wrong.' David's lips were a tight line of anger.

'I won't. That's a promise.'

'I'll need more than that, Livvy. Would you consider couples' counselling?'

David was right. She needed to banish her demons. 'Yes. Anything you want.'

His mouth relaxed into a smile. 'That's good to hear.' Olivia sensed they'd turned a corner.

'I want us to have children,' David said 'Once we're back on an even keel.'

Olivia sucked in a breath. Well, that was a turnaround. 'Are you sure? You've never seemed that bothered.'

'You're wrong. I've always wanted kids, but at the right time. What with me gunning for promotion, you getting established in your business—I thought it better to hold off. Until we're both more settled.'

'Why the change of heart?'

David smiled. 'I was talking to my dad about it. He says the perfect time to have a baby doesn't exist. That you're never fully prepared, so why wait? Over the course of a few pints, he convinced me.'

'Can I come home?' Olivia's words startled her. She hadn't intended to ask that, not yet anyway. Her heart, however, had other ideas. She stared at David, afraid. What if it was too soon?

He reached across the table to clasp her hand. 'I'd like that.'

CHAPTER 31

Elena couldn't repress a smile. Olivia and Connor sat at a window table in Club Coffee, the likeness between them unmistakable as they chatted while Elena placed their orders at the counter. They were all getting on well, despite such a shaky start; Connor was more relaxed now around his sister and mother, although still a little guarded. Give it time, Elena told herself.

'Three lattes, please,' she said to the barista. She also asked for triple slices of salted caramel cake.

Back at the table, she informed Olivia and Connor about the update she'd received that morning from the police. 'Amy Sutcliffe's in a bad way. Her broken leg will heal, but her spinal injuries won't. I've been told off the record she'll never walk again. As for her skull injury, a depressed fracture's a serious matter. The police still haven't been able to interview her.'

'She should be in jail,' Connor said, his expression grim. 'The bitch murdered my adoptive mother. Wanted to kill both of you.'

Elena cleared her throat. Here came the hard part. 'The thing is, darling, there's no firm evidence. The hit-and-run that killed Rebecca Brady happened fifteen years ago. As for her plan to burn us alive, it'll be her word against ours.'

'I'd say she got her comeuppance anyway,' Olivia said. 'Her injuries sound bad. Enough to stop her meddling in our lives ever again.'

'I want nothing to do with her.' Connor's voice sounded decisive. 'Dad—my adoptive father, I mean—was devastated when I told him the full story. He realised she was obsessed, but not how dangerous she could be.'

'Amy Sutcliffe is evil,' Elena said. 'She plotted to keep the three of us apart. I know she's unhinged, delusional. But I can't forgive her for that. Nor for threatening to burn the house down with us inside.' She shuddered.

Connor nodded. 'I feel the same way. What about you, Olivia?'

'Me? I just want to put it all bchind me. David and I have talked some more. I'm moving back home once the notice period on my flat is up. It's early days, but I have high hopes for our marriage.' She smiled. 'I'd like the two of you to meet him sometime.'

Elena glanced at her daughter, love in her heart. Olivia sounded so happy. The darkness under her eyes had gone, along with the tension around her mouth.

'I'd like that too,' said Connor. 'Got a photo of him I can see?'

'Sure.' Olivia busied herself with her phone. Elena fell silent as her son and daughter talked. How wonderful it felt to have everything out in the open at last.

Well, not quite everything. Some things Elena would never tell. Like how she'd never been sure who'd fathered her children. In every way that counted, Harry was their dad. He'd done a wonderful job with Olivia, and he loved spending time with

Connor. Besides, Olivia had shown her the photo she'd taken at Harry's nursing home. The resemblance between Harry and Connor was strong—similar jawline, same hooked nose. She was more convinced than ever whose DNA ran through her children's bodies.

Likewise, she owed it to Sonia's memory never to mention how her former friend had blackmailed her. Elena shuddered as she remembered Sonia's threat to lie to the police about Gerry Baxter's death. Olivia had adored Sonia; why tarnish their relationship?

Besides, Olivia had Elena for a mother now. She'd love and cherish her darling girl forever, and Olivia would never know the ugly truth about Sonia.

Or about Elena.

*****

The morning Elena encountered her former friend after thirty years was seared into her memory. She'd paid no attention to the footsteps descending the stairs as she entered her block of flats. All she wanted was a cup of coffee and a chat with Olivia. Maybe today was the day she revealed her true identity. Her heart beat faster at the thought.

'What the hell are *you* doing here?' Even after three decades, Elena would know that voice anywhere. Her eyes flitted to her former friend. Sonia had aged well, she thought.

Sonia stalked up to Elena, causing her to take an involuntary step backward. 'I'm guessing it's no coincidence you're here. Have you told her?'

Elena shook her head. 'Not yet.'

Sonia spotted Elena's grocery bags. 'Oh, my God. You live in one of these flats, don't you? In the same block as Olivia.'

'Yes. I can explain—'

'Like hell you can. I should have known you'd be back one day to sniff around my daughter. *My* daughter, you hear? You might have given birth to her, but she's mine, in every way that matters.'

Elena gathered her courage. 'She has no idea she's adopted, does she? You should have told her, Sonia. Olivia needs to know her true parentage.'

Sonia stepped closer. 'No, she doesn't. And that's how it'll stay. I won't have you turning up here, unannounced and unwelcome, ruining everything.' By now, she was almost shouting.

Elena pushed away from the wall, causing Sonia to move too. 'Let's go upstairs. We can't talk here. I'll make us some coffee, and we can chat.' She gathered up her groceries.

A look of hate crossed Sonia's face, but she followed Elena up the stairs. Once inside, Elena dumped her bags in the kitchen and reached for the kettle.

'Don't bother on my account,' Sonia said, her voice thick with contempt. She strode into the living room, where she stood, arms crossed, legs akimbo, mouth tight, her back against the mantelpiece. She was as feisty as ever, Elena noted. 'I won't be staying long. Where's Cameron?'

Elena hadn't expected Sonia to ask so soon. 'He's fine. You don't need to worry about him.' Even to her own ears, the words sounded false.

'He's the son I should have had. Of course I'm going to ask about him. I'll say it again. Where is he?'

Elena dropped her gaze, ashamed. 'I don't know,' she said, which was a lie. The tracing agency she'd used had located his address, but so far fear had prevented her from contacting Connor. What if he rejected her?

'You don't *know*?' Elena cringed at the scorn in Sonia's voice. The woman would worm the truth from her soon enough. Best to get it over. No need to tell her everything, though.

'He was adopted.' Shock filled Sonia's face. 'A couple in Newcastle took him.'

If she thought Sonia was angry before, it was nothing to the fury in her expression now. She stepped forward, raised her hand, and cracked a resounding slap across Elena's right cheek.

'You bitch,' she said. 'You despicable cow. I would have loved that boy as if he were my own. He could have grown up alongside his sister. Instead you shunted him off to the other end of the country? Why, for God's sake?'

'I'm sorry. But I had severe postnatal depression. I was ill, not functioning well—'

'Do you realise the hell you put me and Harry through? Well, do you?' Specks of Sonia's spittle landed on Elena's cheek. 'I should never have trusted you. Anyone who sleeps with their best friend's husband is no better than a whore. When Harry got home and told me you'd stolen Cameron, I was beside myself. The community midwife was due the next day, and there we were, minus a child. I wanted to call the police, but Harry persuaded me not to. He said we couldn't risk the authorities taking Olivia from us once the truth came out.' She wiped away a tear. 'I couldn't bear losing her. We might have been blacklisted against future adoptions. Then what could we do? All I wanted was a child.'

Elena's heart ached for her former friend. Back then, she hadn't considered the pain Harry and Sonia must have suffered. No wonder this woman loathed her.

'We had to leave Bristol,' Sonia continued. 'Harry called the midwife and lied to her. Told her his mother was dying, that we'd be in France for a few months. He said she sounded inexperienced, stressed—I'm guessing she was probably overworked and underpaid too—because all she said was to seek midwifery care in France until we returned to the UK.'

'You lived abroad? For how long?'

Sonia snorted. 'Of course we didn't. We ended up in Manchester.'

'Why Manchester?'

'Harry's company had a branch there. I had a suspicion you might cause us trouble. Never, in my wildest dreams, did I think you'd steal Cameron.' Her expression filled with hate, so much that Elena shrank away in fear. 'Instead, I suspected you'd hang around, try to sink your hooks into my husband again. So two months before the birth, I asked Harry to request a work transfer. Figured that a new start, somewhere you'd never find us, was best all round.' Sonia blew out a breath. 'Thank God I did. We went to Manchester, registered both babies' births to allay suspicion, then lay low.'

Elena didn't need to ask the reason. How else could Sonia and Harry have explained why Cameron was missing?

'It's easier to disappear in a big city, especially when both Harry's and my parents were dead. He's an only child, and I rarely see Isobel. Everyone else we lost contact with. We had no choice, thanks to you. We paid privately for Olivia's vaccinations to avoid any nosy health visitors, and dreaded every knock on the door. '

'But you ended up back in Bristol?'

'I missed my home city,' Sonia said. 'When Olivia reached school age, I told Harry I wanted to return. We bought a house in Stapleton, registered with a different GP, saying we'd been in France for the last five years, which explained the gap in our medical records. Nobody twigged, thank God.'

She eyed Elena with loathing. 'We'd already agreed never to tell Olivia she wasn't my child. How could we explain she had a brother she'd never met?'

Footsteps sounded outside Elena's flat. A knock. Olivia's voice. 'Elena? Fancy a quick coffee?'

Elena froze. 'Don't say a word,' Sonia mouthed at her. After a few seconds, they heard Olivia going upstairs. The door to her flat opened then closed.

'I never thought I'd need to hide from my own child.' Sonia's words were filled with fury. She tossed her head, one hand flicking her hair, and Elena glimpsed a flash of gold fall from Sonia's lobe. An earring breaking free and heading towards the thick pile of the carpet. She tried to tell her, but Sonia spoke, and the moment was lost.

'We can't talk here,' Sonia said. 'I'm too angry. I don't want Olivia to overhear.'

Elena agreed. They needed to discuss how best to tell Olivia, and that required careful consideration.

'Meet me tomorrow,' Sonia said. 'Vassals Park, by the old snuff mill. I walk there every morning.'

They arranged to meet at seven the next day. After that, there was nothing to say. Sonia, her expression still thunderous, left, and Elena was alone, the earring long forgotten.

It's for the best, she told herself. Olivia had to discover the truth sometime, and this way was perfect. Elena promised herself she'd write to Connor later; with any luck he'd reply, meaning the twins might soon be reunited. She'd been lucky to be granted a second chance with her children.

*****

Elena slept well that night, but was awake long before her alarm clock. The summer sun pierced her curtains, and when she pulled them back, the sky was cloudless. A good omen, she decided. Today would mark a new chapter in her relationship with Olivia, once she'd agreed with Sonia how to tell their daughter the truth. Maybe she'd soon hear back from Connor; she'd written him a letter the previous evening. Now she just had to post it, and pray he received it okay. For the first time in ages, she was hopeful for a brighter future.

She dressed quickly, then hurried out of the door. It was too nice to drive; instead, she elected to go on foot. The Snuff Mills section of Vassals Park was a ten-minute stroll from her flat, and it had already turned six-fifty. Elena walked at a fast pace, the sun on her skin, a smile on her face. Once at the park, she made her way past the cafe towards the old mill. Sonia was waiting opposite, her back against the wall that bordered the river. Her expression wasn't friendly. When Elena drew near, Sonia pushed away from the wall and strode past her.

'Let's go down here,' she said. Between a nearby ornamental garden area and the wall, a short path, only a few yards in length, led to the river. Sonia walked down it to stand on the stone platform built a foot or so above the water, before shifting to her right. They were out of sight of the main path now, shielded by the ornamental garden's wall. The river ran shallow here, its bed rocky, the stones green and slippery with algae. A pungent water smell tainted the air. Elena came to stand beside Sonia, and for a few seconds there was silence.

'I used to come here as a child,' Sonia said. 'Mum would give me an empty jam jar, and I'd buy a kid's fishing net from the cafe. She'd watch me while I caught minnows and the occasional stickleback. Always made me return them before we left, of course. Happy times.' She grimaced. 'Back then Isobel hadn't been born, and I had no idea I'd been adopted. When Mum told me, I was gutted.'

Elena stayed silent, aware Sonia needed to vent. Besides, what could she say?

'It messes with your head finding out your birth mother was a fifteen-year-old future junkie,' Sonia continued. 'That's why I craved a child of my own. I hoped a baby might take away the hurt.' She dipped the toe of her shoe towards the water, poking at a rock. 'When Harry admitted he'd got you pregnant, my world collapsed. Until I saw a way out. One I believed best for everyone.'

'You blackmailed me. Told me you'd tell the police I killed my father.'

Sonia snorted. 'Of course I did. You were flaky as hell, remember? Not capable of being a mother. I'd have done whatever it took to get those babies.'

'I wanted to care for them. How could you think I didn't? You've no idea how awful postnatal depression is.'

'Don't rub it in that I couldn't have kids. Haven't you caused enough hurt?'

'I'm sorry—'

'If you reckon I'll allow you to wreck Olivia's life, you're dumber than I'd thought.'

'What do you mean?'

'Olivia believes I'm her mother. She's vulnerable at the moment, her marriage shaky. You think I'll let you ruin everything by telling her the truth? No way.'

'She has a right to know—'

'You've got a damn nerve. You turn up here thirty years after putting us through hell with Cameron, and now you want to play happy families?

Not going to happen.' Sonia folded her arms, her gaze forged from steel. 'There's no trick I won't pull to keep Olivia from discovering the truth.'

Elena believed Sonia. Her former friend had already proved herself capable of blackmail. Who knew how low she'd stoop? Hardly surprising, though. Both Sonia and she would fight like mama bears, each in their own way, to protect their daughter.

'You're such a hypocrite,' she said, her voice a snarl. Shock registered in Sonia's eyes at Elena's uncharacteristic anger. She took a step backward, almost losing her footing.

'All this talk of protecting Olivia is bullshit. Not keen on her finding out you've lied all her life, are you?'

Sonia's face was very pale. 'No,' she said. 'I'm not.'

'At least be honest. You're saving your own skin, not hers.'

Sonia dragged in a deep breath. 'I meant what I said. Where Olivia's concerned, there's no lie I won't tell if it's for her own good. None.'

Memories flooded over Elena. Sonia's words from decades ago. *I'll say you got drunk, told me his death's been on your conscience for years… that you shoved him off the balcony after he raped you…. I'm not prepared to cover up a murder…*

'Perhaps I should tell Olivia the truth,' Sonia continued. 'My version of it, anyway. First, I'll reveal how you slept with my husband. Seeing how you want me to be honest.'

'I—'

'Then I'll move on to your drug-taking, the prostitution. How you threatened to sell your newborn daughter to the highest bidder.'

Elena's jaw fell open with shock. Sonia couldn't be serious, surely?

'You remember your addiction to pills, right? Along with the men you shagged for a few quid down dark alleyways. How you demanded money from me. Said you wouldn't tell Olivia the truth provided I transferred fifty thousand pounds to your bank account.'

'That's all a pack of nonsense. I didn't… I would never…'

'Your word against mine. Like I said, there's no lie I won't tell for Olivia's sake.' Sonia's expression turned smug. 'Any guess as to whom she'll believe, you or me?'

Elena didn't think, just acted. She shoved Sonia with such force that the other woman lost her footing, her arms flailing in an attempt not to fall off the stone platform. A second later, Sonia's body lay limp in the river bed, blood streaming from her head, the damage inflicted by a large rock lodged in the mud. Her nose and mouth were under water; bubbles streamed from her lips. The river was shallow at that point, but still deep enough to drown someone.

Sonia's arms twitched, as though she hoped to drag herself upright, then went still. If Elena acted fast, she could save her friend's life.

She didn't, however. Sonia's words resounded in her head. *No lie I won't tell. Drug-taking, prostitution. Sell your newborn daughter.*

Elena peered over the wall to the ornamental garden and beyond, to the main path. Only dog walkers and runners were likely to be around so early, and she didn't spot either. What concerned her was the house that overlooked the river, close to the old snuff mill. Elena's breathing speeded up, her chest tight. She had no idea who lived there—she presumed a member of the park staff—but might someone have seen her from the upper story as she shoved Sonia?

Her eyes scanned its bulk. Blinds covered the windows, and the house was still, with no sign of movement. Elena released a shaky breath, and glanced at Sonia, whose mouth and nose remained below the water. She was dying, yet Elena stayed immobile.

Five minutes passed before she hurried back to the main path. She walked as fast as she dared without attracting attention, her head bowed. A man walking his dog passed, but didn't glance her way Once home, Elena collapsed on her bed and wept for the grief her darling Olivia would soon suffer Really, though, she'd had no choice. Blood, as the saying went, was thicker than water.

*****

No, Elena would keep quiet about what happened a Vassals. She'd also never reveal how, as she dragged Connor to safety from the balcony, she'd shoved Amy Sutcliffe through the gap onto the concret below. Olivia, her focus on Connor, never noticed thank goodness. Fair's fair, Elena reckoned. Th woman had killed Rebecca Brady, would hav burned Olivia and Elena alive. She deserved everything she got.

Besides, it was all in the past. The future was here. Now. At this table, amid the warmth of Club Coffee. With her children, the way she'd always wanted.

'More cake?' Elena asked.

POSTSCRIPT

I hope you enjoyed *She'll Never Tell*! If so, please consider leaving a review on whichever sales platform you bought the book from, and/or Goodreads.

Please note that this book conforms to British conventions of spelling, punctuation and grammar. You'll see favourite not favorite, tyre not tire, maths instead of math, etc., none of which are incorrect, just different.

If you've enjoyed this book, why not visit my website at www.maggiejamesfiction.com, where you can also find my blog - I post regularly on all topics of interest to readers, including author interviews and book reviews. While you're there, why not sign up for my Special Readers' Group, and receive a free copy of *Blackwater Lake*? The newsletter is sent monthly and when a new title is released, so you won't get bombarded with emails. It includes fiction recommendations, news about my latest books and personal life, and discounts on my novels.

You can also connect with me on Facebook (Maggie James Fiction) or via Twitter (@mjamesfiction).

ACKNOWLEDGEMENTS

Thanks to: Mark Dare, Primrose Batehup, Robin Sykes, Jackie Wride and David Gilchrist for allowing me to use their names in *She'll Never Tell*.

Big thank-yous are also due to Mary Moss, Colin Garrow, Deb Day, Donna Morfett and Stephanie Mackell for being top-notch beta readers. Your input proved invaluable in helping me weed out inconsistencies and typos to make *She'll Never Tell* a better book.

ABOUT THE AUTHOR

Maggie James is a British author who lives near Newcastle-upon-Tyne. She writes psychological suspense novels.

Before turning her hand to writing, Maggie worked mainly as an accountant, with a diversion into practising as a nutritional therapist. Diet and health remain high on her list of interests, along with travel. Accountancy does not, but then it never did. The urge to pack a bag and go off travelling is always lurking in the background! When not writing, going to the gym, practising yoga or travelling, Maggie can be found seeking new four-legged friends to pet; animals are a lifelong love!

Find out more at Maggie's website and blog: www.maggiejamesfiction.com.

Printed in Great Britain
by Amazon

66490107R00208